I0608007

REVIEWS

"From the unspeakable, to the ghostly and angelic, author Joy Ross Davis immediately captured my attention by masterfully bringing her characters to life, one by one, generation by generation, in this heartfelt gem of wonder and intrigue.

Surrounding the reader with a most unique setting within the rolling hills of Tennessee, the author opens the doors of The Playhouse Inn—a bed and breakfast full of secrets, as it breathes magic and mayhem amongst the peculiar and eccentric, and leads its guests on a journey where good and evil exist under one roof, where love and forgiveness are genuine, and the romantic and adventurous walk hand in hand. A journey of the best kind!

With a treasure trove of meaningful characters, a whirlwind of suspense, and vivid descriptions throughout, I not only fell in love with this story as I became emotionally attached, but *Countenance* became the story I hadn't realized I was missing, until now...

The haunting, the heartwarming, and heroic, are the very elements which make this mystical, paranormal narrative a delightful blend of the charming and captivating!"

—**WILD SAGE BOOK BLOG**

"The story was a good read before, but now it is even better. I recommend this book to other readers."

—**JUDYANN LORENZ**

"This story has ghosts, an angel, a Scottish hound name Lulu, and some serious magic with some serious bad guys. Loved this book."

—**ROXANE TWISDALE**

"I love a good mystery, and Davis did well to entice readers with the secrets that Sylvie is about to share with her niece. Before her death, Nealey's mother made her daughter swear not to go back to Playhouse Inn. Intriguingly, something happened to her mother when she and Nealey spent the night at the inn.

The prose is evocative; the description of the inn is wonderful and it makes me want to go there myself...the twists and turns of the central characters will keep readers engrossed.

It's a great mix of good versus evil and a ghost story. The prose is evocative; the description of the inn is wonderful and it makes me want to go there myself. Some parts of the story progress at an unhurried pace, but the twists and turns of the central characters will keep readers engrossed.
★★★★★ 5 Stars"

—**READERS' FAVORITE**

"Great read. Hard to put down. Characters were well developed, story took twists and turns that held my attention and ending was quite a surprise."

—**LITA LYNN**

"At this point I don't know if this author could write a bad book. I've read everything she has published and each one is wonderful and truly delightful. She touches your heart with the characters and delights you with plot and settings. The Playhouse Inn is a place I would love to visit, and I'll admit I've reread the book several times to do just that."

—**TIFFANY SEACHRIST**

The

GHOSTS OF PLAYHOUSE INN TRILOGY

Countenance

Book One

JOY ROSS DAVIS

Countenance
BOOK ONE
Joy Ross Davis

ISBN: 978-1-954332-57-7
Library of Congress Control Number on file.

Wyatt-MacKenzie
www.WyattMacKenzie.com

His countenance was like lightning,
and his raiment white as snow.

MATTHEW 28: 3

Prologue

In their new home in Tracy City, Tennessee, boxes still unpacked, Nealey Monaghan set three bowls of cheese grits and three peanut butter and jelly sandwiches on the kitchen table then slumped into a chair. She rubbed her back with one hand, her growing belly with the other.

Only three more months, she thought. September, only three more months.

"Not much of a dinner," she said. "I just didn't have the energy to cook. This little one seems to be draining me."

"It's a fine dinner," Hank said. "I'm a southern boy, remember. I love cheese grits."

Nealey massaged her temples then took in a deep breath and let it out.

"Tell me what's wrong," Hank said. "Please. You've been out of sorts for days, honey, and I'm worried about you. Is it the baby?"

She covered her face with her hands.

"No, it isn't the baby. I don't know what it is. It just won't go away."

Hank slid close to her and pulled her hands away from her face. "What, sweetheart, what won't go away?"

She pushed herself up from the chair then reached for Hank and slid into his lap. She hugged him and kissed his forehead then his lips. "I love you," she whispered and kissed him again.

"Whew," he said and smiled at her. "Don't start something you can't finish, girl. The kids will be here any minute."

"Shh," she said and nibbled at his ear.

"Oh, God," he whispered. "You've done it now."

He closed his eyes and gave her a long, lingering kiss. Then he stroked the sides of her face.

"You're still a great kisser ... for a cop," she whispered and nuzzled against his neck. "Guess you want me to move so you can dig into those cheese grits!" She chuckled.

Hank rubbed his hands down her back. "Feel good?"

"Um, feels wonderful," she whispered.

"I'll keep rubbing while you tell me what's bothering you. Maybe I can help."

"Promise you'll keep rubbing?"

"If it helps you, I'll rub 'til my hands fall off!"

Nealey pressed herself close against him. "That's one thing I love about you, Hank. You'd rub 'til your hands fell off. Not many men would …."

"Tell me," he interrupted.

"It's this terrible feeling, honey, like a black cloud hanging over me. No matter what I do, it won't go away."

"Do you have any idea what it's about? You're not worried about money, are you? We're doing fine, and with your new job at the parish, we'll be even better."

"It's not money. I know we're okay, better than okay."

"Are you worried about the kids? They're healthy, aren't they, and happy?"

Nealey nodded. "They're fine."

"Hm," Hank said and pulled her away so that he could look at her face. "Perhaps you forgot our anniversary. That's it, isn't it? Fifteen years tomorrow."

She raised an eyebrow. "If I'm not mistaken, I'm not the one who usually forgets. That would be you."

Hank pulled her close to him and whispered to her belly. "Your mom's just in a bad mood right now. She'll be fine once you get here."

She stared down at him. "Hank, do you think Brian would hurt Naomi?"

"Is that what you're worried about?"

Nealey nodded.

Hank took her hands in his and kissed them. "I can't say for sure what Brian would do. He's unpredictable and full of rage. Add in a little booze, and you've got a guy who slams his fist through a wall like he did at the last pool party."

Nealey grimaced. "Remember that benefit for the homeless at the Henson's? I thought Brian was going to kill that guy for brushing up against Naomi. He made a laughing stock of himself and scared that poor old man half to death."

"First time I've ever had to haul a family member to jail."

"He's not family. We just tolerate him when we have to be around him."

"He's gone now, sweetheart. Divorce is final. Don't worry."

Hank patted her arm. "I know you're worried about your sister's safety. Brian is greedy, selfish, and he's got a hair-trigger temper. No one ever knows what sets him off. But he's moved out now. So, try not to worry."

He kissed her cheek. "I'm keeping an eye on things. We've got the restraining order. I'm checking her house next door every night."

Nealey held his hand to her cheek. "You're such a good man, Hank Monaghan."

Hank smiled, his cheeks gaining a slight pink glow. "Aw, geez, Nealey."

She planted kisses across his fingers. "What did I ever do to deserve you?"

"Well, for one thing," he said, "you make me these gourmet dinners. And for another ...."

Ten-year-old Nicholas bounded in from outside, his face pale and troubled, his little sister Lauren's hand in his. When Nealey saw the panic in her son's eyes, she cupped his face with her hands.

"Oh, honey, what's wrong? What happened to you?"

She wrapped her arms around him and hugged him. The boy didn't say anything.

"Come on, buddy, tell us what's wrong," Hank said. "Daddy and Mommy will take care of it."

"Aunt Naomi," was all he managed to say.

Nealey lifted his chin and said softly, "What's wrong with her, honey?"

The boy slid his arms around her. "There's blood, Mama. I couldn't wake her up."

"I'll go," Hank said. "I'll call the station and get a car over there."

He buckled on his holster. "Call the paramedics, just in case."

Before he left, he kissed Nealey on the forehead, tousled Nicholas's hair, and ran his finger along Lauren's cheek. "I love y'all. Stay put 'til I get back."

The glass door banged behind him.

She dialed 911, gave the address, and said that Officer Hank Monaghan might need backup.

"We can be there in five minutes," came the response.

Nealey hugged her son close. "It's okay, sweetie. Here, why don't you sit down and try to eat something? It'll make you feel better."

But in her gut, Nealey felt certain that nothing would ever be the same after this day. There would be no feeling better for any of them.

She shook it off. "Come on, you two. Let's eat. I made your favorite, peanut butter and jelly."

Lauren clapped her hands.

She helped Lauren into the booster chair and slid the sandwich close to her. "Mmm, peanut butter and jelly. Eat up."

She popped the two bowls of grits into the microwave, stirred them, then set in front of the children. Then she poured two small plastic glasses of milk, put a sippy lid on Lauren's and placed them on the table.

"Okay, are we all set?"

The kids were already eating. *Cheese grits and peanut butter sandwiches. You'd think I'd served them a feast. God bless 'em.*

She looked at her watch. *What is keeping Hank?*

Her hands began to tremble.

After thirty minutes, the kids had eaten every morsel.

"Nicholas, are you feeling better, honey?"

He nodded.

With her shaky fingers, Nealey tried Hank's cell phone but got no answer.

"Is Daddy okay?" Nicholas asked.

"He didn't answer. He's probably just busy. You know your daddy, always rescuing other people."

But Nealey knew that something was wrong. She smiled at the kids, but the smile covered a gnawing fear that welled inside her.

She put the dishes in the sink and stared out the kitchen window into the fading daylight. She wiped dots of perspiration from under her nose and sighed.

In a few minutes, it would be dark. She tried Hank's cell phone again. No answer.

"Okay, you two, would you like to watch a movie before bedtime?"

Lauren yelled, "Lion King!"

Nealey put on the DVD and arranged the blanket and pillows on the sofa. Satisfied that help was coming, she tried Hank's number again. No answer.

The kids raced to their places as the movie started.

"Okay, guys, I'll be right back. The Emergency Team is here." Nealey said.

A gnawing fear gripped Nealey.

Both of them nodded but neither of them took their eyes off the movie.

As soon as the door closed, Nealey dashed across the yard. She ran, with her arm cushioning her belly, across the lush carpet of last year's new sod.

God, please let her be all right. Please, please.

In less than two minutes, she crossed her own cushioned lawn and stepped onto the dry earth of Naomi and Brian's yard. Every sharp twig and rough stone dug into her bare feet, but she ran. She had to get to her sister, her twin, her lifelong companion.

The door stood ajar at Naomi's house, so Nealey stopped just inside the foyer and listened. When she heard nothing out of the ordinary, she felt a momentary sense of relief. The Emergency Team pushed their way in front of her.

"Stay right here," one of them said.

"No! That's my family down there. My whole family! Hank? Where are you? Is everything all right?"

"Please, ma'am, just stay right here for a minute. Let us make sure it's safe first," another of the emergency workers said.

The team of three walked down the steps and into the den, Nealey quietly following behind.

Nealey followed the team through the living room and into a dark hallway.

She felt nauseous and rubbed her belly.

"Deep breath," she whispered and inhaled, counted to three, then exhaled.

With the team advancing in front of her, she stood at the top of the stairway that led to the lower floor. It looked like a dark, gaping hole.

Her heart pounding now, she eased her feet along the carpeted steps and held tightly to the handrail.

Then she heard three rapid-fire gunshots, like those from a machine gun, and froze.

When she reached the squared landing, she let out the breath she'd been holding. The landing meant a left turn and only three more steps. One ... two ... three, and she was down the stairs.

Moonlight filtered in from the sliding glass doors at one end of the master bedroom. Nealey tried to focus her eyes. She squinted to make out the forms in the room.

"Hank?" she called, her voice trembling and barely above a whisper. She heard the police inside the house now calling out to Officer Monaghan.

"We're down here," Nealey cried out.

She took a step forward and blinked her eyes as they adjusted to the darkness.

And then, she saw them. All of them.

The three Emergency workers lay sprawled on their backs on the floor.

Naomi and the children were stretched out on the bed. Hank was sitting in the recliner. For a moment, she felt relieved.

A rustling noise from upstairs made her gasp.

Oh, God, he's here. Brian's here.

Her heart pounded in her chest.

The noise was on the steps now.

He's coming.

"Mommy, where's Daddy? Is he okay?"

Nealey let out a breath and put her hand to her chest. *The kids.*

"Come here," she said, managing to conceal her fear and keep her voice from cracking. She was furious that they'd left but relieved that it wasn't Brian.

"Hold Mommy's hand tight. Don't let go. It's okay."

Even as she said it, she felt sick to her stomach, felt that sense of dread that had been nagging her for days.

But maybe I'm wrong, she insisted. *Maybe they're just napping.*

Her shoulders relaxed. Her back straightened.

"It's okay," she whispered to Nicholas, "I think they're just napping."

Then Nealey's bare feet squished through something warm and wet on the carpet.

"Oh, gross," she said and looked down. A pool of blood cupped her feet. She blinked her eyes and saw a trail of droplets that led to the bed.

God, oh God.

Nealey's mouth felt dry. A pervasive darkness spread through her body and soul. She braced herself on the wall.

"Hello there, Nealey," a deep voice called to her. "You and the kids come on and join us. We're having a blast."

Nealey inhaled a sharp breath. A sickening feeling overwhelmed her when she recognized the voice.

"Brian? Where are you? You're scaring us."

The closet door flew open. "Boo!" he yelled and jumped in front of them.

Nicholas yelled, Lauren screamed, and Nealey felt her knees turn to rubber.

"Brian, what are you doing?" She resisted the urge to scream at him. "You scared my kids."

"Hi, kids. Sorry about that," he said. "Just playing hide and seek."

Nealey swallowed hard. "The children, Brian."

The tall, wild-eyed man in front of her held a gun in one hand, phone in the other. He turned toward the bed.

"Well," he smirked. "No need to worry. The cops are already here."

He pointed to the chair beside the bed.

"There's Hank sitting right over there, and I hear your backup shuffling around upstairs. Too late."

When Nealey took a step forward, Brian stuck out his arm. "Nope," he said, "not so fast. Sit down on the bed."

Nealey hesitated.

"Move it!"

Startled, she grabbed the kids and plopped down on the edge of the bed. "Don't worry," she lied and gathered them close to her. "It's going to be all right. I promise."

Brian tapped the screen on his phone with his thumb, keeping the gun aimed directly at them.

Nealey glanced at the steps. *Could we make it? I can't just sit here and let him shoot my kids!*

"I wanna go sit with my Daddy," Lauren said and began to cry.

"Quiet!" Brian's voice sounded like booming thunder.

The children huddled as close to their mother as they could get. Lauren scrambled onto her lap. "I'm afraid, Mommy," she said.

"Shut up!" Brian yelled. In an instant, he was bending down in front of them, the gun pointed right at Lauren's face. "Didn't you hear me, you little brat? Be quiet so I can make this call."

Nealey bit her lip to keep from screaming. She kissed the top of Lauren's head and wrapped an arm around her. The little girl didn't cry. Nealey could feel her trembling. In a whispered monotone, Lauren said, "I pee-peed in my pants, Mommy. I'm sorry."

The smell of baby shampoo, that precious clean smell, brought more tears to her eyes, but she refused to cry in front of her children. They needed her strength. "It's okay," she whispered, trying to sound reassuring. "You're my brave little girl."

She gathered Nicholas close. "I love you, my sweeties. It'll be okay."

Brian covered the phone with his hand. "Shut up, I said!"

Then, in calm, cool tone, he said, "I need to report a murder/suicide at 701 Charming Lakes Drive."

Brian tapped his phone off.

Nealey hugged the children and rocked back and forth. *No. No. Oh God. Oh God. Help us, please.*

"Drop your gun!" someone shouted. "Drop it!"

Before she closed her eyes, Nealey saw a flash of white light haloed in gold. It swirled at her feet. Lightning quick, the swirl grew and travelled upward until it wrapped the three of them in a tingling blanket of warmth.

All her fears melted away, and she heard her children giggle.

The rounds of shots sounded no more ominous than a low roll of thunder.

Chapter 1

June

The Playhouse Inn stood serenely atop the cliff-lined canyons of the Cumberland Plateau in a tiny town called Highland, Tennessee. The back balconies of the inn overlooked one of numerous, deep canyon gorges whose icy waters tumbled over ancient stones and teemed with rare species of wildlife. Native hardwood trees, centuries old, arched across the river-carved valley in a dense canopy. Roaring waterfalls sprung from the sides of the cliffs and cascaded into rushing waters of the Highland Rim River. Although it was well over a hundred and thirty years old, the inn had remained relatively unchanged.

Sylvie Wolcott, owner of the Playhouse Inn and a world-renowned chef and cookbook author, stood in her kitchen at the Inn and sliced the last of her juicy white apples, gathered the peels, and dropped them into a pot of boiling water sweetened with a bit of clear corn syrup. In a smaller pan, she poured a half cup of Glenlivet scotch, taking a little nip first to test its taste. A second sip confirmed her choice.

"Delightful," she said.

Into the pan with the scotch went a stick of softened butter. From a tin on the shelf by the window, she withdrew a pinch of golden powder.

"Ah, my special ingredient," she said and sprinkled it over the simmering mixture.

She leaned forward and inhaled the delicious aroma.

"Perfect," she said. "Double crust apple butterscotch pie."

She squeezed her hands together and smiled. "Oh, I believe my readers will adore it."

Sylvie walked to the pantry to get the brown sugar and opened the big double doors. From one of the two head-high built-in shelving units, she spied the sugar and lifted it off the shelf. When the subtle scent of flowers wafted into the pantry, she hesitated. *Jasmine?*

Sylvie shrugged then closed the doors.

Something on the floor by the kitchen entrance caught her attention: her suitcase, her favorite Louis Vuitton. The bulges in the sides told her it was fully packed.

"What on earth is *that* doing down here?"

Atop the suitcase was a cream-colored envelope with the word "*Sylvie*" written in script.

Sylvie picked up the envelope and took out a sheet of paper.

"*Sylvie,*" it read, "*you must go to Nealey. She needs you. Go quickly.*"

"My sweet Nealey," Sylvie said. "What could be wrong?"

Sylvie turned the paper over but found nothing on the back. She glanced around the room for any sign of who could have left both her suitcase and the message.

The aroma of the cooking apples brought her to the stove again.

"Oh, dear, I hope they're not overcooked," she said as she turned off the burners.

Once again, she read the message.

"*Go to Nealey. Go quickly.*"

A rap at the kitchen door startled her.

"Miss Sylvie," her driver said, "the car is parked out front. Whenever you're ready, we'll leave."

For a moment, Sylvie simply stared at him.

"But how did you know I needed to leave? Who told you to bring the car around?"

He hesitated for a few seconds.

"Well, you did, Miss Sylvie, about an hour ago. You said we needed to go immediately to Kentucky to see Miss Nealey."

"No, I didn't tell you that. I'm certain I didn't."

"But you phoned me," he said, then pointed to the envelope. "There's another one of those on the back seat of the car, Miss Sylvie."

Sylvie wrung her hands.

"I've been in the kitchen since dawn working on this new recipe. Don't you think I would remember if I'd phoned you? Something is not right."

The driver lowered his head.

"It sounded like you, Miss Sylvie."

Sylvie took off her apron and laid it across the chair.

"Mercy," she said. "I wish I knew what was happening. If there's the slightest chance that my Nealey is in harm's way, I must go to her. So, I will simply trust this message. It certainly isn't the first time the unexplained has happened at this inn, and I'm quite sure it won't be the last."

"I'll take your bag," the driver said.

"Thank you," Sylvie said and fished in her purse for her cell phone. She dialed Nealey's number but got no answer.

"What is going on, here?" she mumbled to herself. "What could be wrong with my precious niece?"

She dialed another number.

When her friend answered, Sylvie said, "Can you come right away? I have guests, but I need to leave. Something's happened to Nealey, or at least, I think it has. I'll explain later."

She tried Nealey's number again with no success.

Nealey, darling, what is wrong?

"We need to leave, Miss Sylvie," the driver said.

"Yes," she said and brushed a stray strand of hair from her forehead. "Yes, I suppose we do."

On her way out, she glanced up the stairs.

"They must still be sleeping, thank goodness," Sylvie mumbled.

She climbed into the car and picked up the second envelope.

"Sylvie, dear, there has been a terrible tragedy—a heinous act—a shooting by the man named Brian."

"Brian?" Sylvie said. "Nealey's ex-brother-in-law? Oh, she has always been terrified of him!"

She read on.

"Brian has shot and killed Nealey's husband, Hank, and their two children, Nicholas and Lauren. He killed her sister, Naomi, and her little boys, as well, before the police could fell him. Nealey was present at the shooting in Naomi's house. She is wounded, but she is alive."

Sylvie gasped. Her heart raced.

"Oh, no, no," she said. "Not my Nealey's family."

Sylvie covered her face with her hands and sobbed, then straightened herself and finished reading the message.

"Nealey will need you now more than ever, dear Sylvie. She will need your strength and your guidance. Do all that you can for her."

The letter was signed with only one word: *Worthy.*

Chapter 2

November

"Careful, Nealey, don't get too close to the edge," Aunt Sylvie called from the balcony of the Playhouse Inn. "I don't usually let people walk out there. One little slip is all it takes. I'm on my way to a book signing, darling girl. Please stay away from that edge," Sylvie said. "But first, let's unload the car and get your things."

One little slip, Nealey thought as she imagined herself falling headlong into the wild pink dogwoods and purple azaleas that sprouted magically from the rocks, as if they needed nothing but stone to sustain them.

She inched her right foot closer to the edge of the cliff, leaned over ever so slightly, and peered down at the water.

So this is what a thousand feet high looks like.

She spread out her arms. *How I wish I could fly, just fly away, up and away from this most unbearable life.*

A powerful set of arms grabbed her from behind and moved her away from the cliff's edge.

"Excuse me, but you're a little too close to that edge for my comfort."

She stared wide-eyed at the chest of the towering man beside her.

Nealey shielded her eyes with her hand and looked up and up until she saw his face.

His blue eyes, broad shoulders—broader than any she'd ever seen—and black hair resembled Hank's. He wore spotless, sharply-creased khaki pants and a clean white pullover shirt underneath a windbreaker with The Playhouse Inn monogrammed on the front pocket.

"Name's Benton Aimes. I'm the custodian here," he said, his deep baritone voice soothing in her ears.

He stepped back and stuck his hands in the pockets of his jacket. "Sorry if I overstepped my boundaries, but you scared me. Just an instinct to pull you back."

"You thought I was going to jump?" Nealey asked.

"Well, no, but I thought you might fall," he said. "Aunt Sylvie is waiting at the car, and she would tan my hide if something happened to you. Besides, people don't usually come out to the back like this, especially newcomers like you."

"Like me?"

She lowered her head and moved pebbles around in random patterns with her foot.

"Like you," Benton said. "Not familiar with this place. That's all," he said softly. Then he turned and walked toward the front of the inn. "I'll get your bags out of the car."

"I can get them," she said, still looking at the ground. "Don't trouble yourself."

She turned to tell him, but he had already rounded the corner to the front of the house. The mountain air seemed unusually cold, even in August, so she wrapped her arms around herself as tightly as she could and followed after him.

Aunt Sylvie stood beside the car in her usual attire: a broad-brimmed floppy straw hat; her long dark auburn hair pulled back tightly from her face and tied at the back of her neck with a dangling red ribbon. A scattering of freckles dotted the bridge of her nose on an otherwise smooth and glowing complexion. A pair of black trousers, a bright red, printed tunic with bell sleeves, and black tennis shoes completed the "Aunt Sylvie" look.

"I'm off," she said, her voice like a melody. "You'll be fine won't you, darling?"

Sylvie walked toward Nealey and hugged her.

"It's only overnight. There will be people around in case you need anything."

"I've already met one of them," Nealey said. "No worries, I'll be careful. I'm not a stranger here, you know. I practically grew up at the inn. I know this place well. But your Mr. Benton ...."

"Benton?" Sylvie interrupted. She cocked her head to the side. "You've seen him today? He must have come back early. Good, where is he now?"

"Is something wrong?"

"No, of course not. Benton's a jewel, one of a kind. I thought he was on a camping trip in the mountains." She patted Nealey on the shoulders. "Now, I'll only be gone one night. And darling, remember it's been a long time since you were here last. Some things have changed."

"It looks almost the same on the outside."

Sylvie chuckled. "I'm afraid the inside has undergone numerous incarnations. I can never seem to make up my mind about decor. Always trying to figure out what looks best in which room."

Sylvie waved her hand.

"Benton's here, but if there's anything you need, you have my cell phone number, right? I'm only a few hours away. After the signing, I'm meeting friends for dinner. You can call me anytime, though, for anything, and I'll come scootin' back."

"Now, Aunt Sylvie, I wouldn't have you disappoint your fans."

Sylvie smiled and kissed her. "Do me a favor?"

Nealey raised an eyebrow. "Favor?"

"Before our guests arrive, see if you can find something a little more elegant than fleece pants and a sweatshirt. But even if you don't, you're such a stunner it won't really matter. Look at that hair," she said and ran her fingers along the top of Nealey's head. "Red as ever, and those eyes, still as vivid green as they were when you were a child."

She put her arm around Nealey's shoulder. "Just look at you, honey. You're skin and bones, fragile as a porcelain doll. Oh, by the way, I put a little surprise in your room. Hope you like it."

"Mrs. Wolcott, we need to go," the driver called.

"I'm so sorry I have to leave just when you're arriving. That's timing for you, isn't it?" Sylvie plopped onto the back seat. "But I'll see you tomorrow night."

"Oh, wait! I need to get my bags." Nealey said. "Can you open the trunk again?"

The trunk popped open, but when Nealey peered inside, she saw nothing but Aunt Sylvie's overnight bag. "Where are my bags, Aunt Sylvie?"

A familiar voice said, "I took them to your room."

Benton stood on the wide front steps. "Isn't that where they belong?"

Nealey knitted her eyebrows together. *How did he do that so quickly?*

She shrugged then closed the trunk.

"How are you, Aunt Sylvie?" Benton asked. "Off for another book signing?"

"I'm just fine. I thought you weren't due back for another day or two. But I'm glad you're here. You can watch over Nealey for me while I'm gone, won't you?"

"I'll do my best. Everything is taken care of."

He smiled and winked at Aunt Sylvie. "Don't worry yourself."

Sylvie waved from the back seat. "I love you, Nealey. Don't forget that. Oh, and by the way, did I tell you I remodeled all five bedrooms on the second floor? You'll adore yours. It's so ... so you!"

"What about the third floor?"

"Oh, it's a disaster up there! Only a few weeks into the renovation, it's a holy mess, so don't go rummaging around or you might end up falling through the floor! I've had to turn down more than a few guests because of it. But I have word that since the second floor is completely finished and inspected, I can call some of my regulars and book rooms for them. So, there's no one here but us for right now, but all of that will change in a couple of weeks."

Nealey chuckled and waved.

The wide front steps of the inn were flanked by two enormous columns. Freshly painted in a brilliant white, they almost glowed. The long porch, white trim around new windows, shining oak, double doors with bright gold handles made the 1880s inn sparkle in the sunlight. Six hanging baskets filled with flaming red begonias hung at intervals along the porch.

"It's too cold for begonias," she said and started up the steps.

"Ah, but your Aunt Sylvie has a way with flowers," Benton said. "Why don't you go in and get settled? There's a nice warm fire in the living room."

"Thanks for getting my bags," she said. "I'm not a stranger to the Playhouse Inn. I know about the cliffs, and I wasn't going to jump."

Benton rubbed his hands together. "You'd better go in before you freeze."

Nealey put her hand out to open the door.

Promise me you'll never go back there, Nealey. Promise me you'll never set foot in the Playhouse Inn again.

Her mother's voice. The last words she said before she died three years ago.

Her hands trembled. *Swear to me you'll never go back there. Swear it!*

Chill bumps crept along Nealey's spine.

She tightened her grip on the door handle. She pictured herself and her mother driving in the old Nova. Her sister Naomi hadn't wanted to come, so she spent the weekend with the Simpsons next door, mainly to putter in their three lush gardens and see Johnny, the Simpson's youngest. When she and her mom had pulled into the driveway, Aunt Sylvie had run out and greeted them with bear hugs. They were all so happy. But after the first night there, when the very first ghost appeared in front of her mother, her mother gathered her up in her arms and sped out of the driveway so fast that gravel went flying and tire marks blackened the road behind them.

After that night, thirty years of anger, fear, and hatred turned the once-lovely woman she knew as her mother into a lonely, paranoid recluse given to crying jags, drunken stupors, and temper tantrums. Someone cold, frightened, and angry had replaced the elegant, smiling, tender woman.

"Are you all right?" Benton called.

She pushed, and the doors swung open.

"Forgive me," she said.

"Maybe," Benton called to her from the bottom of the steps.

She turned in surprise and looked at him.

"Maybe you should forgive yourself."

He saluted Nealey with his index finger. "I'll be in the guest house if you need me."

"What?"

He'd taken only a few steps when he said, "Tell Lulu I said hello."

Before she stepped inside, Nealey stopped. She didn't remember Aunt Sylvie mentioning anyone named Lulu.

"Who's Lulu?"

Benton was gone. All Nealey saw in the fading sunset was the silhouette of a man seated on a large rock at the top of the hill. Storm clouds rolled above him, the sound of thunder echoed throughout the plateau. When two thin bolts of lightning seemed to strike near him, she winced.

But the man didn't move. Instead, his enormous hands began to rise and fall in graceful waves, like an artist's as he released and caught two fluorescent, spinning beams.

Nealey felt acid rise into her throat. When her knees began to tremble, she caught hold of the door to steady herself.

She remembered the haloed swirls of light, but when had she seen them? Where? Vivid images overtook her: her life before the murders, a happy life filled with family dinners, picnics, hugs and kisses, a life filled with love.

Why would I want to survive this? Why?

Nealey slumped to the floor of the porch. *My children, my sweet sister. My husband, my wonderful Hank. Gone, just like that. All of them gone.*

She closed her eyes and drifted into a welcomed semi-consciousness.

Chapter 3

From her room at The Playhouse Inn, sunlight streamed through the large picture windows on each side of the antique, four-poster bed where Nealey yawned and snuggled into luxurious silk sheets. She pulled the down comforter over her head and closed her eyes. *Just a few more minutes. Then I'll get up and get Hank and the kids ...* she forgot, momentarily, that Hank and her kids were gone.

Nothing mattered to her then except that they were gone, her whole family, even her unborn child, dead. She had no enthusiasm for living and spent weeks doing nothing but sleeping, wandering around the empty house in a fog, crying, then sleeping. She'd felt cut off from the world, as if an invisible barrier separated her from everyone and everything, a cast away, drifting alone on a sea of tears.

And then, Aunt Sylvie visited a second time and changed everything. In only a month or so, their little house was sold, Nealey quit her job, and Aunt Sylvie moved her into The Playhouse Inn. It had happened, but Nealey remembered so little of it. Then as now, her grief consumed her.

She drew the comforter up under her neck and sobbed until she felt she had no more tears. She wiped her eyes and surveyed the surroundings. A crystal chandelier hung from the high ceiling, brocaded wallpaper covered the top portion of each wall separated from the lower portion by a chair rail painted gold. Built-in bookcases covered two walls, each one filled with books of all shapes and sizes. A light scent of jasmine wafted throughout the room. A hint of a smile slowly made its way to her lips.

My bedroom. I remember it now, different, more elegant, but the same.

The bed, flanked by two marble-topped nightstands, reminded her of something she might see in a magazine: four shining posters, a lovely white silk scarf draped through them; an ornate headboard crowned with delicately carved cherubs.

Nealey traced the carvings with her fingers.

How did I get here?

Two separate seating areas, one in front of each window, held overstuffed, navy-blue leather chairs and marble-topped side tables. To the right of the double doors stood a gilded, full-length cheval glass mirror.

Nealey dangled her legs over the side of the bed.

"Who is it?" Nealey called. "Who's out there?"

No one answered.

Nealey stood up, her heart beating faster. "Who's out there?"

No answer came.

But lumbering through the door was the biggest, ugliest dog Nealey had ever seen. She gasped and sat back down on the bed.

The size of a small pony, the dog had long, thin legs, wide shoulders, and a massive head, all covered in grayish-brown wiry fur. The eyes were almost hidden by the hair growing on the face. And all around the chin, fur hung like a scraggly beard. A pink collar studded with multi-colored rhinestones hung around the neck, with a heart-shaped tag that read, "Lulu."

The dog sat at Nealey's feet and stared at her. Never afraid of any animal, and with a special fondness for dogs, Nealey lifted her hand and patted its head.

"So, you're Lulu," she said, her voice barely above a whisper.

The dog stood up and wagged her tail, creating a substantial breeze.

"You are, without a doubt, the biggest dog I've ever seen," her mind jumping to an image of Paul Bunyan and his big ox named Blue.

"You and Benton," she said then shook her head. "Nah," she whispered, "he's too handsome to be Paul Bunyan, and you're much too pretty to be an old ox!"

Lulu's bark, surprisingly gentle and soft, reminded Nealey of a human mother's cooing, almost as if Lulu understood.

Nealey made the bed then stood in front of one of the huge windows.

I used to stare out these windows while Aunt Sylvie cooked. Good days.

The Great Smoky Mountain chain surrounded the grounds,

yet in the distance, it wasn't a mountain but something else that caught her attention. An enormous rock sat atop the lone hill that sloped toward the main guest house. When the door of the guest house opened and Benton emerged, Nealey stepped away from the window.

Benton! Of course! He must have brought me up here. Who else could have done it?

Nealey glanced around the room.

"Ah, the closet. Yes, I remember it," she whispered.

As she moved toward it, she caught her reflection in the mirror and stopped dead still.

"Girl, you look awful." She ran her hands along the dirty sleeves of her sweatshirt, then down the legs of her pants, both of them hanging loose on her small body. She pushed back her stringy hair with her hands and leaned in close to the mirror. No makeup, dark circles under her eyes, pale lips, sallow, blotchy skin.

She shook her head in disgust.

Lulu again barked that soft and feminine little bark.

"I'm a mess from head to toe."

Nealey turned the doorknob. An enormous closet abundant with hanging space, shelves, built-in cabinets, and a mirrored back wall greeted her. On one of the shelves sat her large duffle bag. On the other, her two smaller bags. Nealey exhaled.

"My bags," she said. "Thank goodness."

She opened one of the small bags then stared for a moment at the other. She ran her hand across its surface.

Never again.

She turned her thoughts to the bag in front of her and carefully retrieved her treasures: five framed photos, her favorite of which was of her wedding, Hank tall and proud beside her, both of them smiling as if that cherished moment would last forever.

How could we have known? How could anyone have known?

Her eyes misted, but she took a deep breath, swallowed hard, and sent the tears away. A large chest of drawers and a vanity table graced the opposite wall, so Nealey walked across the huge room, photos in hand, to give them a perfect place to rest. The closer she got to the furniture, the stronger the scent of jasmine became.

She chose the top of the ornate mahogany chest of drawers

and carefully set the photos so that she could see all of them from the bed. She and Naomi as toddlers, Aunt Sylvie and their mother behind them, all smiling; Nicholas at his second birthday party; Lauren at her first; the wedding photo, and a family portrait taken only a month before the murders.

Nealey picked up the photo with her mother and Aunt Sylvie in it.

For a moment, she looked puzzled. She'd seen the photo every day for years but it was only now that she noticed her own resemblance to Aunt Sylvie. The hair color was different, but the facial features—even the freckles—seemed almost identical. She wondered why she'd never noticed it before.

She shrugged and set the picture back in its place.

Then something else caught her attention. She lifted her chin and sniffed. The jasmine scent was almost overpowering. On the vanity table, an overturned perfume bottle, the stopper askew, solved the mystery. Nealey picked up the glass bottle and saw the word, "Heavenly," engraved in gold across the front. She set the bottle upright and replaced the stopper.

She waved a hand across her nose.

"Whew, strong stuff."

She walked back to the small bag in the closet. Aunt Sylvie had told her there was a surprise waiting for her in her bag. So, she dug down to the very bottom, and pulled out a shaft of blue paper folded into three sections. Aunt Sylvie had attached a note:

Darling,

It's been one year since that horrible night. It is time for you to begin to heal. You can do that by taking on extra responsibilities. I wouldn't trust just anyone with my precious inn. My book signings and tours, not to mention writing new books, take so much of my time. I simply cannot manage all of my responsibilities alone any longer. My deepest wish is that you will grow to love the Playhouse Inn, even with all its little eccentricities. I will teach you all you need to know to be the perfect innkeeper, and I shall enjoy every moment of it. It is a gift for you, my darling girl, and such a joyous blessing for me. All my love, Aunt Sylvie

Nealey gasped and sat down on the bed again, shocked by what she'd just read.

What? Co-owner?

Nealey covered her mouth with her hand.

No, no, she thought, that can't be right.

Lulu licked her hand.

Nealey jerked it back, startled, then let it fall again. Her heart raced and she could hear her own heartbeat thrumming in her ears.

Co-owner? Me? I know nothing about running an inn. Nothing.

"Sorry, girl," she said to the dog, her voice trembling. "I'm a little bit nervous. Lick all you want. I need a shower."

The bathroom door, right next to the chest of drawers, had no knob, but its hinges gave it away. Nealey pushed the door open and entered a room filled with light. Large windows, a huge skylight, white marble floors, a crystal chandelier, and frameless shower doors enclosing a tiled walk-in-shower.

She scrubbed and rinsed, and then relaxed under the warm water. Afterward, she pulled on a pair of jeans, buttoned up the new lace-trimmed blouse that Sylvie had bought her, and ponytailed her long red hair. A touch of makeup, a white ribbon around the ponytail, clean tennis shoes, and a splash of her perfume gave her a sudden lightness of heart.

"I can do this. I can learn to run an inn and take pleasure in meeting new people."

She fairly galloped down the winding staircase that led to the first floor. She was hungry, for the first time in longer than she could remember, so she headed for the kitchen, Lulu right beside her.

They passed the library, the parlor, the living room, and the dining room, all elegant and newly-refurbished in the grand style of her bedroom.

Sylvie's right. The inside is totally different.

Toward the back of the inn, Nealey saw double metal swinging doors with large glass panes in them.

She reached to push open the door, but Lulu sat solidly in front of her and would not let her move. Even sitting, the dog was tall enough to impede her actions. When she reached a second time for the door, Lulu nudged her away and whined.

"Lulu, move girl. I want to see the how Aunt Sylvie's redone the kitchen. Besides, I'm starving."

Why am I talking to this dog as if she understands what I say?

She tried to step around Lulu, tried to get in back of her and to scoot her out of the way, but nothing budged the enormous dog.

Maybe she knows commands.

"Heel, Lulu," Nealey said and snapped her fingers.

Lulu eased her large head between the doors, turned it this way and that then gazed up at Nealey. She got up and sat at Nealey's heels.

"What were you doing, making sure the coast was clear?" The words frightened Nealey even as she said them. "Come on, let's go get something to eat."

It seemed perfectly natural to talk to the dog now. Nealey felt certain that somewhere in that doggy brain of Lulu's, the language cylinders were firing full blast.

She took the first step through the door.

Aunt Sylvie's decorating style didn't extend to the kitchen with its lime green cabinets, black and white linoleum floor, yellow wallpaper with a rooster and chicken motif, a red and chrome table with six chairs, an old refrigerator, an even older stove.

"Yuck, just as I remember it." She scrunched up her face and moved forward until she saw the new apron sink, a lovely picture window above it with interior and exterior window boxes filled with various kinds of herbs. There were new stone countertops, a second shiny stove with double oven, and even a dishwasher.

Nealey ran her hand along the smooth countertops. "Nice."

She opened the fridge and found it fully stocked, almost overflowing with food.

"How about some bacon and eggs, Lulu?"

When she turned around, she didn't see the dog anywhere.

She shrugged and assembled her cooking arsenal.

On a shelf beside the cabinet, a myriad of books stood like ready soldiers. Nealey scanned the titles: *Earth Magick for the Beginner, Magical Scents, Beginner's Guide to Spellcasting,* and *The Healing Power of Plants.*

She wiped her hands on a dish towel and slipped one of the books from its place. It showed no creases or signs of wear but didn't seem to be new, just unread. On the inside was an inscription. "To our delightful Sylvie. From Noble and Worthy."

Noble and Worthy?

Nealey flipped through some of the pages but her stomach growled again, so she replaced the book. She'd ask Aunt Sylvie about it later.

"I've seen those books before," she mumbled.

A vivid scene played out in her mind, a scene from long ago.

"They're dangerous," her mother warned. "Don't you dare touch any of those books!"

The words made Nealey all the more curious.

She sneaked in while her mother and Aunt Sylvie were talking and climbed up on the counter. She reached for one of the largest books, but it was so heavy that it fell from her hands and onto the floor with a loud thud. Mother and Aunt Sylvie came running.

When her mother saw the book, her face turned bright red, but before she could begin the ranting, Aunt Sylvie picked up the book.

"For God's sake, Charlotte. It's just a book. It can't hurt the child."

Aunt Sylvie replaced it, took Nealey's hand and helped her off the counter, then issued an order to her sister.

"Charlotte, loosen up and climb down off that high horse. There's nothing there that can hurt this child. She's my niece. I'd never allow any harm to come to her. Now, let's go into the parlor and finish our tea."

"It's a good thing I'm her mother!" Charlotte snapped. "Otherwise, she'd be just like you."

Nealey shook her head and brought herself back to the present and her rumbling stomach.

The smell of frying bacon soon filled the kitchen. Nealey popped two pieces of bread into the toaster, fumbled in the drawers and found an egg whisk. She drained the bacon on a paper towel then poured in the eggs.

But instead of eggs and bacon, she smelled a light floral scent.

Nealey cocked her head, sniffed, and caught the subtle fragrance only briefly. *Jasmine?*

She sniffed again but smelled only bacon and eggs.

She stepped to the window above the sink and scanned the selection of potted herbs and plants. No jasmine.

I smelled it. I know I did.

She shrugged it off when her stomach growled. Salt and pepper shaker in hand, she seasoned the eggs and stirred, watching carefully so that they wouldn't burn.

"Hey, don't forget about us. We're hungry, too," the voices said.

Children's voices.

Nealey gasped and whirled around.

Two little girls sat at the table.

They smiled at Nealey and smoothed their yellow dresses.

Then, they vanished.

Chapter 4

"Smells like something's burning," Benton said.

He stood in the doorway, a hulking silhouette awash in morning sunlight. Nealey could barely see his face, but she recognized the voice and the sheer size of the man.

He was beside her before she could blink. "Need some help?"

Nealey opened her mouth to speak, but no words came.

Benton turned off the burner, removed the pan, and scraped the blackened eggs into the trash.

Nealey watched him go to the fridge and retrieve more eggs. "Why don't you have a seat and let me fix these for you. I make a mean omelet."

"N-n-no, thank you." Her voice came back, but she could hear the fear in it. "I'm not really hungry now."

Benton pulled out one of the chairs. "Sit. You look like you could use some food. Please?"

She felt Lulu's cold nose on her back nudging her forward.

"I thought you ran out on me," Nealey said to the dog. "Now, here you are. I didn't even see you come in."

"She usually sits by the door. I saw her when I came in," Benton said. "She always knows when someone's coming. Irish wolfhounds are like that."

"An Irish wolfhound, oh, no wonder she's so big," Nealey said.

"As long as she's around, you don't have to be afraid of anything."

"Afraid?" she asked, the images of the two little girls still crystal clear in her mind. Benton whisking the eggs almost drowned out her trembling voice.

He took the pan, wiped it out, then took it over to the sink. He pinched off several bits from the fresh herbs in the window boxes and sprinkled them liberally into the pan.

Nealey watched the way his big hands delicately worked with the herbs.

After he'd beaten the eggs again, he poured the herbs into them.

In only a couple of minutes, Benton set an omelet with a side of bacon on the table. "So, how does it look?"

Lulu whined.

"Don't worry. I made enough for you," Benton said and filled the dog's bowl.

She lapped it up in a few bites.

"You're not going to eat?" Benton asked.

"I just don't, I just can't," she said and moved the omelet around on her plate with her fork. "I appreciate your trouble, but ...."

"Won't you at least try it?"

Nealey took one bite. The eggs were firm but not hard, just right. The omelet melted in her mouth, the taste of it unlike any she'd ever had before. *Delicious.*

"What did you do to these? They're wonderful."

She took another bite, and it was even better.

Benton chuckled as she finished the omelet, scraping every last bite off the plate.

Nealey sighed and leaned back in the chair. "You didn't tell me what you did to make those eggs taste so good. I don't think I've ever eaten so fast in all my life."

Benton smiled. "I'm a fan of your Aunt Sylvie's cookbooks. I got the recipe out of the first one: *The Magical Art of Breakfast*.

He took her empty plate and set it in the sink. "You ever read one of her books?"

Nealey shook her head. "I'm not much of a cook. I just never got interested in ..." She stopped. Her heart felt suddenly so heavy that she could barely breathe. *Cheese grits with peanut butter and jelly sandwiches, their last dinner. What kind of wife and mother would fix that mess and call it dinner?* Tears ran down her cheeks and her knees felt almost like rubber, ready to give way at any moment. A great sob came from her as she braced herself on the counter.

Benton moved close to her and wrapped his arms around her.

"I'm so sorry about your family, Nealey. So very sorry."

When she'd cried for several minutes and finally stopped and moved away from Benton, she went to the sink and splashed cold water on her face then dried it with the nearest hand towel.

"You'd think I'd be a little better by now," she said. "But sometimes, the grief just washes over me in waves. I can't control it. It just comes when I least expect it."

"Grief is a harsh taskmaster," he said. "It will get better in time, but it won't go away, so you just do the best you can one day at a time."

Nealey nodded.

"Thanks," she said.

"By the way, I'm not a great cook, either," Benton said. "Most of the time, it doesn't really matter about how good the eggs taste. It matters more that I made the effort. That's what counts, isn't it? That we care enough to make an effort?"

The prickly sensation in her nose warned her that she was about to cry again.

You are not going to cry!

Nealey stood up beside the table. "So, you're saying that the eggs tasted good just because you tried your best?"

"Lord, no!" Benton slung a dishrag over his shoulder. "They tasted *good* because I used Aunt Sylvie's recipe, but they tasted even *better* because I made them especially for you."

"Well, thank you," she said, a slight smile forming on her lips, "for going to all that trouble just for me."

Benton stood with his back to her, rinsing off the dishes. "No trouble."

Nealey saw the way the fabric of his shirt strained against his broad back and tightened against the heavy muscles of his arms. Her eyes followed the breadth of his shoulders then the middle of his back and down to his fairly narrow waist. *There's probably not an ounce of fat on him.*

"Did you ..." she hesitated. "Was it you who carried me upstairs last night?"

Benton nodded.

Nealey brushed a stray wisp of hair off her forehead and looked down at the floor.

"Thank you," she said, wanting for some reason to avoid his eyes. "I can't remember much except saying goodbye then waking up in a strange bed."

Benton dried his hands on the towel, folded it, and draped it across the sink divider. "You needed help," he said, a huge smile on his face. "I couldn't leave you out there in the cold. Your Aunt Sylvie would've killed me!"

Nealey felt her face flush.

He has such a beautiful smile, so genuine, caring. His eyes are as blue as the sea, and look how they sparkle when he smiles.

She almost formed a smile of her own until the voice inside of her yelled, *'You two-timing cheater! Hank's only been dead a year, and here you are thinking about another man.'*

The smile never formed on Nealey's lips.

The bright one on Benton's face disappeared. He went back to drying the dishes. "One of your guests is already here," he said, "on the front porch."

"What? I didn't hear the doorbell."

"No, you wouldn't. Noble's always the first to arrive. He sits on the porch and waits for his brother. Won't come in without him."

Nealey walked toward the swinging doors but stopped just before she pushed them open. "Benton?"

"Yeah?"

"Have you ever seen, I mean, did you ever see anything strange in here?"

"There's usually always something a bit strange in Sylvie's kitchen," Benton said and winked.

Nealey didn't respond. Instead, she gave him a serious look.

"This morning, I saw, no, I *thought* I saw two little girls, red-headed twins."

Lulu barked her soft but strong bark.

A sharp pain shot though Nealey's right eye then traveled across the top of her head. She closed her eyes and massaged her temples.

No, no. Not a migraine. Not now.

Lulu licked her right hand and whined. She kept licking until Nealey felt as if the skin might come off. She pulled her hand away.

"Need an aspirin?" Benton asked.

"No, it wouldn't help. The girls were sitting right there," she said and pointed at the table. "Then all of a sudden, they just vanished."

Benton looked puzzled. "Vanished?"

"You don't believe me?"

Her head throbbed. Then, without warning, the pain subsided. Within a few seconds, it had gone. "I don't blame you," she said, her voice barely above a whisper. "I must sound like a lunatic. I don't know why I told you about them."

Benton stood beside her. "Nealey," he said and put his hands on her shoulders, "you're not crazy. What you saw was real enough, wasn't it?"

Nealey nodded her head.

The doorbell rang, and Nealey jumped.

"There's nothing here that will hurt you, so no worries," Benton said. "I'd better get that door. I'm sure it's the Gates brothers."

Benton looked at his watch. "As usual, they're here early, but old Noble beat his brother again. He'll be thrilled that he was the first again this year. Come on. You'll love them."

"Again this year, so they've been here before?"

"Yeah, they came last year, at about this same time, the beginning of October."

Lulu plopped down in front of Nealey and blocked the doorway. She looked up at her with her big brown eyes and whined.

"Is something wrong, girl?"

Benton clapped his hands. "It's just the Gates brothers. They mean no harm."

Lulu sat with her huge paws covering her head, whining with each breath.

Nealey bent down and stroked her head. "It's okay. I promise."

She had heard her own voice saying the same thing to her children many times, even on the day they were murdered. She was always telling them that every outing would be wonderful and that they would have such a good time, they'd never want to leave. Pangs of guilt shot through her like jolts of electricity. Nealey whimpered.

Lulu was up immediately, nudging her with her head. One soft bark alerted Benton, and he kneeled down beside her on the floor.

"Nealey, you did the best you could," he said and lifted her to her feet.

"What did you say?" Nealey asked. "How did you ...."

Benton shrugged and repeated, "You did your best."

"No, I let them down," Nealey said. "I lied to my babies. I lied to them. The last thing they heard from me was a lie."

Lulu put a cold nose to the inside of Nealey's elbow and purred like a cat.

Something strong surged through Nealey, and instantly, she stood straighter. The urge to cry left her. She took a deep breath, looked up at Benton, then wrapped both arms around Lulu's neck.

"Good dog," she said. "Are you hungry?"

Then a barely audible knock came to the door.

Benton opened the door just as two little girls' voices called, "The bad man's coming."

Chapter 5

Nealey was still trembling as they made their way into the entrance hall. The girls' voices rang in her ears.

The bad man's coming.

When the doorbell rang a second time, she cowered. Too afraid to move, she hoped that Benton would open the door and greet the guests.

I can't do this. What will I say to them? "Oh, by the way, there are two ghosts in the kitchen, little girls who told me they were hungry then told me ...."

Nealey couldn't bear to think about it.

When the doorbell rang again, all she could do was cover her face with her hands. She wished she could transport herself back to her house, the one she and Hank had lived in. Aunt Sylvie had come right after and stayed with her, but Nealey hardly noticed her. Once she left, Sylvie called daily, and to each inquiry about her mental and physical health, Nealey replied, "I'm fine."

Aunt Sylvie came back a few days later and stayed a month, and this time when she left, she said, "Nealey, darling, we have a buyer for this house. I've taken care of everything. I'll fetch you in a week, but while I'm gone, you'll be looked after. No more worries, my precious child."

Nealey had heard the words, but they made little sense to her. Adrift in her waves of grief, all she wanted was to be with Hank and the children.

Hank, she thought. *Please, come back for me.*

A hot breath on her cheek jerked her out of her reverie.

Nealey moved her hands away from her face. Two large dark eyes stared at her.

"Lulu," she moaned.

The dog nudged her shoulder with its head and cooed.

The doorbell rang three times in succession, the sound of it harsh in Nealey's ears.

Benton came to her side.

"How are you feeling?" he asked.

"Better, I think."

"You're about to have some visitors," he said and walked to her. He put his hands on her shoulders. "You're going to be fine, Nealey. You're surrounded by people who care about you. We'll all help you to heal. I can promise you that."

Nealey smiled up at him.

"I'll get the door," he said. "Come on. They're waiting."

Lulu trotted beside her and Benton, then seated herself to the side of the door, her tail swishing back and forth across the gleaming marble floor. Three barks later, the door opened and in walked the gang. The wind chime on the porch sounded softly.

Nealey watched as Benton opened the door. Standing in front of several people, Aunt Sylvie ran to Nealey and hugged her tight.

"Surprise, darlin'," she said. "I'm back! And look who I found standing on the porch. You're going to love them. Are you all right, Nealey? You're trembling, honey, and you look pale."

"I'm fine, Aunt Sylvie. I'm so glad to see you."

Two men stood behind Aunt Sylvie. One of them waved at Nealey.

"Now, let me introduce these brilliant folks. They're guaranteed to make you feel better," Aunt Sylvie said.

"Ah, there he is. Benton, dear. How have things been?"

Nealey leaned in close to her and whispered, "He made me an omelet using one of your recipes."

Aunt Sylvie smiled and raised her eyebrows. "Really? He certainly must like you."

"He was just being nice."

Aunt Sylvie hugged her again. "Whatever you say, dear."

Lulu wagged her tail and whined for attention.

"Oh, you precious girl," Aunt Sylvie said. "Did you take good care of our Nealey?" Sylvie patted the dog on the head then lifted her chin and kissed her on the mouth.

Nealey winced.

Aside from the color of their clothes, the two guests looked as different as any two brothers could possibly look.

The short, plump man with curly dark hair wore a white three-piece suit, a striped blue shirt underneath. He stepped beside

Nealey and stuck out his hand. "I'm Worthy," he said, "and this is my brother, Noble. He beat me here again this year. Takes great pleasure in it, too."

"Noble and Worthy," Nealey said and smiled at them.

"Our father's idea," Worthy said and winked at her. "We've fought our share of battles over those names, haven't we, Noble?"

The man nodded once.

Tall and thin, with long, pure white hair tied back at his neck, white shorts, matching shirt, socks and tennis shoes, and leaning on a silver cane, Noble not only had not waved at her, but he said not a word. The way the sunlight shone on him made his unlined face almost glow. Nealey imagined that his eyes would be deep blue, like Benton's, and she waited for him to remove his sunglasses. When he didn't, she stuck out her still-trembling hand.

"I'm pleased to meet you, Mr. Gates," she said.

He took her hand in his. The touch was so light that Nealey could hardly feel it, but she did feel the tingling warmth spread through her body. It relaxed her.

Noble nodded at her and turned toward the living room.

"You'll have to forgive his terrible manners," Worthy said. "He rarely says a word. Just an old reprobate."

"Come," Sylvie said. "Let's have a seat in the living room. There's so much to talk about. Nealey, see if you can find Benton and grab that basket off the kitchen table. Our guests need some refreshments."

"What basket?"

"I passed the delivery man as I came in, darling. God bless his soul, drove all the way out here from town just to make sure my gift basket would be here in time. You must have been distracted. I'm sure Benton let him in."

She'd taken only a couple of steps toward the kitchen when the doorbell rang again, two rings in quick succession. They sounded insistent.

"Should I get that, Aunt Sylvie?" Nealey called.

Lulu bounded forward and plopped down at her feet.

"Honestly, Lulu, you can't block me every single time I go into a door," Nealey said. She sounded exasperated but managed a smile. "Aunt Sylvie, this morning, she wouldn't let me into the kitchen. I've never seen a dog so intent on keeping me in one place!"

Aunt Sylvie bent down and whispered into Lulu's ear. "You're upsetting our Nealey, darling. Must you keep blocking the door?"

Lulu barked.

"I think that means yes," Sylvie said. "Lulu is a very smart, intuitive creature, honey, so please, just indulge her. She'll move eventually. She's protecting you the best way she knows how."

"From what?"

Sylvie stood up. "Well, perhaps she senses that you're frightened. I know all of this is new for you, and you're bound to be a little nervous. But, has anything frightened you? Anything our Lulu might perceive as a threat?"

Before she could answer, someone banged on the door. Nealey jumped.

"Goodness gracious, you're a bundle of nerves, darling. Let me get the door."

Lulu moved so that Sylvie could open the door, but the dog didn't budge from her side.

A sudden tumble of clouds blotted out the sunlight and swept a gust of wind across the front porch, strumming the wind chimes in a deep, melancholy song.

From the doorway, a well-dressed man smiled at her and held out his hand.

"Hello," he said. "The parking lot looks pretty crowded, but I wondered if you had a vacancy."

Nealey watched the man as he talked to Aunt Sylvie. For a second, he looked over at her and caught her staring at him. He smiled, reached over, and offered his hand.

"Hello," he said. "I'm Max Leighton."

Nealey felt the power and strength of his hand. Hers seemed so small in his. She let her eyes wander from the bright gold cufflinks in the crisp white fold of a French cuff shirt to the subtle dark stripe in the fine Italian suit, cut elegantly to fit his broad shoulders. The dark suit and paisley tie complemented his blond hair, thick, shoulder length but not in the least feminine.

He resembled statues she'd seen of Greek gods, their hair always long, the source of their strength. His brown eyes, speckled with hints of gold flecks, held her gaze as if in a hypnotic spell.

"I need a place to stay for a few nights, but if you're full then I'll try to find another place," the husky voice said.

Have I heard that voice before? I have. I know *I have. It's ....*

Nealey wasn't quite sure, but she knew it was familiar.

"Yes, of course, we have a room," Aunt Sylvie said. "Please, come in."

"Thank you," he said and set his leather bag down next to the desk.

Lulu trotted up beside him.

The man stepped away from her. "I'm not very fond of dogs," he said, "especially big ones, and this is the biggest one I've ever seen."

"Lulu," Aunt Sylvie said and snapped her fingers.

Lulu circled the front desk then sat down at Sylvie's feet. "She's an Irish wolfhound. She looks fierce. She was bred to bring down wolves, after all, but she's quite harmless."

As if to prove her wrong, Lulu stood up, lowered her head, and snarled at the man. "Harmless?" Max asked. "By the size of those teeth, I wouldn't say she was harmless."

"Oh, nonsense," Sylvie said. "She's a sweetie pie."

Max leaned over the desk. "How tall is she?"

"Average height, about, um, thirty-four inches at the shoulder, weighs 130 pounds, still svelte for a woman of her age," Aunt Sylvie said and chuckled. "This is my niece, Nealey Monaghan, and I'm Sylvia Wolcott. Everyone calls me Sylvie."

"Surely, not THE Sylvia Wolcott, author of those charming cookbooks?"

"Oh, my," Sylvie gushed. "You've seen my books?"

"But, of course!" Max said. "Your *Magical Arts* series is one of my mother's favorites. She'd be lost in the kitchen without them." He unzipped his leather bag. "Thanks to you, we have herbs growing in every conceivable spot so that she can follow your recipes."

"Well, I'm delighted that she likes them."

"I know you'll find this strange, but I just purchased your newest one for her. Would you mind signing it?" He pulled the book from his bag and held it out.

"I'd be happy to. I just got back from a signing, in fact." She dug a pen from her purse and looked at Nealey. "Will you fetch Benton, darling? He simply *must* meet Max and say hello to the guests."

"No need to fetch me," Benton said. "I found this on the table, thought you might need it." Benton ducked a bit and stepped from behind the dining room door carrying the basket of goodies.

"Ah, there you are!" Aunt Sylvie said. "Benton Aimes, this is Max Leighton, our newest guest."

Nealey watched Benton nod at him, but he didn't offer to shake hands.

"Excuse me," Benton said, "I'll attend to the guests. Nealey, why don't you join us?"

"Oh, yes, yes," Sylvie said. "I'll show Max to his room and let him get settled. Go ahead, darling. Go mingle!"

Nealey glanced up at Max. He was smiling.

Benton touched Nealey's elbow. "Allow me," he said and offered his arm.

Nealey let him lead her into the living room, but as she walked, she glanced back at Max. His smile had faded but his dark eyes shone with an intensity that frightened her. She felt as if he could see right through her, all the way to her soul.

Tiny hairs prickled on the back of her neck. The children's warning came to her mind.

The bad man's coming.

Chapter 6

In the formal living room of the Playhouse Inn, a five-tiered crystal chandelier hung from the twelve-foot ceiling, blue silk draperies graced two bay windows, and blue toile fabric covered the sofa and side chairs. The mantel above the fireplace held cherub figurines, brass candlesticks, and family photographs. Above them all stood an antique gilded mirror so large that it hung over the sides of the mantel and towered almost to the ceiling.

Nealey walked immediately to the mantel and picked up a photograph of her mother and Aunt Sylvie as teenagers. She ran her thumb along the ornate frame.

"The unspeakable," Nealey whispered.

In the photo, the two girls wore matching red dresses with white belts and white pumps. Their bouffant hairstyles matched, as well. Aunt Sylvie's finely-chiseled nose dotted with freckles made her mother's plain, slightly wider one look a little drab by comparison.

Nealey had inherited her aunt's freckles, a fact that somehow made the two of them a united front against everyone else, even Naomi, who had her father's olive skin. When they were very young children, Naomi and Nealey had spent hours with Sylvie while their mother worked. Nealey often sat cross-legged on the floor with Sylvie looking in a handheld mirror, talking about their freckles, laughing at first this one, then that one, Nealey cuddled against her, entranced by her tales of childhood antics in the mountains of Tennessee.

Sometimes, Naomi would sit with them, but most of the time, she preferred to play with her dolls or draw pictures of trees with her crayons. She never cared much for Aunt Sylvie or the inn. In fact, most of the time, when she knew Aunt Sylvie was coming to get them, she begged to stay with the neighbors next door who loved her deeply and had made Naomi her own garden patch to the side of their lush plantings. They'd even furnished a spare bedroom for her, and they had a Steinway piano that Naomi loved to play. Their son, Johnny, was her best friend.

But then, she agreed to come on that one visit to the Playhouse Inn. Everything changed that night, especially their mother. No more hugs, no more laughing over silly little jokes, no more laughing about anything. It was almost as if their mother had died the night they left.

If Nealey tried to play with her, the woman simply said, "Shh."

If Naomi brought her fresh flowers from her garden next door, her mother would stare at them as if they were demons. Then, she would put her fingers to her mouth and say, "Shh."

The twins named their mother's condition, "the unspeakable."

Naomi, my sweet Naomi, Nealey thought. *The unspeakable robbed us both of our mother, and now, I am robbed of you by a maniac. What kind of God would allow such a thing? God? Just a name, a useless name for something that doesn't exist.*

Nealey had tried to help her mother, to find out the source of her misery, but the woman refused to speak of it. She said, over and over, "Promise me you'll never go back into that house."

Now, not only was Nealey back in the "dreadful place," as her mother called the inn, but her name was on the deed, along with Aunt Sylvie's. She didn't know why Aunt Sylvie had chosen to do it, why she'd given her this gift and taken not a penny for it. Sylvie had made her co-owner of every inch of property, every stick of furniture. Nealey knew of the many promises she'd made to her mother, swearing that she'd never enter the place again, and she felt guilty, as if she'd lied to her, even on her deathbed.

She felt that unwanted sensation that she was about to lose it, so she sniffed and swallowed hard, then replaced the photograph.

A sudden cold sensation at her midriff startled her and she gasped.

Lulu nudged her with her nose then stretched her massive head forward toward Nealey's chin. Nealey thought for sure that as it neared her face, she saw a hint of mischief in those sparkling brown eyes.

"There's no use telling you to go away," she said and patted the dog's head. "You'll just come right back."

"I'm like a bad penny, I guess," Benton said from beside her. "I just keep showing up."

Nealey smiled and put her hand lightly on Benton's arm. "No, I wasn't talking about you, really. But now that you mention it."

"Oh, great, thanks," he said. He swirled the iced tea in his glass, adjusted the napkin underneath it, and stepped in front of her. "It's good to see you smile. Now," he said as he took her arm once again, "shall we go to the sitting room and have a chat with the brothers Gates?"

She glanced down at Lulu. "Well, do *you* mind?"

Lulu barked then eased away from her.

"If I didn't know better," Nealey said, "I'd swear that dog understood every word."

"She's taken quite a shine to you," Benton said and led Nealey toward the sitting room.

"There is something a little unusual about her, though."

He bent down close to her and whispered, "Perhaps she thinks the same thing about you."

From across the room, Lulu barked, not her soft feminine bark, but a deeper one, almost a snarl that Nealey had not heard from the dog before.

The sound of it made her shudder.

Chapter 7

Noble and Worthy sat side by side on the blue leather sofa in the quaint sitting room as Aunt Sylvie told the story of a horrifying encounter years ago at The Playhouse Inn.

Seated in a plush antique high-back chair, her feet resting on the matching ottoman, Aunt Sylvie relived the experience.

"Well, I didn't know what to do," she said. "I didn't know anything about ghosts then, but there she was not five feet from me, her skin that horrid gray pallor, hair a tangled mess, dress torn, her hands reaching toward me. I was terrified, I tell you." Aunt Sylvie brushed a few strands of hair from her forehead. "I write herbal cook books, for God's sake. I certainly didn't know how to deal with a ghost!"

Worthy scooted forward and put his hand on Aunt Sylvie's clenched fists. "Tell us, Sylvie," he urged, his dark eyes focused on hers. "Did you use earth magick?"

"But of course I had to, you see," she said, unclenching her fists and wiping away dots of perspiration from her upper lip. "What choice did I have?"

Worthy waved his plump hands in the air, "Oh, do continue, my dear. We want to hear it, don't we Noble?"

With his long, pale index finger, Noble adjusted his sunglasses. He nodded in Sylvie's direction.

"You see, Sylvie, Noble is on the edge of his seat. He can't wait to hear it. Please, dear, please continue," Worthy exclaimed. "We practitioners must support one another. It's why we're here."

Slapping his hand and raising one eyebrow in mock contempt, Aunt Sylvie purred in her best exaggerated Southern drawl, "You're such a good *liar*, Worthy."

Worthy sucked in a breath. "My word, Sylvie!"

"Very well." She straightened in her chair and put her feet on the floor. "I had to think fast. I was terrified, even though she wasn't the first ghost I'd ever seen. But the look in those eyes of hers sent chills all over me. Thankfully, I'd been sipping on a glass of water, and there was a scented candle lit on the table next to some freshly-potted rosemary, so I had what I needed."

"Ah, yes," Worthy said. "The four elements of earth magick: earth, air, fire, and water."

Sylvie stood up and braced herself against the back of the chair.

"She came closer and moved her lips as if she wanted to speak. Her arms were only two feet away from me. I fumbled with the rosemary, broke off some leaves and sprinkled them around the candle. Then I dropped some onto the flame itself. I was so afraid that I couldn't remember what to do next, so I picked up the glass, and poured the water on the floor in front of me. I tried for a circle, but my hands shook so badly, I made a messy splatter. Then I grabbed the candle and poured the wax into the water, chanting the whole time, '*do no harm, do no harm.*'"

Worthy stood and clapped his hands. "How exciting! Now, what happened next?"

"She just kept coming, Worthy, until her feet touched the rim of the water. Her eyes, those terribly sad eyes, suddenly looked beyond me, as if she'd seen someone behind me. I whirled around, my heart pounding in my chest so hard I could barely breathe, but there was no one. By the time I turned around again, she'd vanished."

Sylvie shuddered.

"Powerful earth magick," Worthy said. "The water stopped her. Earthbound ghosts cannot cross over water. And the rosemary, brilliant! The most healing of all scents. It kept you safe."

"I handled myself much better the next time I saw her," Sylvie said and lowered her head. "I wasn't nearly as afraid. And now? Now, I just want to help her."

From the sofa, Noble turned his head toward the window.

Twilight fell across the sitting room like a warm blanket.

"And those precious little girls, of course," Sylvie whispered.

Chapter 8

Max Leighton fingered the silk draperies that framed the large window in his room and studied the portrait that hung above the antique bureau. The plaque affixed to the bottom of the frame read: *Lady Sylvia Wolcott, The Cotswolds, England, 1888.*

The woman in the portrait stood with her back to her audience, her head turned, lips smiling at her artist, one hand propped daintily on a chair. She wore an elegant, dark green gown with a long train cascading behind. Her blonde hair was swept up in the back, with curling tendrils falling against her shoulders. The profile of her face reminded him a little of the Sylvie Wolcott he'd just met.

"Nothing changes," he murmured.

Above his bed hung another portrait of the same woman, together with a man dressed in a dark suit, and a priest dressed in white and gold vestments. The woman, flanked by two men, sat in a dark velvet chair inside a strikingly familiar foyer. The plaque on the frame read: *John Wolcott, Anna, and Father Maxwell Madison, The Blessing of the Playhouse Inn, Tennessee, 1889.*

"Now, *there's* a story," he mumbled.

A Bible on the dresser caught his attention since several extra pages seemed to be sticking out. His curiosity compelled him to pull on one of the errant pieces. As he pulled it out, he found that it was an old newspaper clipping. A smile spread across his face as he picked it up and read the words aloud.

"Local police chief and family slaughtered by crazed gunman."

Max scanned the article and found the words he was searching for: "lone survivor" and "Nealey Monaghan."

He ran his finger over her picture. "Ah, Nealey," he whispered. "You were my favorite."

Three raps on the door startled him. He folded the article carefully and stuck it into his jacket pocket.

"Yes?" he called. "Who is it?"

The door inched open and Aunt Sylvie stuck her head in.

"Mrs. Wolcott, how nice to see you," Max said as he straightened his jacket.

"Oh, please, call me Sylvie. Dinner will be served shortly. We're having drinks in the sitting room. Perhaps you'd care to join us?"

"Certainly," Max said. "I'd be delighted. Allow me to escort you down."

He crooked his arm and offered it to her.

"Is the room to your liking so far?"

"Perfect," he said. "It's quite elegant. You've done a wonderful job of decorating this place."

"Oh, goodness," she said, "most of this is just as it was left to me. Some refurbishing here and there, that's all." She took his arm. "I hope that's sufficient."

"It's splendid," Max said and patted her hand. "Actually, coming from me, I'd say it's a genuine compliment. I'm a bit odd in my taste of furnishings sometimes, perhaps even a little snobbish."

Sylvie waved her hand in the air. "Who can say what's odd in this world? We all have our little idiosyncrasies! A handsome man like yourself is bound to have a few, well, let's just call them preferences, shall we?"

A hearty laugh came from Max.

Sylvie stopped on the stairs beside him. She focused on his eyes.

"Have we met before, Max?"

He urged her down the stairs. "I don't think so. Surely, I would have remembered meeting a famous author like you."

She stopped a second time. "I'm certain that we've met. It's not that you look familiar as much as you sound familiar. Your voice, your laugh. I know them from somewhere. I'm sure of it."

The smile left Max's face. "I must insist that you're wrong. I've travelled abroad for most of my life and only within the last year have I settled here in the States. So, the chances of our having met are quite slim."

"Aunt Sylvie," Benton called from the foyer, "your wine is waiting. Dinner in fifteen minutes. And Mr. Leighton, what can I get for you?"

"Wine would be lovely," he said, a thin smile on his face.

"Please, call me Max."

"Red or white?"

"He'll have red," Aunt Sylvie said. "It suits him."

Max glanced at Sylvie then back to Benton. His thin smile faded into a tight line. "Actually, I prefer white, a crisp Riesling, if you have it. Pear or apricot would be lovely. So much lighter and more refreshing than red."

"Of course," Benton said. "We can offer you the apricot, if that will suffice."

"Oh, yes," Max gushed. "Yes, indeed. It is a delicious wine."

"Aunt Sylvie prides herself on her fine stock of wines," Benton said and left the room.

"I'm surprised at your offering of such a gem, Sylvie," Max said, the smile returning to his face.

Sylvie looked up at him and smiled. "I think you'll find that the Playhouse Inn offers much that will surprise you, Max."

Max laughed, then suddenly cocked his head as if he were listening to something no one else could hear.

"Whatever is wrong, Max?" Sylvie asked, a concerned look on her face.

"My own stupidity amazes me at times, Sylvie. Please, if you'll pardon me for just a few moments, I must get something from my car."

"Benton will be glad to do that for you."

"No, no, how silly of me not to bring my hostess her gift. Now, I'll be back before you can say boo!" Then he laughed and walked out the door.

A hostess gift? Sylvie smiled at the thought of such a little treasure.

She walked to the mirror in the hall and put on some fresh lipstick. She pushed back the stray wisps of hair that fell across her forehead, pinched her cheeks for a bit of natural blush, and straightened her large loop earrings. She was pleased with her porcelain-like complexion, still smooth, unwrinkled, and with a hint of a glow.

"Not bad," she said and smiled.

A shrill scream and the sound of breaking glass wiped the smile off Sylvie's face.

Chapter 9

Benton knelt beside Nealey as she tried to scoop up the large pieces of broken glass from the picture frame.

"What on earth is wrong?" Sylvie asked, obviously shaken.

"I'm not sure," Benton said.

Sylvie bent down next to Nealey. "Darling, did something happen? Was it you who screamed?"

Nealey nodded, the girls' voices still running through her mind.

The bad man's coming.

Benton moved her hands away from the glass. "I'll get that. Don't worry about it. Why don't you sit down over there and relax?"

Worthy and Noble walked in from the parlor. "What is wrong, Sylvie? We thought we heard a scream."

Sylvie looked up at them and nodded her head toward Nealey.

Worthy bent down and helped Nealey to her feet. "Come dear," he said. "Sit beside me and tell me what frightened you so." He led her to the sofa.

"Now," he said. "I'm all ears." He held her hands in his.

Nealey took a deep breath.

The bad man's coming.

"The window," she said, her voice faint and weak.

"Yes, dear, tell me about the window," Worthy said in a soft, melodious voice. "Noble's standing guard there now. Nothing can hurt you, I promise. You're safe here."

"Hideous man," Nealey said, her voice hollow. "A man with a hideous face stared at me, tried to reach through ... reach through the window. The bad man's coming," she muttered.

"Noble?" Worthy called. "Do you see anything? Nealey says a man was staring at her."

Noble said nothing.

"He didn't see a thing, dear. Can you tell us more about this man?"

"Of course he can't see anything," Nealey said, her voice a monotone. "It's dark out there now."

"But *you* saw something. Tell me about it, as much as you can remember." He leaned close to her. "And dark or not, Noble could see. He has extraordinary night vision. Now, what were you doing when this man appeared?"

"This morning while looking at the photograph of my mother and Aunt Sylvie, I remembered coming here years ago—Naomi and me—then being taken away early the next morning by my mother. She was scared to death. She was never the same afterwards."

"Oh, dear," Sylvie sighed. "Oh, my sweet dear. All those terrible memories."

"And these memories," Worthy said, "do you think they upset you so much that ...."

Nealey stood up. "You don't believe me?"

She turned and pointed. "I saw him right out that window. His face looked like a mass of burned flesh with only a black hole for a mouth. He had fangs and matted hair. He was horrible looking at first. Then, his face changed—I knew that face. He grinned at me, and I know he wanted to kill me. I watched him try to reach through the window."

Nealey stopped and covered her face with her hands.

Benton stood beside her holding a glass of red wine. "Here, try a sip of this. It will help you feel better."

Nealey stared up at him. "Do you believe me?"

Worthy, Sylvie, and Benton gathered round her. "We all believe you, darling," Sylvie said. "If you say you saw that monster, then we absolutely believe you. You're our precious girl."

The front double doors opened and closed.

After a few seconds, they opened and closed again.

"I'm back, Sylvie," Max called. "Sorry I was delayed. I couldn't find your gift, but I brought this for you."

Max walked into the living room carrying a large gift-wrapped box and stopped dead still.

Nealey, Benton, Sylvie, and Worthy stared directly at him. Lulu sat in the corner and growled.

"What has happened?" Max asked. "What on earth is wrong?"

No one spoke.

Max stepped toward the group, but Lulu brushed by him so quickly that it caught him off guard. Max took a step back, and Lulu seated herself in front of Nealey.

"Well now, Max," Sylvie said. "You were just outside. Did you happen to see anyone who might have been looking in the window there?"

Max lifted his chin. "Are you implying something?"

Sylvie cocked her head. "Implying gets us nowhere. I'm merely asking if you happened to see anyone else out there?"

"I was at my car. From that vantage point, I couldn't possibly have seen anyone on that side of the house," Max said, his hands locked in front of him. "If you'll be so kind as to tell me who or what I was supposed to have seen, I think we can resolve this situation. And for that matter, it seems that one of your other guests is missing. Where, might I ask, is the other Mr. Gates?"

"He left directly before you came in," Worthy said. "He went to check out the grounds."

"He couldn't have walked past me without my seeing him," Max said. "I saw no one."

"Perhaps," Sylvie said and moved closer to him, "you were occupied in the car. Our Noble moves quickly."

Max shrugged. "Anything is possible."

Sylvie took his arm. "Come, Max. Let us explain what has happened. Perhaps you can help."

Max let out a sigh. "My dear Sylvie, you had me worried. I couldn't imagine what would have happened that would cause you to think ill of me. Perish the thought."

He put the box on the table and followed her to the chairs in the living room.

"Please, sit. Let's all have a glass of wine and try to figure out what happened. Our Nealey needs us. Agreed?"

Benton disappeared and returned a few moments later with a large silver tray topped with wine glasses, napkins, and a cheese ball with party crackers. He disappeared again and brought out a bottle of white wine chilling in an ornate silver ice bucket.

"Thank you, dear. I don't know what we'd do without you," Sylvie said to Benton.

"My pleasure," he said and smiled as he poured a small glass of wine for everyone, including one for Noble. When the wine was poured, the cheese and crackers within reach, Noble walked into the room and sat down on the sofa next to Worthy.

"Find anything, Brother?" Worthy asked him.

Noble said nothing, looked at no one.

Worthy shrugged. "I'm sorry," he said. "He found no one."

"Now, Nealey darling," Sylvie said, "if you can, tell us one more time about that creature you saw at the window. Sit next to her, Benton. A broad shoulder to lean on is always helpful."

Benton clumsily wedged his large body down next to Nealey. Lulu remained at Nealey's feet and didn't even lift her head when he sat down.

"Please, share with us, dear," Worthy said.

Nealey took a deep breath.

"I was standing by the window looking at the photograph. After that terrible visit, my mother changed. Naomi and I used to call her condition 'the unspeakable.' We lost our mom after that day. Lost her." Nealey stopped and stared at the window.

"I looked out and thought I saw," she hesitated.

For a moment, no one spoke.

"Come, dear, whom did you see?" Worthy asked, his voice calm and melodious.

"No one," she mumbled.

Sylvie narrowed her eyes and looked at Benton. Then, she nodded at him.

"Nealey," Benton said and inched closer to her. "Don't be afraid. We won't let anyone hurt you. You are safe here."

"Safe?" Nealey said through her sobs. "Safe in a place where I see ghosts, where I see some grotesque form of the man who murdered my family trying to get in here and kill me? I don't feel safe, not one bit."

Sylvie gasped and stood up.

"You saw Brian, darling? I thought you said ...."

"At first, it was just some hideous monster. Then it changed into someone that looked like Brian, then into something so terrible I could barely look at it. That's when I screamed and dropped the photograph."

Benton put his arm around Nealey and drew her close to him. Sylvie knelt between her and Lulu.

"Sweetheart, please believe me," Sylvie said. "You are safe here. Nothing will hurt you here in this house. Nothing. Seeing things is frightening, but they're only images. Images can't do physical harm to you, darling. I've learned that the hard way."

"Sylvie's right," Worthy said. "They can scare the bejesus out of you, but they can't hurt you. Isn't that right, Noble?"

Noble adjusted his sunglasses.

"See? Noble agrees. We all agree, dear girl, that you are safe here with us. We will protect you from harm. You have our solemn vow. Why, you're the very reason we're ...."

Benton cleared his throat and frowned at Worthy.

Then he turned to Nealey. "Would you like to take a short walk? How about if I get our coats and we take a stroll outside? How about it?" he asked and held out his hand.

He took her hand and gently pulled her up off the sofa.

She looked again at the window. "What if he's out there?"

"Then we'll just have to make him sorry he scared you, won't we?"

Lulu barked, this time a loud deep bark with nothing feminine about it.

"Uh oh," Benton said. "Lulu's got her A-Game on. She's ready for anything. And if she can't protect you, then I can."

As the two of them passed into the entrance hall, Benton got their coats from the rack and helped Nealey on with hers. Then, he opened the double doors and whistled.

"Come on, Lulu. You don't want to miss all the fun, do you?"

"Benton, would you like one of us to go with you?" asked Worthy. "I'll be happy to accompany you. Don't let my size fool you. I'm quite the fighter if need be."

"We'll be fine, Worthy. Lulu and I can look after Nealey, but thank you all the same."

"Don't forget Lulu's little hat, Benton," Sylvie called. "Heaven forbid that she catch cold. She looks tough, but deep down, she's a softie, and she needs her ears covered. Oh, and get her booties, too. She likes the pink ones best."

Benton grimaced and pulled the pink hat off the rack. "Sorry, girl," he whispered as he slipped it over her head and adjusted the strap under her neck. "Let's forget about those booties, okay?"

When Nealey saw it, she covered her mouth to stifle a chuckle.

"Careful, you'll hurt her feelings. I'm not sure what she thinks of the pink hat, but Sylvie insists."

Nealey bent down and patted her head. "You look gorgeous," she exclaimed. "Simply gorgeous."

Lulu barked that soft feminine bark, stopped in front of the large mirror in the foyer, and turned her head toward it. Then she trotted ahead of them.

"Did she just check herself out in the mirror?" Nealey asked.

Benton shook his head. "Women!"

As soon as the door closed, Sylvie announced, "Let's seat ourselves in the dining room. Dinner is ready, and by the time those two get back, we can have the food on the table. Max, would you be a dear and make sure we have enough chairs?"

"Most certainly. I'll see to it."

When Max got up and left the living room, Sylvie looked at Worthy and patted his hand. "You must be careful, dear. Our Nealey is still in a fragile state. We have to be mindful of that and be gentle with her. She'll learn all she needs to know when she needs to know it."

"Correct as usual, Sylvie. I got a bit carried away. I apologize," Worthy said.

"Oh gracious, no need for an apology. Let's get dinner on the table."

They stood up together and went toward the dining room. Sylvie stopped at the entrance and gazed up at Noble.

"I'm counting on you," she said. "Just as the ancients chose champions to protect them, I have chosen you. Nealey needs your strength."

Noble smiled.

Chapter 10

Lulu bounded in the door and stood perfectly still while Benton fumbled with the tie strap and finally removed her pink hat.

"Mm," Nealey said. "Something smells good."

"Indeed, it does," Benton said. "Perfect timing."

Sylvie sat at the head of the table with Max seated opposite her. Noble and Worthy sat on one side, while Nealey and Benton took the other.

"Is someone else joining us?" Nealey asked. "Three empty chairs, three place settings. Who's coming?"

Sylvie waved her hand. "No one, darling. But I like to be prepared just in case. Extra place settings come in handy if guests drop in. And of course, since I run this wonderful inn, I can never tell when someone might need hospitality. Lesson number one in the rules of operating a first-class establishment."

"Exactly right," Worthy said. "You must always be prepared for unexpected guests."

Nealey raised an eyebrow. "Should I be taking notes?"

Sylvie opened her mouth in surprise.

"Well, listen to you! My, my, I was right, Benton," she said and smiled at him as she passed a plate of homemade yeast rolls. "Broad shoulders to lean on have let loose our Nealey's sharp tongue and quick wit."

Nealey blushed. The rest of them chuckled.

"And yes, dear," Sylvie said to her, "keep that notebook handy. Never pass up an opportunity to *pretend* to learn from those with more experience ... and the generosity to bestow gifts. Now, let's enjoy this sumptuous fare."

"Max," Sylvie continued, "would you be so kind as to pass along my famous broccoli casserole? Then, the pork medallions—those are portabella mushrooms on top. Then, if you will, help yourself to the pole beans and candied yams, all fresh out of the garden."

"I'd be charmed, Sylvie," Max said as he scooped out a large portion for himself and handed the dish to Worthy. "It all looks delicious. I can't imagine when you had the time to do all this."

From her place next to Nealey, Lulu whined.

Sylvie chuckled. "Well, a woman has her secrets, especially in the kitchen." She took a porcelain saucer and as the casserole came her way, spooned out a helping. "I'm sure your mother would agree."

Max nodded. "Indeed, she would. After dinner, please allow me to give you your hostess gift."

With her head at Sylvie's eye level, Lulu stood beside her and whined.

"She dearly loves broccoli," Sylvie said and set the dish on the floor. "Eat gently, now, and try not to make a mess on the new rug."

"Aunt Sylvie, what is this topping on the mushrooms? It's spicy but delicious and such a vibrant purple."

"It's called Nard, my dear, or Spikenard to be more exact," Sylvie said. "I use it in many dishes, but sparingly. It's one of my little luxuries, very expensive. Used primarily in Medieval times as a fragrant healing oil. But, like all herbs and spices, it has many uses."

"It used to be a medicine, didn't it?" Max asked. "A sedative, I think. Highly toxic."

Sylvie looked surprised. "Why, you're exactly right, Max! How intriguing that you know of it."

Max stared directly at Sylvie. "Pharmacy school," he explained. "Isn't it a little daring to use such a poisonous ingredient? Even an extra spoonful could cause intestinal pain. Or so I've read."

Sylvie dismissed the notion with a wave of her hand. "Pish tosh. Most of our favored spices are toxic if overused, but chefs all over the world use them, dear Max. Surely, you've noticed it in your travels. The secret," she said with a sly grin, "is in knowing how much to use, as with all ingredients."

The group quieted and finished their meal.

"Well," said Sylvie, "I don't think we'll have many leftovers!"

"It's your delightful cooking, Sylvie," Worthy said.

"Oh my, how you flatter me, Worthy. And how I love it!"

Everyone laughed.

"Shall we take dessert in the parlor?" Sylvie asked. "We have a zesty lemon tart with whipped cream and pure vanilla, in the proper proportion, of course," she said and smiled at Max.

"I'll help," Benton said.

"You're such a dear, Benton," Sylvie said. "Nealey, darling, why don't you help Benton? I'm sure he could use an extra pair of hands."

Nealey smiled a weak smile as she moved toward the kitchen.

The others, led by Sylvie, took their seats in the elegant parlor.

Max stood in front of Sylvie, bowed gallantly before her, and placed the gift-wrapped box in her lap. "It isn't what I'd intended. Nonetheless, please accept this gift. You are a most gracious hostess," he said. "I hope it pleases you."

A broad smile spread across Sylvie's face.

"My goodness," Sylvie said as she untied the bright blue ribbon. "Whatever could be in this beautiful box?" She peeled back several layers of embossed tissue paper and found the treasure: a straw hat trimmed with bright blue ribbon that encircled the brim and spilled over the back for a least a foot. She held it up and admired it.

"It's wonderful," she said as she stood in front of the mirror and tried it on. "I couldn't have picked out anything better myself."

Max smiled and nodded at her. "I'm delighted you think so."

Sylvie turned this way and that, admiring herself in the mirror.

"It suits you, Sylvie," Worthy said. "Don't you have a blue tunic to match it?"

Sylvie looked quizzically at him and cocked her head. "I do, yes. In fact, I bought it only a week ago."

Sylvie put the hat back in the box. "Well, now, let's have a bit of wine, shall we?"

Worthy poured a glass for everyone except Noble who indicated with a shake of his head that he didn't want any.

"Max," Sylvie said as she took a sip of wine, "thank you so very much for the hat."

"You're quite welcome," he said and held up his glass to her.

Sylvie sat back in her chair and propped her feet on the ottoman. "It is a bit odd, don't you think, Max, that even though you had no idea you were coming here, you chose a perfect hostess gift, something that suits me to a tee."

Worthy knitted his eyebrows.

"Seems quite the coincidence, I'd say."

All of them turned to Max, their faces indicating a degree of suspicion.

"How did you manage that? Hostess gifts are normally so generic, a bottle of wine, a round of cheese, a set of napkins. For someone who stopped here at random, it does seem a little too coincidental."

Max's cheeks colored slightly. He set his glass on the coffee table and put his hands together as if in prayer. He touched them to his lips and stared down at the floor.

"Actually," he began, his voice barely above a whisper, "I purchased the hat for my mother."

"What was that, Max? I'm sorry, but I couldn't hear you," Sylvie said.

Benton and Nealey suddenly walked in carrying silver trays of coffee.

"Coffee anyone?" Nealey asked.

"Oh, yes," Sylvie said. "I could certainly do with a fresh cup."

"Me, too," Worthy said. "There's nothing quite like a cup of just-brewed coffee. Coffee for you, Max? Now, please continue."

Max held up a hand, "None for me." Then, he took a deep breath and straightened in his chair. "My mother saw a photo of you and wanted a hat like yours. When I arrived here and found out that you were Sylvie Wolcott, knowing your fondness for straw hats, I decided it would make a lovely hostess gift."

Sylvie's eyes narrowed as he spoke. "Do tell," she said. "But I insist that you keep this for your dear mother. I'll sign the inside with a personal note to her."

"You're declining my gift?"

Sylvie waved a hand. "Don't be silly," she said. "I wouldn't dream of declining such a gift. Heaven forbid. I'm simply offering to make it an extra special one for your dear mother."

Max stood up. He clenched his fists but smiled. "Whatever

you say. Now, if you'll excuse me. I think I'll retire for the evening."

"Do you feel that?" Nealey asked, her eyes wide.

"Feel what?" Benton asked.

Nealey got down on her knees and put her hands flat on the floor.

"It moved," she said.

"What is it, dear? What moved?" Sylvie asked.

"The floor," Nealey said, her voice shrill. "It trembled."

Sylvie glanced at Benton. He shrugged his shoulders then shook his head.

"But you must have felt it," Nealey said. "I couldn't have been the only one." She stood up and called, "Max, wait!"

He stopped in the doorway, his fists still clenched, his jaw set.

"Did you feel the tremor?"

Max relaxed his fists and clasped his hands behind his back. A thin smile formed on his lips.

"Rest well," he said and left the room.

Chapter 11

Sylvie sat next to a pajama-clad Nealey on the side of the bed.

"I *did* feel that tremor in the floor, Aunt Sylvie. Are you sure you didn't feel anything?"

Sylvie patted her arm. "Well, I can't be perfectly certain. This is a very old house. It has its share of aches and pains. An occasional rumbling isn't unusual."

Nealey leaned closer to Sylvie and put her head on her aunt's shoulder.

"I know I felt it. I didn't imagine it."

"No, of course you didn't darling. But it's over now, and you're safe."

"Do you think there's something odd about Max?"

"Odd? In what way?"

"Well, for one thing, he didn't answer my question when I asked him about the tremor. He just smiled and said, 'Get some rest,' or something."

"Perhaps he was just being courteous, although he appeared quite put off that I offered the hat to his mother."

"Yes," Nealey said and sat up straight. "And he was outside when that horrible face appeared in the window. Then, there's just something really familiar about him, too. I know I've never seen him before–I'd remember a man that striking–but I've heard his voice before. I'm almost sure of it."

Sylvie stood and smoothed the wrinkles from her tunic. "I will admit that I felt the very same way. I would have sworn that I'd met him before."

"He makes me feel funny inside, Aunt Sylvie, as if I should know him, almost as if I've been ...."

"Been what, darling?"

"I can't tell you. It's too embarrassing."

Sylvie put her hands on Nealey's shoulders. "No, honey, never let embarrassment keep you from doing anything." Sylvie stroked the side of Nealey's face. "There are some things in this life that are simply beyond our control. Now, tell me what is bothering you about Max."

Nealey looked at her, then lowered her head. "The way he looks at me, the way he sounds. It's almost as if he ... he knows me ... in an intimate way. But that's impossible."

"Ah," Sylvie said, "the realm of the impossible. I believe that Max fits somewhere on that line between possible and impossible. You're right, of course. There is something about him that is unmistakably familiar in quite an unsettling way. But enough of that. Come now, it's time for you to crawl in and get some sleep," she said. "You've had a memorable day. You must be exhausted."

Then she gave Lulu a pat on the head. "Bedtime for you, too."

The dog stretched, yawned, and flopped onto her side.

Nealey fluffed her pillows and got into bed. "Aunt Sylvie?"

Sylvie stepped to the cheval glass mirror and eyed her reflection. "Oh, my, what a fright I look!"

Nealey shuddered as the image of the face at the window came to her mind. Those horrid fangs, the gaping mouth, the charred flesh, then almost immediately, the face of the murderer of her family, Brian.

She clutched her stomach and moaned softly.

"Are you all right, dear?" Sylvie asked as she brushed back stray strands of hair then dabbed at the circles under her eyes. "What is it? What's tormenting you so?"

Nealey hesitated.

"I don't mean any disrespect. I know it was you who supported us after Mom ... got sick. You were the one who kept food on our table. But I wondered ...."

"Come now," Sylvie said, "it does no good to stifle feelings or let questions go unanswered."

Sylvie stood beside the bed and motioned for Nealey to move over.

"For goodness sakes, what is it that's been such a mystery, darling? You have but to ask."

Nealey smiled and moved over so that her aunt could sit.

"I love a good mystery. Please, please," she said and rubbed her hands together, "tell me what has been running around in that clever mind of yours all these years."

Nealey inhaled then let out a long breath.

"Dear me," Sylvie said as she tightened her hair ribbon. "It must have been burdening you for a long time. Tell me about it."

"Aunt Sylvie, my mother told us ...."

Sylvie's shoulders slumped. "Yes, I can only imagine."

Nealey fingered the comforter. "She blamed you for all of her troubles. She said this place was evil and that it was your fault. She said you practiced black magic."

Sylvie looked startled.

"Black magic?"

"Yes, that's what she thought. She said you used spells and brought some plague into the house."

"She thought that long before your last visit here, honey. Even when we were teenagers, I didn't have those fundamentalist beliefs that your grandparents and your mother had. They were so strict, so close-minded about religion. I've always been a little different. And in my younger days when I explored other religions, your mother thought I was possessed by the devil."

Nealey cocked her head to the side. "But if you wanted her to accept you, why were you so obvious with it? You kept those totems on the front porch. You always wore that amulet. You had books in the kitchen about magic. You sort of flaunted it, Aunt Sylvie."

Sylvie nodded her head and smiled, "You say I flaunted it. I say I didn't hide it. In my own home, I was free to live the way I wanted."

Nealey said nothing.

Simultaneously, the two women parked strands of hair behind their ears.

When they realized it, they both smiled.

"Oh, mercy, enough of this," Sylvie said and waved her hands.

"Well, will you tell me why you have so many books on magic in the kitchen?"

"Oh, honey, I'm an adventurer at heart. I love exotic herbs and spices, things outside the normal, those special delights that give an indescribable touch of magic to fruits and vegetables. I learned all that from those books. They're delightful reading. I don't cast spells, darling. I dig for information."

"That's it?" Nealey asked. "You use them for cooking?"

"Certainly not! I use them for everything. Cooking's just a by-product. Those books tell me what to plant and when to plant it, how to use herbs and spices, how to tell when they've reached their prime, and how to call forth the healing aspects and weed out the poisons. The magic is in knowing how to tweak them to perfection!"

Nealey laughed. "Well, from all the fan mail I see piled on the table downstairs and that photo of you with the Iron Chef, I'd say you've learned to do that fairly well."

"I love hearing you laugh," Sylvie said. "One last thing, honey, and we'll call it a night, okay?"

Nealey smiled at her.

"I loved your mother with all my heart. If I could have fixed her, I would have, for your sake and Naomi's. But I couldn't. I tried, but I failed, and now, she's where she wanted to be. She's in Heaven."

Nealey lowered her eyes.

"I don't think so," she whispered.

Sylvie looked at her with a puzzled expression on her face. "I'm afraid I don't understand."

"My mother is dead, Aunt Sylvie. My sister is dead. My husband." Tears welled in her eyes. "My babies, gone."

Sylvie hugged her. "I know, precious. They're in heaven now."

Nealey struggled out of Sylvie's hug. "With God?"

Sylvie looked startled.

"You mean the God who let my mother be driven insane while her two little girls needed her?"

Nealey wiped tears from her face. "Or maybe the one who let my family be murdered?"

Sylvie inched close beside her and wrapped her in a loving embrace.

Nealey sobbed onto her shoulder.

"I don't believe in God anymore, Aunt Sylvie. As hard as I try, I can't."

Sylvie ran her fingers through Nealey's hair and held her close. "It's all right, my sweet," she whispered. "He still believes in you."

Nealey sniffed and wiped her face with her hands. "Please,

Aunt Sylvie, please don't say that. God doesn't exist for me anymore."

Sylvie held the girl at arm's length. "All right, honey. It's all right."

Tears still flowed from Nealey's eyes.

Sylvie grabbed a tissue off the nightstand and blotted Nealey's face with it. "Do you remember your years at St. Mary's, darling? You were so happy there, weren't you?"

Nealey lowered her head.

"I lost Naomi there," she whispered.

"What darling?"

"Naomi stopped speaking to me once I went to the convent. I wrote her letters, but she never answered a single one of them."

Sylvie hugged her.

"You must realize that Naomi was so much like your mother. She held the same strict beliefs, sweetheart, and she saw your entry into the convent as a betrayal of those beliefs."

Nealey nodded.

"It seems so long ago now, a different world."

"Yes, but after you left," Sylvie said, "you continued your studies, remember? You've always been drawn to theology and to the study of things of a more spiritual essence. We have that in common, you and I."

"I suppose," Nealey said in a barely audible whisper.

"You're not the same person now, darling, but I want you to remember how you felt, Nealey, your heart so full of love then. Hang on to that feeling if you can. It will give you peace."

"There is no peace for me now," Nealey said. "I've lost everyone and everything I loved. I don't know how to make this pain go away."

Nealey sniffed and put her arms around Sylvie.

"I didn't mean everyone, Aunt Sylvie. I still have you. You were like a mother to me for so many years. I remember that."

"And I want you to remember that I love you, and I believe in you. Now," Sylvie said and patted her on the back, "how about a bit of red wine to help you sleep?"

Nealey shrugged.

"Good!" said Sylvie. "You climb in bed, now," she said and

gave Nealey a little scoot. "Go ahead. Snuggle up, and I'll be back in a jiffy."

Sylvie opened the double doors and clutched at her chest.

Benton stood before her, one hand raised as if to knock. In the other he carried a small silver tray which held two crystal stems of red wine.

"Oh, my goodness, you gave me a bit of a fright!"

"I thought you and Nealey might appreciate a sip before bedtime," he said.

"Certainly," Sylvie said and moved so that he could bring the tray inside.

Nealey bunched the covers under her chin.

Benton set the tray down then turned and walked back to the door.

Lulu whined as he walked by her, so he bent down and patted her head. "None for you, I'm afraid," he said.

He reached into his pocket and drew out a dog biscuit.

Her long tail thunked on the floor as she wagged it.

"But, I did bring *this.*"

She wolfed down the biscuit, then flopped her head back onto the floor and stretched.

"I hope all three of you ladies will sleep well," he said. "Please let me know if you need anything."

"You're such a dear, Benton. What would I do without you?" Sylvie said and smiled at him. "Good night, my helpful friend."

When she'd closed the door, Sylvie reached into her jacket pocket and brought out a green satin pouch. She opened it and drew out one of the small bottles from inside. Carefully, she poured a measure of the contents into her palm then emptied it into one of the wine glasses.

She smiled at Nealey. "I've infused your wine with a bit of powdered lavender."

She lifted the glass, swirled the contents, and smelled it. "Mm," she said, "wonderful aroma." Then she handed it to Nealey.

"Well, what do you think?" Sylvie asked. "Lavender does wonders for the nervous system. Isn't it heavenly?"

Nealey took in the aroma and sighed. "Lovely," she said after a sip. "I didn't know lavender was gold."

"No, it isn't. That's my secret ingredient." She winked at Nealey.

Nealey sniffed again and put down her glass. "Do you smell that, Aunt Sylvie? That scent of jasmine? I thought it was the lavender, but it isn't."

Nealey threw back the comforter, got up and walked to the dresser, Sylvie right behind her.

"Why, it *is* jasmine," Sylvie said.

She put a hand out and caught Nealey's arm. "Honey, please just relax. You've had a long day."

Nealey shook her head.

"I've smelled this before. I smelled it in here and in the kitchen, right before I saw ...."

"What, sweetheart, what did you see in the kitchen?"

Nealey shook her head. "It was, well, maybe it was just my imagination."

"So, what did your imagination show you?" Sylvie asked.

"You won't believe me."

"Dearest, you'd be surprised at what I'd believe. Now, out with it."

"I thought I saw two little girls sitting at the kitchen table. They had curly red hair and were a few years younger than Naomi and I were when we were last here. And it was only for a few seconds. Then they disappeared."

Sylvie clasped her hands together. "Two little girls," Sylvie repeated. "Were you frightened?"

Nealey let out an exasperated sigh. "Frightened? I was scared to death."

"What did you do, dearest?"

"What *could* I do? Nothing. I just stood there and shook all over."

"Oh, my, and I wasn't here for you. I'm sorry, honey."

"And now, that bottle of perfume. Yesterday, I found it on the dresser. It had toppled over, so I picked it up and capped it back tightly. Now, here it is again, overturned with the cap off. How did that happen?"

Sylvie shook her head.

"It is a mystery, dear, but we shall solve it."

Sylvie picked up the bottle and replaced the stopper. The name on the front read *Heavenly*.

"What is it that frightens you so about this?"

"I don't know," Nealey said. Her shoulders slumped. "I'm tired, Aunt Sylvie, very tired."

Sylvie tucked the bottle into her pocket then got the glass of wine and handed it to Nealey.

"Sip it down, now. You'll forget all about this, and in the morning, you'll awake refreshed and eager to begin your third day. I promise."

Nealey finished the lavender-infused wine in one gulp.

"Sleep well, my darling girl," Sylvie said and kissed the top of her head. "Tomorrow, you and I will have a nice long talk about the inn. I want you to know its history …."

Nealey snuggled into her bed.

"…and all its little secrets," Sylvie said and winked at her.

"Secrets?"

"Oh, yes. This old dear is over a hundred and thirty years old. She's seen her share of troubles and holds some fascinating secrets. I'll explain it all to you in the morning dear, when you've had a chance to rest."

On her way out, Sylvie glanced back at Nealey and smiled. Then she switched off the light.

When she closed the double doors, Sylvie leaned against them and let out a long sigh. She wrapped her fingers around the tiny bottle of perfume in her pocket.

"Stop it, Anna!" Sylvie said, her voice brusque but barely above a whisper, "Don't you dare do to Nealey what you did to her mother!"

Down the expansive hall, far from Sylvie's line of sight, Max quietly eased his door shut and smiled.

Chapter 12

Benton stood shirtless in front of the full-length bathroom mirror in the guest house and ran a bamboo scratcher down his heavily-muscled back.

"Ah," he said, "that feels so good."

Worthy called to him from the adjacent living room, "May we anticipate your presence at any time in the near future?"

Benton stepped into the room. "I'm here," he said, still scratching his back.

"The itchy back has returned," Worthy said. "Have no fear, my friend. Remember it is temporary, the price you must pay for all those—what shall we call them—muscles. They will serve you well when the time comes. Isn't that right, Noble?"

Noble pushed his sunglasses up on his nose.

"See? Noble whole-heartedly agrees!"

Worthy picked up a glass of red wine from the coffee table. "Join us?"

Benton slipped on a t-shirt, covering his defined abs and bulging biceps then sat down in an overstuffed chair near the fireplace.

"You never cease to amaze me, Benton," Worthy said.

Benton looked at him quizzically.

"After all these years, you've managed to maintain that amazing physique. Quite impressive. I, on the other hand," Worthy said with a pat to his belly, "have certainly let mine go. Pray, tell me, what *is* your secret?"

With a chuckle, Benton said, "Secret? It's physical labor. I chop wood for the fireplaces, all eight of them counting this one and the main house. I chop it, gather it, make sure each fireplace is functional, shovel out ashes, keep all of them in fine working order."

"Yes," Worthy said, "and you do a fine job, my friend."

"And if that weren't enough, I'm in charge of all these acres of garden. Flowering shrubs, fruit trees, exotic herbs, little-known plants. Trust me. There's no secret other than hard work."

"Did you hear that, Noble? Our Benton has become quite attached to his—what is a good word for it—ah, physicality," Worthy said, a broad grin on his face. "He thrives on hard work. Should we try it ourselves?"

Noble turned his head toward Worthy.

"No," Worthy said, the smile fading, "I guess not. A couple of old farts certainly can do without physical strain."

Benton chuckled again. "Come now, gentlemen, let's get to the business at hand. We have far more important concerns than whether or not you two want to begin changing your physiques."

"Yes," Worthy said. "You're quite right, Benton. Tell us, if you will, why you've summoned us. What urgent matter awaits our attention?"

Benton scooted forward in his chair, propped his elbows on his knees, and locked his fingers together. "Sylvie's upset," he said.

"Whatever is wrong with her? She made no mention of it."

"No, she wouldn't have. It happened only a few moments ago. She was with Nealey, trying to get her to relax after tonight's trauma."

"Oh, yes indeed," Worthy said and put his wine back on the coffee table. He hadn't taken a single sip. "That poor girl was terrified. Do we know yet who was outside? Perhaps we should call the local authorities?"

Noble adjusted his sunglasses.

"No, I guess not," Worthy said. "It's what *people* do under these circumstances."

Noble moved not an inch.

"Yes, well, I agree. These are rather extraordinary circumstances. Is Sylvie quite bothered about the intruder at the window?"

Benton sighed. "That and one other thing," he said. "Sylvie believes the trouble is being caused intentionally."

"Well, certainly, but by whom?" Worthy asked and shivered slightly. "It's a bit frosty in here. Let's have some heat."

He looked at the fireplace, pointed to it, and immediately, the flames burst to life.

"Ah," he said, "much better."

"I'd appreciate it if you'd refrain from those gestures for the time being, Worthy," Benton said. "You are needed here, but you must avoid being conspicuous or frightening, especially in front of Nealey. We must allow her to call on us for help without fear."

"Yes, yes," Worthy said. "Duly noted. Now, please, continue."

"Though I hate to say it, Sylvie believes that Anna is trying to frighten Nealey away."

Worthy gasped.

Noble leaned forward.

"Oh my, look how you've upset Noble," Worthy said.

"It's what Sylvie believes, Worthy. She thinks that Anna wants ...."

"Anna wants nothing more than to protect herself and her two little girls," Worthy said. "Nealey is no threat to them. Surely, our Sylvie knows this. What on earth would make her believe that Anna is to blame for tonight's events?"

Benton shook his head. "It was the only thing she could think of to explain the face at the window and the tremor in the floor. And there was Anna's bottle of perfume. It was found twice tipped over with the cap off. Nealey says she righted it and put the top on tightly, so she has no idea how it toppled over."

"A bottle of perfume set this in motion? Highly doubtful," Worthy said.

"No, actually, it makes sense."

"Well, perhaps you're right. Perhaps I've grown too attached to them."

He wiped the perspiration from his forehead.

Benton stepped to the fireplace and closed the glass doors. "Sylvie is struggling to make sense of what's happened. She loves Anna and her girls. She is simply trying to put the pieces together to avoid another crushing episode like the one from years ago."

"Yes," Worthy said, his voice calmer, "her poor sister."

"Most people don't take kindly to seeing ghosts, Worthy, especially people as emotionally unstable as Sylvie's sister from what we know of her. The fright was too much. It rattled her brain, made her doubt her faith. Sylvie says she was a staunch fundamentalist. Her faith was the most important thing in the world to her."

Worthy cringed. "Mercy."

"The slightest little chip in her religious armor unsettled her, and she never recovered."

Worthy paced behind the sofa. "Forgive me, my friend," he said, "but I think that something else happened that fateful night."

Benton eased back into his chair. "Sylvie doesn't know what really happened. She's only guessing."

"Ah ha! Then perhaps there is more to it!"

Noble tapped the edge of the coffee table with his cane.

"Why, that's it!" Worthy exclaimed. "Noble is convinced that something else frightened Sylvie's sister! Of course! Now, we simply must determine what or who it was."

"And perhaps it wasn't even Anna," he continued, "who tipped over the perfume, though that is quite clever, don't you think, in a very feminine way?"

Noble tapped the coffee table again.

"Yes, Brother? Do you know who the culprit is?" Worthy asked.

Noble turned his head toward Benton.

"Wonderful!" Worthy exclaimed. "Noble says that you know the answer, friend."

"We do have a new guest," Benton said.

"Max?" Worthy said and rubbed his chin. "Ah, yes. We should keep him well in our sights. There is something quite odd about him."

Benton stared quietly straight ahead and flexed his fingers.

"Well?" Worthy prompted. "Am I alone in my thinking? What are your thoughts, Benton?"

Benton closed his eyes and rested his head on the chair.

"Oh, my. Sorry to disturb," Worthy said.

He turned to Noble and put a finger to his lips. "Shh, we mustn't distract him."

Orbs of golden light formed beneath Benton's hands.

Worthy smiled.

His eyes still closed, Benton turned his palms up and cupped the shimmering lights. When he spread out his fingers, the orbs swirled along them, and when he lifted his hands a few inches into the air, the lights danced above them, then settled back into his palms.

Benton opened his eyes.

The dancing lights disappeared.

An icy gust of wind blew open the front door and slammed it against the wall.

Two identical curly-haired girls in yellow dresses and white patent leather shoes stood hand in hand in the doorway of the guest house and glared at Benton.

Chapter 13

Lulu whimpered, pawed at the covers, and crowded next to Nealey.

"Geez, you scared me half to death," Nealey mumbled and tried to shove her away, but the big dog didn't budge.

Nealey glanced at the clock on the nightstand: 4:04 AM; she turned over and pulled at the covers that were bunched up under Lulu.

"Go back to sleep," she said. "I'm exhausted."

A thought made its way slowly into her fading consciousness.

What if she needs to go outside?

Nealey groaned and sat up.

"All right," she said, slipping into her thick robe and slippers.

"Brr, it's cold in here." She tightened the robe around her and tucked her hands under her arms. The chill jerked her out of her sleepiness. Now, she was wide awake.

"Come on," she said. "Let's get this over with."

At the double doors, she stopped and sniffed.

Jasmine?

Lulu gave a delicate little bark.

"Okay," Nealey said, "let's go."

Lulu locked her teeth around the door handle until it clicked and opened. The bright light of the hallway poured in.

Nealey squinted against it.

"If you could open it by yourself, why did you wake me up?"

Instead of heading down the steps to the first floor, Lulu sat at Nealey's feet and turned her head as if to survey the expansive hallway.

Nealey watched as the dog looked toward Aunt Sylvie's door, then glanced across the hall to the room where Max was staying. She seemed to be focusing on his doorway. With a low growl, Lulu stood, her head still turned to Max's door.

"What's wrong?" Nealey whispered.

Lulu took off down the corridor, Nealey following quietly behind. The dog stopped in front of a doorway. In only a few seconds, she'd pushed down the handle in her oversized mouth and nudged the door open with her nose.

"We can't go up there," Nealey whispered, even as she watched Lulu climb the narrow stairs. "Too much construction."

Nealey tightened her robe again, felt for a light switch, and flipped it on. Then she followed Lulu to the third floor.

Aunt Sylvie said it was dangerous up here.

She distinctly remembered her aunt saying, "You might fall through the floor."

Nealey sighed and shook her head. "What is that crazy dog doing?"

She hadn't seen the attic rooms in years, so she prepared herself for the mess she might find if the rooms were being renovated. Sheetrock dust, loose boards, peeling wallpaper, buckets of paint, drop cloths, a scaffold or two.

But when she reached the top of the stairs and stepped onto the spacious landing, she found no such mess. Instead, she saw three doors, one in front of her and one on either side, all of which looked brand new. Not a single one had a handle or knob.

Nealey pushed open the door in front of her and peered inside a large, fully-finished dressing area and bathroom. On the far wall opposite her was an arched stained-glass window flanked by two similarly arched clear-glass ones. Nealey turned on the light, then walked to the windows to find that they overlooked the cliffs of the Highland Plateau.

From the hallway, Lulu whined.

Nealey found her standing in front of one of the doors. Lulu pushed it open, turned her head from side to side, then stepped in and with her nose, flipped on the lights.

An elegantly furnished bedroom awaited them, one with antiques similar to those in Nealey's room. On the far wall stood a grand four-poster bed draped with white chiffon. A soft blue nightgown was folded neatly at the bottom of the bed. A large dresser graced a corner of the room, and on top of it, something that looked familiar.

Above the dresser hung a painting entitled *Family Portrait 1890*, which showed a beautiful young woman seated in a Queen Anne chair, three children surrounding her, a tall young man standing a ways apart from the others with a queer look on his face, and in the center of the portrait, a handsome, bearded red-haired man standing directly in back of the young woman, his hands resting on the chair back. Nealey stared at the children, particularly at the two smallest girls—twins about six years old—with curly red hair.

Then, Nealey sucked in a breath.

The two girls ... the ones I saw in the kitchen.

Nealey felt as if her heart had dropped into her stomach.

It can't be. No, it can't be the same ones.

Nealey stood on her tiptoes to get a closer look.

The woman, obviously the mother of the girls, had light-colored, swept-up hair and an almost pale complexion. In direct contrast, the man behind her—the father of the girls—had a rugged look, slightly unkempt but in a well-tailored suit. What struck Nealey the most was that not one of them was smiling. The bearded man looked worried, while the lovely woman and two girls looked ... frightened.

"Family portrait," Nealey whispered. "But, who are they?"

Nealey opened the dresser drawer quietly. Inside was a collection of pieces of costume jewelry: brooches, pins, earrings, and several necklaces. Nealey picked up one of the necklaces and stared at it. She held it up to the light from the window.

It wasn't costume jewelry. It was real, a heavy gold chain stationed with pearls, rubies, sapphires, and one large emerald in the center.

"Oh, it's lovely!" Nealey said.

She looked at the portrait again, then down at the necklace. Standing on tiptoes, she held the necklace as far up to the portrait as she could.

The fair-haired woman wore the same necklace.

The room grew suddenly much colder.

Nealey shivered and closed her hand around the beautiful necklace. She heard a strange whispering and whirled around.

In front of her, an oval shape began to ripple the air like water.

A woman's voice rose from the ripples.

"It belongs to me. Put it back!"

Chapter 14

The twin girls in Benton's doorway floated an inch or so off the ground. Their dark eyes narrowed, and they scowled at him.

"You're saying bad things about our mother!" they said in unison. "We don't like it."

Worthy clutched his hand to his chest. "My goodness, children, you gave me a fright! Come in here and close that door. It's freezing outside."

Almost immediately, the door slammed shut, and the two girls stood in front of Benton.

"Well, now, that's better, isn't it, Mae?" Worthy asked the taller of the two and straightened his white silk tie.

Benton opened the glass doors of the fireplace, then knelt in front of the girls.

"Does your mother know you're out here by yourselves, Maggie?" he asked the child.

The girls looked at each other, then back at him, then immediately vanished.

"No, I didn't think so," he said.

They reappeared in front of the sofa. "Are you angry?" Mae asked.

Benton shook his head. "You can have a seat by Noble for a few minutes. Then you must go back. If your mother finds you gone, she'll be very upset."

Noble turned his head and smiled at them. He draped his arm across the back of the sofa, as Maggie and Mae hopped onto the couch.

"I want to sit next to him," Mae said, stray red curls peeking out from the identical yellow headbands they wore. She scooted as close to him as she could get. "I love Noble!"

"Please don't tell our mother," Mae said.

Maggie sat quietly beside her.

"Don't worry, children. Noble won't tell. He and I are much like the two of you."

"But, we're girls!" Mae said and the two of them giggled.

Worthy wiggled an index finger. "But of course, you're girls. What I meant was that one of us is rather quiet by nature." He nodded toward Noble. "The other—yours truly—seems to love the fine art of chatter."

The girls just looked at him.

"No matter," he said and brushed the sleeve of his white suit coat. "Pardon me, dearies. My mind must be occupied elsewhere. I don't believe I heard that promise. Did you hear it, Benton?"

Benton shook his head.

The little girls sighed. "Okay," they said, "we promise."

"Now, children," Worthy said, "that sounded a tad, shall we say, *shallow*, though I'm assured that you did not intend it so."

The girls inched closer to Noble.

"We absolutely, positively promise!" Mae exclaimed.

"Wonderful!" Worthy said, his voice full of enthusiasm.

Benton spoke up. "All right, time to 'fess up. Quickly before you get too tired, tell us about the bad things you heard."

Simultaneously, the girls twirled long stands of curly hair between their fingers as they whispered to each other.

"Girls," Benton said, "Let's get on with it."

"We're not tired," they insisted. "We promise."

"Very well, continue," Worthy said.

Mae cleared her throat. "Well," she said, "we heard Aunt Sylvie talking in the hall. She was mad at our mom for playing tricks on Nealey. She doesn't remember us, so she's scared."

Benton stood up. "Yes, her name is Nealey. She's Aunt Sylvie's niece. She's had a rough time of it, so you two need to be extra nice around her."

"We *were* nice," Mae said. "But the food smelled so good."

"Girls, remember that you're a little different from other children, and if people aren't expecting you to appear, then they might be frightened, especially when they are alone in a room," Benton said and smiled at them. "You must follow the rules."

"We *did*. We sat at the table, we put our napkins in our laps, and we cleaned up first," Mae said. "We thought we looked pretty."

"Oh, we have no doubt that you looked every bit as beautiful as you do this minute," Worthy said. "You're such precious girls.

Isn't that right, Noble?"

Noble nodded. The girl smiled up at him.

"Yes, you're quite right, Noble," Worthy said. "I don't think we followed *all* of the rules, now did we?"

The two girls frowned.

"We cannot appear unbidden to people who don't know us," Mae said. "Ever."

Maggie nodded her head.

"Excellent!" Worthy said and clapped his hands. "Truly excellent."

Benton got up and sat on the arm of the sofa. "Girls," he began.

"Ooh, you're gonna get in trouble!" Mae said. "Aunt Sylvie will be mad."

"Why is that?" Benton asked.

Maggie pointed to the arm of the sofa.

"You're sitting on the arm of the sofa, Benton. That's a no no."

Mae said in her best imitation of Sylvie, "You must respect other people's property. Otherwise, you will not be invited back. Ever!"

Benton smiled then got up. "Let's go," he said. "It's late. You're tired, and your energy is leaving you. Want me to walk you back?"

"Would you?" Mae asked. "It's scary now."

Benton knelt beside the sofa.

"Scary? You mean scary outside because it's dark?"

They shook their heads.

"Do you mean it's scary *inside* the inn?"

They nodded, then shivered.

Noble and Worthy leaned forward.

"What's scaring you inside the house?" Benton asked.

The front door creaked slowly open.

The little girls screamed and wrapped their fading arms around Benton's neck.

"The bad man's coming! He found us."

Then, with a whimper, they vanished.

Chapter 15

Nealey stood frozen in place.

The rippled air in front of her had disappeared, the voice gone, but Nealey couldn't move, and she still clutched the necklace in her hand.

She replayed the woman's command in her mind.

It belongs to me. Put it back.

When Lulu nudged her and whined, she gasped and dropped the stunning necklace onto the rug.

"Lulu," she whispered. "I'm okay, really."

But Lulu nudged her again and whined.

With trembling fingers, she stroked Lulu's head.

"I'm fine," she said. "Just my imagination again."

Her knees felt rubbery, but she bent, picked up the necklace, and put it back into the drawer. She was about to close it when a sheaf of papers in the back of the drawer caught her attention.

She took a deep breath and lifted out the yellowed papers. Carefully, she placed them atop the dresser. The first sheet was blank, so she removed it. Handwritten in beautiful script on the second page was a title and date: *The Collected Stories of Anna S. Wolcott, 1890.*

Nealey glanced up at the portrait again and stared at the woman.

"Anna?" she whispered.

She flipped to the third sheet and read the beginning sentences.

"They played, the three of them, on black and white linoleum, their dainty hands in their laps, rumpling the skirts of their frilly yellow dresses. Matching head bands held back red curls from their angel faces. Thick lashes protected the eyes, so dark brown that they looked black ... black, wide, and lifeless. The straps on their shiny patent leather shoes left indentations on their lacy white socks. They could have passed for sisters, these three. Their memories haunt me still."

The soft bark that came from Lulu startled her.

"Let's go, girl," Nealey said. "It's freezing up here, and I've got a bad case of the jitters."

Nealey tucked the papers back into the drawer.

"I'll come back for them later," she whispered.

As she eased the drawer closed, she saw a single small bottle of perfume in the middle of a lace doily. *Heavenly.*

Nealey put her hand to mouth. "The same bottle," she whispered.

Her head ached now. Her hands and feet felt uncomfortably cold, but she was fascinated by this room.

In the middle of the back wall was a fireplace with an ornately carved mantel above it. On the far side of the room were two twin beds with down comforters. A pair of flannel children's pajamas, folded neatly, lay at the foot of each bed.

Two child-sized rocking chairs, a fluffy stuffed animal in each, sat between the beds.

She rubbed her arms and walked to where Lulu sat: in between the two small rocking chairs. Lulu inclined her head to the right, then to the left.

That's exactly what she does when I rub her head.

Nealey clapped her hands softly. "Come on, girl."

But Lulu didn't budge. She moved her head about and cooed.

Nealey walked to the door, looked over her shoulder at Lulu, then shrugged.

She left the room and stepped out onto the landing. Freezing but curious about the other room, she hunched her shoulders together, rubbed her arms briskly, and eased open the door. The light from the hallway landing didn't filter well into the room, so Nealey waited until her eyes adjusted to the dimness before she took her first step.

Inside, she found nothing except drop cloths, unpainted sheetrock, a couple of ladders and several cans of paint. *Ah, the construction.*

Nealey wandered around the empty space.

"Another bedroom, I guess," she said.

On the far side of the room, the front of the house, was the only window, a small arched one that matched the arched pattern of those in the bathroom and other bedroom. Nealey gauged the size of the room compared to the one she'd just left and wondered why this one was smaller.

She pictured the back of the Playhouse Inn. Three sets of windows, the large set in the middle and two matching ones on either side, came clearly into her mind.

Why would Aunt Sylvie block them?

"Oh, well," she said. "I'm going back to my warm bed."

As she turned to leave, a slight movement in front of the window caused her to stop.

She stared for a moment, then took a few steps across the room, avoiding the numerous paint cans, and keeping her eyes focused on the window.

The ladder beside her jiggled. A paint can toppled off and landed with a loud thud onto the floor.

Nealey gasped.

She tried to turn and leave, but her feet felt glued to the dust-covered floor.

The room seemed even colder now, and each breath streamed out in vapors before her. She opened her mouth to call for help. Nothing escaped except the distinct, barely audible sound of raspy wheezing.

Two little voices called, "The bad man's coming. Go away!"

Her heart pounding in her chest, Nealey grabbed her leg and dragged it forward. She did the same with the other until she could take a step.

For the first time, Nealey noticed the jagged floorboards and the large hole only a yard or so in front of her. Her entire body felt like rubber, but she took a deep breath and strained to see into it.

"Too late. He's here." The girls' voices came from deep inside the hole.

Instead of turning away, Nealey stared down into the darkness.

When she did, a different voice spoke.

"Help me, honey. I'm trapped in here."

Her quickening heartbeat drummed in her ears. Her hands trembled.

"Hank?" Her voice cracked as she spoke. "Is that you?"

She inched forward.

He's dead. Dead and buried.

Her mind pushed away the thought.

Then, without warning, she felt a tugging at her arm.

Nealey inhaled a quick breath then looked down. Lulu scooted backwards, dragging her away.

Nealey lurched her arm from the dog's mouth. She scrambled closer to the jagged edges of the floorboards and peered over into the hole.

A faint flicker of daylight shone in through the window.

As she watched, a face smiled back at her, Hank's face.

"Oh, Hank," Nealey said and stretched out her arm, but as she did, she heard Lulu's vicious bark.

A sudden force slammed into Nealey and knocked her sideways. She rolled over onto her back and moaned.

Lulu's frantic barking almost drowned out the two trembling voices that yelled, "Too late. He's here. He's here!"

When the floor began to quiver, Nealey turned her head and gazed open-mouthed at the form rising from the hole.

It wasn't Hank at all.

Chapter 16

Sylvie's heartbeat quickened as she realized that the god-awful noise she'd just heard was actually two sounds: Lulu barking an unusually vicious bark and Nealey screaming.

Sylvie pulled on a robe and headed for the doorway. She eased open the door and surveyed the hall. No other doors were open ... except the one at the far end, the one that led upstairs.

"Mercy!" Sylvie said and ran as quickly as she could down the hall.

"Oh my good mercy," she said, taking the steps two at a time. "Nealey, where are you, honey? Aunt Sylvie's here. Everything's going to be all right."

Help us, Benton. Something's terribly wrong.

When Sylvie reached the landing, she paused. Both the barking and the screaming had stopped. The only sound she heard was a low, frightening growl.

She stepped into the door of the room to her right and gasped. She stared wide-eyed at Nealey lying on the floor, Lulu sprawled atop her, and Benton on one knee beside them both.

"What on earth?" she asked and moved forward.

Benton held up his hand to stop her. Then he pointed to the hole.

Sylvie covered her mouth with her hands when she saw the sickly-green vapor rising from the edges of the jagged boards.

"Get Worthy," Benton said.

Sylvie looked at him, puzzled.

"Ah, yes," she whispered and closed her eyes.

Quickly, Worthy, help us.

A sudden and inexplicable gust of wind swept across the room and swirled around Sylvie.

"Quickly," she whispered.

After a few seconds, Sylvie heard the faint sound of a wind chime somewhere far away.

"Well, I certainly hope this is important," Worthy said from behind her, his curly dark hair dripping wet. "I was enjoying a leisurely shower." He wrapped his plush robe tightly around him.

"Oh, my goodness," Sylvie said. "That always startles me a bit."

She moved away from the doorway so that Worthy could see beyond her.

Benton nodded in the direction of the window.

Worthy stared for a moment then put his hand to his nose and said, "Gracious, those vapors smell quite putrid, don't they?"

He walked to the edge of the hole and called down, "There is no need for all this show. I demand that you stop stinking up the house and scaring our precious Nealey. If you are who I *think* you are, then show yourself and let's be done with it."

He stepped back a few paces and fanned his hand in front of his nose. "Terrible smell."

He called once more into the hole. "You cannot win. You are outnumbered, and we will never let you harm her."

With a loud whooshing sound, the vapors disappeared.

Worthy smiled.

"Is that it?" Benton asked.

Worthy shook his head. "Hardly. Just a temporary fix, I'm afraid. We must be prepared for another attempt at any moment. Nealey, darling, are you all right now?"

She sat propped against the wall with Benton at her side, Lulu at her feet, and Sylvie on her knees with one hand on Benton's shoulder, the other on Lulu's back.

"Where are the little girls?" Nealey stared straight ahead.

"The girls?" Benton asked.

"Children. I heard them," she said, her voice a hollow monotone. Her cheeks flushed a bright red. Beads of sweat dotted her upper lip. She trembled all over. "They were afraid. They warned me."

Suddenly, Lulu sprang to her feet, lifted her head, and howled.

Benton grabbed Nealey into his arms.

"I'm taking her downstairs," he said. "This can't be good."

With her arm draped over Benton's shoulder, Nealey whispered into his chest, "Where are the children?"

"We're here," two voices called. "We're over here."

Hovering above the hole was a pulsing green mass.

Something formed inside it.

Sylvie gasped and clutched at her chest.

A small hand covered in a slimy green substance appeared at its edge.

A moaning sound escaped from Sylvie's mouth when the hand became two, then three, then four.

The mass hummed and throbbed until finally, two small forms that resembled little girls in dirty yellow dresses appeared—their arms outstretched, their faces dead white, their eyes solid black as they hovered atop the hole.

"Help us, Mama," they said. "We're afraid."

Nealey scrambled out of Benton's arms. "The children," she said as she tried to make her way forward. She stumbled and fell but got to her knees. She held out a hand to the two girls. "Don't be afraid. Everything will be all right. I promise."

The little girls smiled and reached for her hand.

But Lulu intervened. Her legs straight and wide apart, the giant dog blocked Nealey's way and took a guard's stance in front of the hole. She snarled, then issued three loud barks in rapid succession.

Worthy called to them in a not-so gentle voice, "Hello, children. Come, stand beside me. I'll keep you safe."

The smiles on their faces disappeared. They glowered at him.

Lulu snarled and barked again, three barks.

Benton scooped Nealey into his arms once again. "I must get her out of here."

"No, no!" the two girls screamed. "No, no! We're afraid."

Nealey strained to reach out to them, even when their voices changed to deep growling sounds.

In a smooth, quiet but authoritative voice, Worthy said, "Let us be done with this game!"

The two enraged girls growled and snapped like ravenous wolves. The thunderous sound reverberated around the room.

Lulu snarled and lunged, landing squarely in front of Worthy, just as the furious forms flew at him.

With a yelp, Lulu dropped to the floor.

"Lulu!" Sylvie screamed.

With a sharp, quick movement of his arm, Worthy pointed at them and scowled. "Unimpressive," he said.

From the end of his finger, a slender ray of light shone.

"Leave us," he said.

The room quieted.

Then, the girls vanished.

Chapter 17

"Dear me," Worthy said and slipped into one of the kitchen chairs. "Is nothing sacred anymore?"

He held out one hand, fingers facing him. With the thumb of his other hand, he cleaned his nails. "Using the images of our sweet girls to entice Nealey into his deadly trap. It's almost unforgivable! How is she? I trust Benton delivered her safely to her room."

Sylvie rummaged through a large drawer. "She's fine, of course. I gave her one of my special infusions. Where did I put that egg whisk?" She shook her head, "There's no telling what I did with it. Oh, it might be in the dishwasher."

"I must say, dear, that you're taking this much better than I expected," Worthy said.

"I found it!"

Sylvie went to work. She measured flour, vanilla, eggs, and milk into a large stainless steel mixing bowl. Then she grabbed a bottle off the shelf of the window box. "The magical ingredient," she said as she sprinkled gold-colored bits into the mix.

She washed and drained a bowl of fresh blueberries, another of fresh strawberries.

"Now, if I can just find my favorite paring knife."

"Sylvie," Worthy said. "Talk to me, dearest. You must have been frightened out of your wits."

Sylvie opened one drawer, fingered several utensils, and slammed it shut. She opened the drawer next to it, picked up a small knife, then tossed it back into the drawer.

"Fiddlesticks!" Sylvie yelled. "Where *is* that knife?"

Worthy got up from the table, tightened his white, fluffy robe around him, and walked to the counter where the mixing bowl sat.

"This knife?" he said as he held it up.

Sylvie brushed a few stray hairs from her face.

"That's it," she said and let out a long sigh. "I thought I'd misplaced it."

Worthy smiled at her.

"You're Sylvie Wolcott. You don't misplace things, my dear. You run the most organized kitchen, and the most beautiful B & B, I've ever seen. A place for everything, and everything in its place. That's you."

He gave her a gentle hug. "I appreciate you, Sylvie."

Sylvie sniffed.

"Yes," Worthy said, "go ahead. I promise not to tell a soul."

"I was so frightened," she said, her voice trembling.

"Yes, of course. As was I. We must hold out hope for our Wayfarer's Sky to appear before more damage is done."

Sylvie sniffed again and after two tiny sobs, covered her mouth with her hands. Then, just as suddenly, she straightened her shoulders, blotted under her eyes with her fingers, and patted Worthy's arm.

"I have berries to slice," she said. "Berry pancakes are one of my specialties, you know."

"Sylvie, dear, you must tell Nealey the truth," Worthy said. "She deserves to know everything, even the one thing you want to keep from her."

Sylvie grimaced but made no response.

Lulu whined for attention.

Worthy walked over and squatted next to her. "It was an awful thing, wasn't it my dear? But you were brave, yes indeed, you were."

He rubbed the top of her head.

"Why, Sylvie, have you ever seen such a brave dog as this?"

Sylvie grinned. "No, never," she said. "I think our Lulu is a warrior true to her Irish roots. Her ancestors would have been proud of her."

Lulu purred and flopped over onto her side.

"Now, Worthy," Sylvie said, "you must go and get dressed appropriately for my delicious breakfast. Can't have you sitting at the table in your robe, for goodness sakes. Whatever would people think?"

"Yes, of course, you are right," he said, drawing the thick robe around him. "But isn't it a bit early? If my watch is correct, the hour is now six o'clock. Breakfast is usually at seven, isn't it?"

Sylvie ignored him and sliced strawberries into a colander in the sink.

"Yes, well, I shall take your advice, dear Sylvie, and outfit myself in a grand style befitting your fine establishment. And Sylvie?"

"Yes?"

"We will not allow harm to anyone. We can't prevent the fright—my word, he was hideous, wasn't he?—but we will not allow harm to anyone in this house. You must once again put your trust in us."

Worthy turned to leave.

A chill swept through the room as two little girls appeared in front of him.

"Those other little girls upstairs weren't us, Aunt Sylvie. Honest," Mae said.

Worthy caught his breath. "Oh my, children, you startled me! And, of course, we know those girls were not you two. Why, I could tell instantly simply by looking at their dresses."

Maggie nodded.

Mae smiled. "We'd *never* wear such dirty old dresses!"

Sylvie tossed the drained strawberries into the batter then went to work washing the blueberries.

"Girls!" she said with a smile on her face. "Right on time to help with breakfast."

Worthy cocked his head. "Did we follow the rules?"

The girls nodded in unison and held out their hands for inspection.

"I invited them to breakfast," Sylvie said.

"Hmm," he said and narrowed his eyes. With his hands clasped in front of him, he bent and examined their hands.

Maggie and Mae snickered.

Worthy glanced at Sylvie. "They seem to have found something humorous," he said and winked at her.

"Girls, would you care to share the source of your chuckling?" he asked, his eyes still narrowed, his hands still clasped in front of him.

The girls looked at Worthy, then at each other, and snickered again.

Sylvie folded blueberries into the batter.

"Well?" Worthy said.

"You look like ...."

Giggles overtook them.

"Ahem!"

"You look like a fat snowman," Mae said. Maggie's cheeks flushed.

"My word!" Worthy said. "Sylvie, did you hear Mae? She says I look like a snowman, and a fat snowman at that!"

Sylvie stopped folding the berries and turned toward him. "Well, Worthy, you know I love you dearly, but she is not entirely wrong. It's the white robe, I think," she said with a chuckle.

"My, my," Worthy said. "Where are the manners of young people today?"

The girls quit laughing.

"Did we do something bad?" they asked in unison.

"Indeed, you did," Worthy said. "At the very least, you could have said a *chubby* snowman!"

Then he grinned.

"Enjoy your breakfast, darlings. The *fat* snowman must now try to waddle home and make himself presentable for a formal breaking of the fast."

The girls made a face and giggled.

Worthy paused at the door.

"Sylvie, do you think our Nealey is resting comfortably?"

Sylvie took juice glasses from a cabinet.

"Certainly," she said. "She had one of my most soothing infusions, lavender with chamomile, and my extra special ingredient. She was sleeping peacefully when I left her."

She set white porcelain plates on the table.

"Girls, where is your mother? I'm certain she can smell the pancakes, and the berry ones are her favorites."

"Yes," Worthy chimed in, "where is Anna?"

The girls lowered their eyes but said nothing.

"Come on, children, is something wrong? Is your mother upset?"

The two girls shook their heads.

Worthy stood beside them, his hands on their shoulders. "Tell us, dearies. What is your mother busying herself with this morning?"

"Ah," Worthy said suddenly, "I'll bet I know. I think she is attracted to Benton. Perhaps she's primping a bit."

The girls shook their heads.

"No way," Mae said.

"You can never tell about these sorts of affairs of the heart, girls. She might well be ...."

"She's not primping," Mae said. "And she doesn't like Benton. She still loves our papa!"

Immediately, the salt and pepper shakers on the table slid forward an inch and almost toppled over.

Maggie and Mae hunched their shoulders. "Sorry," they said.

"No bother, darlings," Sylvie said. "You know how things happen when you're upset or angry."

"Yes, ma'am," they said in unison.

"And of course, your mother still loves your papa. I'm certain she does," Sylvie said, glancing quickly at Worthy. "But what is she doing? She knows it's time for breakfast."

The girls said not a word.

Sylvie sighed and took off her apron.

"Never mind," she said. "I need to run upstairs and check on Nealey."

"Aunt Sylvie," Mae said, "you don't need to check on her. Isn't that right, Maggie?"

Maggie twirled a strand of curly hair and nodded.

"See?" Mae said.

"Nevertheless, I'm afraid I do need to check, dears. It's been over an hour."

"No, ma'am, you don't," Mae insisted. "She's *fine*."

The salt and pepper shakers jolted backward into their original spot.

Worthy's voice came a little louder.

"Children, I want the truth. How do you know that Nealey is all right?"

Sylvie cocked her head. "Come now, darlings," she said. "You know that our Nealey is not ... she's not feeling well. It is very important for us to make her feel safe here."

The girls nodded their heads.

"Our mother is good at making people feel better," Mae said.

"Yes, she is. But Nealey doesn't know anything about ghosts."

A look of concern crossed Sylvie's face.

"Oh, my word," she whispered and clasped her hands at her chin. "Where is your mother?"

Chapter 18

Sylvie threw open the door to Nealey's room and rushed to her bedside. Nealey slept peacefully and looked as if she hadn't stirred. Sylvie wrung her hands and glanced around the room. She saw nothing out of place, no signs of anyone—Anna most specifically—to disturb her slumbering niece.

Until she noticed the rocking chair beside the window. Empty, it rocked gently back and forth atop the plush new rug.

Sylvie tiptoed to the chair and put her hand on the high back to stop the rocking.

"Anna?" she whispered and glanced back at the bed to make sure she hadn't disturbed Nealey.

The scent of jasmine suddenly wafted around the spot where she stood.

"Anna," she whispered, "you mustn't be here."

The temperature in the room dropped by several degrees.

"Why not?" Anna's voice came from next to Nealey's bed. "She needs looking after."

Though Sylvie couldn't see her, she saw the rippling edges in an oval shape around the spot where the voice came from. Momentarily, the air appeared almost like waves in the water. Inside the oval shape, Anna stood, transparent at first, but then, as the ripples disappeared, Anna stood perfectly formed, looking utterly human.

Tall and slim, in her early thirties, she had a youthful face, a gentle smile, and soft pink lips. Only the dark circles under her bright blue eyes betrayed her youthful vigor. Her floral dress, belted with blue ribbon at the waist and tied in a delicate bow in the back, flowed to barely above the toes of her black lace-up shoes. Some of her wavy blonde hair was swept up to the top of her head, while the rest fell past her shoulders in curling tendrils. Her slender fingers clasped at her waist, Anna watched over Nealey the way she'd watch over her two little girls.

Beautiful Anna, Sylvie thought.

She tiptoed to the door and motioned for Anna to follow her.

But Anna shook her head in a definite "no."

Sylvie raised an eyebrow and extended her hand toward the door.

Anna sighed softly, just as Nealey stirred and turned over.

Sylvie inhaled sharply.

Nealey squinted her eyes, but they fluttered closed again.

Sylvie brushed a wayward strand of hair off her own forehead and stepped to the doorway. She motioned again for Anna to follow her.

With another sigh, Anna trailed behind, her feet just above the floor.

Sylvie nodded her approval.

Stepping into the hallway, Sylvie heard a door creak open and glanced up as Max emerged from his room.

The lights in the hallway flickered then beamed brightly again.

Max straightened his tie and brushed at the sleeves of his suit coat then turned to head down the long stairway.

"Why, good morning, dear Sylvie," he called from across the hall. "I trust you slept well. I'm ravenous this morning. Truly, I believe some wonderful aroma from your kitchen roused me from a deep sleep." He rubbed his hands together. "I cannot wait to indulge in the sumptuous fare!"

Sylvie put a finger to her lips and pointed at Nealey's door.

"Ah," Max whispered, "she's still sleeping?"

Max made a motion as if he were locking his lips together and throwing away a key.

Sylvie stepped gracefully to the stairway and glanced at Max's feet.

"Max, dear," she said, "something seems to be stuck to your shoe," she said softly. "A clump of grass, perhaps?"

Max looked down and grimaced.

"My word," he said then put his finger to his lips. "I'll just go and get this cleaned up," he whispered as he removed the offending shoe. "I'll be along shortly for breakfast."

Sylvie smiled a thin smile and nodded.

When the door to his room closed, Sylvie rubbed her temples

for a few seconds then went into her own room.

"Anna," she called. "Come here, please, and bring the girls. Quickly, quickly."

After a brief shower and change of clothes, Sylvie tied back her hair with a green ribbon, seated herself at the vanity, and dabbed on some makeup.

Lulu sprawled on the floor beside the dressing table, looking up with interest only occasionally.

Anna, Maggie, and Mae sat on the side of her bed, their hands folded in their laps.

"Darlings," she said to them as she applied the finishing touch of blush to her cheeks. "We must have a little chat."

Mae opened her mouth to say something, but a look from her mother silenced her immediately. She folded her arms across her chest. Anna's raised eyebrows brought a sigh from Mae's lips, and she folded her hands appropriately in her lap.

"You're such a perfect little lady," Sylvie said to Mae. "You all look beautiful this morning."

The girls beamed. Anna did not.

Sylvie knelt in front of the twins.

"Girls," she said. "We must do what we can to help our Nealey. Do you agree?"

The girls nodded.

"Yes, I thought you would," Sylvie said. "And that means that we must remember that she doesn't know anything about you. She isn't familiar with ...."

Sylvie stood up, and with a flourish of her hands, said, "Well, here you have it. She simply doesn't know one little thing about our family, especially about the more, shall we say, *spiritual* members of it."

The girls stared blankly at her.

"Ghosts, my little darlings. I'm afraid that our Nealey is quite clueless."

Lulu lifted her huge head, gave a soft bark, then lay back down.

"We will have to help her understand. That is our task, at the moment. We must help her, but we must do it in a way that doesn't frighten her too badly. Do you agree, Anna dear?"

Sylvie heard a whimper.

The vase on the bedside table began to rattle. Sylvie reached for it to keep it from toppling onto the floor.

"Anna? Girls? What is wrong?"

Anna sat sobbing on the bed with her hands covering her face.

Sylvie knelt beside her.

"My goodness, dear, whatever is wrong?"

When Anna did not reply, Sylvie turned to Mae.

"Do you know what is wrong with your mother?"

"Uh, huh," Mae said. "She doesn't like it when you do that, Aunt Sylvie."

"Do what, darling?"

"You know," Mae said. "It's the same as always."

Sylvie hugged Anna.

"I'm sorry, Anna," she said softly. "I didn't mean to hurt your feelings. I love you, dear, love you to pieces."

Anna moved her hands from her face.

"I just don't want to be ..." Anna hesitated. "I can't stand the thought of it, Sylvie. After all these years, I just can't."

"Mama?" Mae said. "It's all right, really. We don't mind. We're happy."

"Truly?" Anna asked.

Mae got up and looked back at her mother. "Watch, Mama, watch."

The little girl picked up the vase and held it in the air. Then she set it back down on the table. Then, she ran over to Sylvie's closet.

"Watch, Mama," she said as she opened the closet door, took out Sylvie's favorite straw hat, and plopped it on her head. She turned this way and that, modeling the hat.

The room had grown colder by several degrees, but Sylvie laughed anyway and clapped her cold hands.

"See?" Mae asked. "Did you see me, Mama?"

Anna nodded.

"Mama, I picked up the vase all by myself, just like a real girl!"

"You were magnificent!" Sylvie said.

Then Mae stood beside her mother.

"Mama, don't cry. We're all right."

Anna smiled and held out her arms.

Mae snuggled into her mother's tender hug. "I'm strong, Mama, almost like a real girl."

Sylvie kissed Anna on the top her head, kissed Mae on the top of hers, and bent to kiss Maggie.

Maggie mumbled something.

"What did you say, my sweet?" Sylvie asked and looked at Anna. "Why, I think Maggie wanted to talk," Sylvie said.

"Tell us, sweetheart, what is it you want to say?"

Maggie cupped her hands around her mouth and motioned for Sylvie to bend down.

"That girl Nealey, she's real," she whispered to Sylvie. "I saw her the whole time. She didn't fade away not even once!"

A sharp rapping sound startled all of them.

"Sylvie?" Max called from outside the door.

Sylvie eased the door open.

"Yes, Max, do you need something?"

"Oh, no, of course not. I just wondered if you would allow me to escort you downstairs."

"Oh yes, it is, indeed, time for breakfast."

Sylvie closed the door behind her and walked to the stairway.

Max didn't budge.

"Are you waiting for something, Max?"

Max shrugged. "Not really. I just wondered about your friends. Aren't they ready for breakfast?"

"Friends?" Sylvie said.

"Well, yes," Max said. "I wasn't eavesdropping, of course not, but I heard you talking."

Sylvie waved her hands in the air. "Oh, pay no attention to that, Max. I often talk to myself, especially while I'm getting ready in the mornings. Heavens, don't give it a second thought!"

"Now, Sylvie," Max said. "Granted, we all talk to ourselves on occasion, but I think you should invite the woman and her children to breakfast."

Max stood resolutely in front of the door.

"I don't mind waiting at all while you get them," he said without a hint of a smile.

Chapter 19

Nealey tossed in a fitful sleep.

"Help me," she heard as the dream played in her mind. *"Help me,"* a far-away voice rising from somewhere dark and deep, *"I need you."*

Her eyes fluttered open only a few seconds before she closed them again. She turned on her side and slid her hand under the pillow.

Tired, so tired.

She drifted toward sleep, the sound of rushing waters her lullaby.

"Mighty Waters," she mumbled, half- asleep.

An image tip-toed into her mind.

As a child, when she was upset or angry, when sleep escaped her, when she imagined hideous creatures stalking her, she sought comfort in something Aunt Sylvie had taught her: water is healing, soothing.

Once, when she and her aunt stood by the cliff's edge at the Playhouse Inn, before the great silence–the Unspeakable–crept into their mother, their lives were filled with playing. All sisters loved each other, and Aunt Sylvie seemed more her mother than her aunt. She had taken Nealey for another weekend while her mother worked a double shift at the library and Naomi stayed with the neighbors ... again. During the evening, a terrible nightmare caused five-year-old Nealey to awaken screaming.

Early the next morning, standing a safe distance from the edge of the cliff, Aunt Sylvie had held her hand.

"Close your eyes, darling, and listen to the waters. Listen to the power of what God has created."

Nealey had closed her eyes, but all she heard was a loud rumbling sound that wasn't soothing at all.

She opened one eye and glanced up at Aunt Sylvie who was staring down at her smiling.

"Try it again," she whispered. "Ask the waters to soothe you."

"But what is their name?"

Her Aunt Sylvie had chuckled. "Just call them the Mighty Waters. How's that? Now, close your eyes and think only of the water. Then, whisper the name."

Nealey did as she was told.

She thought about the water below her, nothing else but the water.

Then, she whispered, "Mighty Waters."

The rumbling sound frightened her, and she felt Aunt Sylvie's hand tighten around hers.

"Mighty Waters, gifts of the Creator, soothe us," Sylvie whispered.

Nealey slipped her fingers out of Aunt Sylvie's hand and raised her thin arms, though she didn't know why. It seemed the right thing to do.

"Mighty Waters soothe us," she whispered. "Mighty Waters."

Suddenly, the rushing waters sang to her.

Nealey smiled but did not open her eyes.

The waters sang a melody of trickling streams and tumbling waterfalls, of softly rushing currents gliding over smooth rocks, of flowing rivers sliding across dark moss, of fishes and birds and flowers, of all things alive and pleased to hear the call of a young girl.

"*Nealey, wake up,*" the far-away voice called again. "*I need you.*"

Nealey pushed herself up and leaned on her elbow. She rubbed her eyes and looked around the room.

"*Nealey,*" the voice came again, this time familiar but demanding. "*Get up. I need you.*"

She threw back the covers and got to her feet. Unsteady, she caught herself on the nightstand. She felt groggy and couldn't think straight, so she sat down on the bed and took a deep breath. She let it out slowly.

Better.

She stood up, brushed through her hair with her fingers, and stretched.

Much better.

In front of the mirror, she noticed the dark circles under her eyes. She leaned forward, closer to the cold glass, and dabbed at them gently.

She squinted and moved even closer.

"God, my eyes look awful," she whispered.

Must be fatigue.

She reached across to the vanity and took her eye cream off the top of it. With a quick squeeze, the cream was on her fingers. She twirled it around on her fingertips and looked back into the mirror. As she smoothed on the cooling cream, she relaxed and smiled.

"Now, all better."

Without warning, Nealey's heart began to beat rapidly. She inhaled sharply. Her hands, steady only a few seconds ago, began to tremble.

Instantly, she noticed that the room was freezing cold. Her body shivered.

Sounds filtered into her awareness, voices she knew.

"Mama, will you help us?"

My children.

"Please come help us, Mama. We're trapped."

"Where are you?" Nealey asked, her voice a hollow monotone.

"At the cliff, Mama."

Chapter 20

Max's eyes widened as the handle moved downward and the door to Sylvie's room eased open by itself.

He cleared his throat and straightened his tie.

"Go ahead, Max dear," Sylvie said, her voice almost like a song.

But as Max stepped into the doorway, he saw Lulu standing just inside the room.

She growled, and he jumped back.

"I'm not fond of dogs," he stammered. "I didn't know ...."

"Yes, well, it seems the feeling is mutual," Sylvie said. "Lulu, darling, are you feeling better now? Come, let's go make breakfast. My batter is probably ruined." Sylvie winked at her. "It will take some special cooking magic to revive it."

The dog brushed past Max, who had to steady himself to keep from being knocked over.

Sylvie paused and patted Lulu's head. "Yes," she said, "we had a nice little chat this morning, didn't we, my precious?"

Sylvie leaned forward and kissed Lulu on the top of the head. "You're such a good girl."

Max coughed, as if he were choking.

Sylvie ignored him and followed Lulu down the stairs.

"Ah, good morning," Benton said and held out his hand to help Sylvie with the last two steps. "How are my girls? Both looking lovely, as usual."

Lulu wagged her tail, then jumped up on Benton, her long front legs draped over his shoulders, her head above his.

"Just look at how she loves you," Sylvie said and glanced at Max, a smile on her lips.

Max wasn't smiling.

Benton rubbed Lulu's sides vigorously. "You're quite a charmer, girl. Now, get down and let's see if Sylvie needs help. Shall I set the places, Sylvie?"

"Would you?"

"Which pattern would you like me to use?"

Sylvie tapped her nose with her forefinger. "Hmm, let's see. I think we'll use the Haviland this morning. You know, Benton, that set of china was first purchased in 1850. It has made its home here ever since and still looks new, doesn't it, as if we'd just unpacked it. Yes, it will look splendid with the berry pancakes."

"An excellent choice," Benton said. "And shall we pair it with the Grand Renaissance sterling with the Lismore stemware?"

Sylvie did a soft little clap. "Oh yes," she said, "something ornate to celebrate this beautiful morning."

"Three extra places as usual?"

"Certainly! Ah, our table will be lovely!" Sylvie said.

"Max, would you like to take coffee in the sitting room?" Benton asked. "I believe you'll find Noble and Worthy already there."

Max bowed his head slightly.

"I'll bring it right away," said Benton. "Just make yourself comfortable."

Sylvie walked into the kitchen with Lulu right behind her.

"Oh, dear," she said as she looked at the mixing bowl.

She ran the whisk through her thickened pancake batter. "No, this won't do. It just simply won't do!"

Lulu looked up at her, the large face seeming almost sympathetic, then flopped down.

"Don't you worry," Sylvie said. "We'll have this place in order and fresh batter ready before you can say ..." she leaned forward and wiggled her fingers at Lulu, "boo!" she said, and laughed out loud.

Lulu whined and put her paws over her head.

"Gracious, me, I was only playing, darling. No need to be frightened. We got a terrible scare last night, eh? No worries, my love. We'll be more careful in the future. Poor baby," Sylvie said and rubbed behind Lulu's ears.

Lulu's eyes drifted shut then popped open. She sat up and looked toward the door.

"Sylvie," Benton said. "I came back to help, not that I can do much."

"How delightful!" Sylvie said. "My first batch of batter sat too long. I'll need to revive it."

As she washed off her hands, a vivid image came to her.

"Benton, do you remember the time—oh, I must have been a child—when I was very ill, and you came into my room?"

"You were four, I think, and burning with fever," Benton said. "I remember well."

"You held your finger in front of your mouth, 'Shh.' Then you sat on the side of my bed and smiled. You put your hand on my forehead."

Benton nodded.

"Oh, I still remember the feel of your hand on my face. I felt as if I were being bathed in cool water. It was quite a heavenly feeling."

"I told you to sleep and that when you woke, you would feel much better."

"Yes, and indeed I did. My mother and father thought a true miracle had occurred! And I must agree with them. Did I ever thank you?"

"Many times over, dear Sylvie," Benton said.

"Did I miss something?" Max called from the doorway.

"Max," Sylvie said, hiding her astonishment, "not at all. What makes you ask?" Before he could speak, Sylvie continued. "Oh yes, yes, you must have overheard me talking, as you heard me talking upstairs. I was simply sharing my ideas with our Lulu and Benton. I thought you were having coffee in the sitting room. Did Benton fail to bring you a cup? I've never known him to do such a thing."

"Need more coffee?" Benton asked. "I was just about to bring around refills."

"I think Max is a bit outdone," Sylvie said. "It seems he's bothered by my incessant talking."

Benton walked over to Max and stood looking down at him. "Is this true? You think our Sylvie talks too much?"

Max smiled a pathetic excuse of a smile. "Of course not," he said. "I was merely curious."

"Ah, curiosity," Sylvie said. "I believe it was Mr. Emerson who said, 'Curiosity is lying in wait for every secret.' Wonderful quote, isn't it?"

"Then, Max, I believe you can return to the sitting room,"

Benton said. "The biggest secret you'll find in here is that Sylvie talks to the dog ... and the chairs, the books, the stove, whatever is handy."

"I see," Max said.

Before he left the room, he said, "I prefer the great French writer Anatole France who said, 'Curiosity is perhaps man's greatest virtue.'"

"If it is so, then you must be quite the virtuous man," Sylvie said.

When the door closed, Benton turned to Sylvie.

"What is going on with him?"

"Slice up a few more strawberries, won't you, dear? This batter needs a bit more."

Sylvie paused momentarily and glanced up at him. *He's heard them.*

Benton knocked the colander against the side of the sink to get out the last drop of water. *I'm afraid he's heard and seen far more than that, Sylvie.*

Sylvie winced and braced herself on the countertop.

Benton moved next to her with the colander of berries, a dishrag underneath in case of a drip.

Sylvie motioned to the large stainless steel mixing bowl she cradled in her arms and nodded.

Benton poured in the berries a little at a time while Sylvie folded them into the batter.

This is his last night, Benton. I'll be glad to be rid of him.

Benton smiled at her.

We will all be glad to see him go.

Lulu gave a sharp bark that startled Sylvie so that she almost dropped the bowl.

With another piercing bark, Lulu jumped up, mouthed open the door, and bolted outside.

"What's that all about?" Benton asked.

"Well, well," Max said from the kitchen doorway.

Sylvie gasped and plopped the bowl down on the counter.

"Yes, Max?" she said, the tension obvious in her voice.

Max steepled his fingers at his chin.

"It would seem that your niece has decided she's had enough

of your hospitality, Sylvie. I wonder why?" he asked, the question sounding like an accusation.

Lulu barked three more times, loudly enough that even from outside they sounded like booms of thunder.

Benton rushed out the door.

Sylvie followed behind him. "Mercy," she said, "oh, mercy."

As Benton rounded the corner of the house, he stopped short.

"What is it?" Sylvie asked, breathless from the run.

Sylvie peered from behind Benton and saw Lulu about six yards away. Beside her stood Nealey, her toes dangerously close to the edge of the cliff.

Benton stepped slowly toward her. "Nealey, is something wrong?"

Nealey laughed out loud, but it wasn't a happy laugh at all.

"Wrong, *here*, in *this* place? Of course not," Nealey said, her voice cracking, her face drawn, eyebrows furrowed.

"Nealey, my child, please," Sylvie begged. "Please, come inside. I've got some wonderful berry pancakes for breakfast."

Even as she said the words, Sylvie realized how utterly foolish they sounded under the circumstances. She wrung her hands and chided herself for thinking that pancakes could erase the trauma of last night's events.

Then, she straightened her back and took a deep breath.

"Nealey, come into the house," Sylvie said, her voice strong and authoritative. "There is much for us to talk about. I'm going back to my kitchen, and I expect you to come with me."

For a moment, Nealey seemed to relax. She made a single step back, then stopped suddenly.

Lulu edged in front of her, her paws gingerly moving around the precarious slope.

Nealey didn't seem to notice when one of Lulu's paws slipped off the edge or when she struggled to get her footing on the unstable ground.

A scattering of rocks trickled down the cliff.

Benton moved forward until he stood within a foot of the two of them.

"Easy, girl," he said to Lulu. "Easy does it. Bring that foot up. Good girl."

"Go away," Nealey said. "I need time to think. I just want to be left alone."

Benton moved closer. Then, he glanced beyond Nealey for a second and smiled. Noble returned his smile with a slight nod.

"Please, step back a little," Benton said to Nealey. "You're scaring me."

"I'm scaring *you*? Well, what about *me*? This house is just as my mother told me it was," Nealey yelled. "It drove her crazy. I heard my children. My dead children!" Lulu stood in front of her nudging her slowly away from the edge.

"Stop it!" she yelled at the dog. "I want answers, Aunt Sylvie. No more secrets. I have a right to know what is wrong here, don't I?"

Sylvie called back. "Then you'll have to come with me, I'm afraid. I absolutely refuse to talk on this dangerous cliff side."

Sylvie stopped and looked back at her niece, but her eyes drifted to a point beyond Nealey.

Noble stood with his hand on the head of his cane, his feet slightly apart, one hand to the bridge of his sunglasses.

"Benton," Sylvie said, "if she wants to be left alone, then leave her alone. She's a grown woman fully capable of making her own decisions."

Nealey stared at Sylvie. The look on her face had changed from anger to shock.

"Fine," Nealey said and folded her arms across her chest.

Benton turned to walk away.

Lulu gave another small nudge at Nealey's mid-section. It was just enough to knock her off balance.

Nealey waved her arms as she struggled to regain her footing, but the waving motion threw her forward.

She and Lulu teetered on the edge of the cliff.

Chapter 21

We're going to die.

Suddenly, just as Nealey had convinced herself that death was imminent, she felt a strong pressure across her midsection, and to her astonishment, she was shoved a step back from the edge.

When she looked at her middle, all she could see was silver shimmering light. Again, she felt its pressure and stepped back away from the edge. She glanced down at Lulu, the shimmering light illuminating her fur and glowing warmly as it separated her from the edge, as well.

It's just light. How can it be strong enough to move us?

Looking to her left, Nealey followed the powerful beam, but the brightness of it was almost blinding. She squinted her eyes against it and tried to make out what appeared to be a human form at the end of the light.

Who is that?

Once more, she felt the pressure at her mid-section and stepped back. Steadied by this silver shimmer, she and Lulu were now safely away from the cliff's edge.

The beam now formed a silvery blanket of warmth around her, and for the first time since she'd been at the Playhouse Inn, Nealey felt at peace.

But almost immediately, the light disappeared, and she felt a powerful arm wrap around her waist. She glanced down and saw Benton grab Lulu by the collar.

Nealey clasped her arms around the dog's neck.

"I'm sorry," she said and nuzzled her face against Lulu's. "I'm so sorry and so glad that you're all right."

Then, she turned her head and looked toward the place where the great beam had come from.

Noble stood there. His face registered little emotion, his eyes hidden by the sunglasses, his mouth with the merest hint of a smile. But with an almost imperceptible nod of his head, Noble turned and, supported by his silver cane, walked silently away from them.

Nealey watched as Benton glanced over his shoulder and bowed his head slightly toward him. The man stopped and looked back.

A warm gust of air that smelled of honeysuckle drifted across Nealey's face.

Benton put an arm around Nealey's shoulder. "Come on," he said, "let's get you and Lulu back to the kitchen. A good meal will give you strength."

"I don't understand what just happened," Nealey said. "The light was so bright. I couldn't see anything except," her voice trailed off. "Did Noble do that?"

Benton lifted her gently, making sure she could stand on her own.

"Noble is a good friend to have," Benton replied without any further explanation.

Then he walked over to Lulu and stroked her head. "You're a great protector," he said. "You've done well today. Now, how about some pancakes?"

Lulu cooed at him.

"I thought that would cheer you up. Let's go."

Nealey trailed after them. Occasionally, she paused and stared back at the place where Noble had been standing.

He saved my life? How?

Each time Nealey stopped, she saw Benton and Lulu do the same. Neither of them made a sound, but they watched her.

When they were almost to the kitchen door, Nealey stopped again. She put her hand on Benton's arm.

"I wasn't going to jump," she said, "but thank you for pulling Lulu and me away from the edge. I don't know exactly how I got there. My mind seems to have gone blank, but suddenly, I was just closer to it than I thought. I'd never wish any harm to come to Lulu. You know that, don't you?"

Benton stared down at his feet. "I know that you're scared, and I know that you're upset. Who wouldn't be after last night? But I also know that there's something else eating away at you, something you're hiding from."

He reached down and patted the top of Lulu's head. "She thinks of you as family, and she needs to protect you. She will go wherever you go. So, if you don't want her life in danger, then …" he stopped and looked down at Nealey.

"I know. I know," Nealey said. "I keep messing things up and dragging her with me."

Benton opened the door and ushered Lulu inside. "Go get some breakfast, girl. We'll be there in a minute."

Lulu gratefully obeyed.

He held out his hand to Nealey. "Care to take a short stroll through the garden before breakfast? It might help calm your nerves."

Nealey furrowed her brow and folded her arms in front of her.

"The garden?" she asked. "How could the garden make me forget about what we saw upstairs? Or the ghosts of those two little girls? Or … my babies."

Benton reached down and picked up a ragged stick from among the hedges that lined the area just in front of the garden's entrance.

"Do you think I can just wave a magic wand and make those things disappear from my mind?"

He looked into Nealey's eyes and as he held the stick, his large hands ran swiftly up and down along its jagged spine. Thorns and twigs flew in all directions, but Benton never once took his eyes off Nealey.

"What are you doing?"

Her voice was softer now, her gaze locked onto Benton's.

"Voila!" he said, his eyes still holding hers. "Your magic wand."

Nealey took it and held it in her palm. The stick was perfectly smooth, all rough edges gone, as if the outer bark had been completely stripped away down to its soft, tan inner core. She rubbed it with her fingers.

"It's so smooth it almost shines," she said. "What did you do to it?"

Benton shrugged. "Nothing much."

"Tell me, Benton. How did you do this? I want to know!"

Benton opened his palm to reveal a small object that looked a bit like a staple puller. "A thorn stripper," he said. "Comes in handy for lots of things."

His eyes focused only on hers.

Nealey felt the tension in her body drain away. For a moment, as she stared into his beautiful blue eyes, she experienced a lightness, as if she could fly away. She laid her thin, white hand on his forearm.

With his finger, he traced the contours of her face.

"Don't be afraid," he whispered, still holding her eyes with his.

Nealey slid her hand up Benton's warm arm, and when she stood on her tiptoes to reach his shoulder, she felt his powerful hand at her back. A delicate fragrance lingered in the air.

Nealey breathed deeply, the aroma almost intoxicating.

As Benton leaned closer to her, she saw a golden light swirling gently around her. Her worries faded away, and at that moment, she thought of nothing except him—his broad shoulders, his large hands, his blue eyes. It was as if she and Benton were the only living, breathing souls that existed.

When he drew her into his arms and their lips touched, Nealey closed her eyes and savored the gentle tingling sensation on her lips. As they lingered there together, it spread throughout her body. All sense of time melted away. The ground beneath her seemed to vanish, and she felt as if she were floating.

And when she felt a sweet breeze across her face, his lips on her cheeks then her forehead, her eyes fluttered open.

Nealey could no longer see the garden entrance way, yet she knew they had not moved from it.

She and Benton stood amidst a rainbow of vibrant colors. Sky blue, sea green, sun gold, and rose pink shimmered around them.

"Beautiful," she whispered.

"Like you," he said and put his lips to hers once more.

Chapter 22

"Benton! Nealey! Where are you two?" Sylvie called.

Nealey shook her head as if waking from a deep sleep. The garden entrance way came into plain view again.

Benton steadied her with a hand on her back.

"Guess we'd better go back inside," he said. "Your Aunt Sylvie will be mightily offended if we refuse breakfast."

Nealey suddenly became aware of the wand in her hand and tightened her fingers around it.

Beside her, the stone pathway that led into the gardens seemed inviting. She took a step toward it.

"Breakfast will be stone cold if you don't get in here," Sylvie called from the kitchen door.

"She's waiting," he said and ushered Nealey forward. "We'll visit the gardens later on, okay?"

Nealey nodded. She didn't want to think about breakfast. Her mind didn't want to be bothered with details. All she wanted to think about was the kiss, the wonderful kiss.

She watched her feet as they moved over the graveled path to the kitchen. She listened to the crunching sound they made on the tiny stones.

As they neared the kitchen, Benton took her hand and rubbed it against his cheek.

"Your skin feels like silk," he said.

Nealey smiled at him.

He opened the door for her. Once inside, they paused for a moment.

Sylvie looked them up and down.

"Nealey, dear, you look more relaxed than I've seen you since you've been here. How delightful!"

Nealey felt her face redden. She thrust out her hand.

"Look what he made for me."

Sylvie rushed to her and hugged her tightly. "Are you feeling better, my darling? Isn't Benton just a genius with wood? He makes the most beautiful things. Remind me to show you some of his pieces later. They're all through the house."

Benton headed to the sink and washed his hands.

"Breakfast smells wonderful," he said. "As always, Sylvie, you've managed to fill the kitchen with the most enticing aromas."

Sylvie brushed a stray hair away from her face.

"Are you hungry, dear?" she asked as she led Nealey into the dining room. "Maybe you can eat a few bites."

"Oh, Aunt Sylvie," Nealey gushed. "The table!"

Two sterling silver candelabra with long purple tapers and a leaded crystal vase filled with colorful fresh flowers formed the centerpiece atop a white lace tablecloth. Gold charger plates held fine porcelain dinnerware—*is that the Haviland?*—and at each setting, Nealey recognized the Waterford crystal stemware and juice glasses. Crocheted lace napkins rested underneath sterling silver flatware.

"It's beautiful," Nealey said.

Sylvie smiled.

"Take a seat, my sweet girl. Yours is right here beside Benton."

Then Sylvie leaned close and whispered in her ear, "And you're right, darling, it is the Haviland."

Nealey stared at her, her mouth wide open.

"How?"

Sylvie winked at her.

"Benton," she said, "yours is next to Worthy."

Noble, Worthy, and Max stood up and waited until Nealey took her seat before they sat down again.

"What gracious southern gentlemen!" Sylvie said. "Their mothers certainly taught them well."

Nealey placed her wand in her lap.

Can she really hear what I'm thinking? No, it's impossible.

"Oh, no, darling!" Sylvie said to her. "All things are possible. Now, show them your little gift. They'll be delighted to see it."

Nealey gasped then coughed.

"My gracious, we'd love it," Worthy said as he handed Sylvie a platter. "We do love gifts! Don't we, Noble?"

Noble made no sound and moved not an inch.

"See, he's delighted! Please, show us, dear. Sylvie, would you like some of your own most delicious raspberry syrup?"

"Now, how on earth could I resist such a temptation?" Sylvie said.

Nealey hesitated then held the wand gently in her small hands for all of them to see.

Max laughed loudly, then wiped his mouth with the white cloth napkin.

"Forgive that outburst," he said. "I simply couldn't contain myself."

He pointed at Nealey. "A stick?" he asked. "That's certainly unique."

"Max," Sylvie said, a thin smile on her lips, "if I didn't know better, I'd swear that you were being a bit critical. Surely, you didn't intend any such thing, not in this house, anyway. Benton, darling, pass that smoked ham, please."

"Oh, I think it's perfectly lovely," Worthy said, "so smooth it almost shines! And just look at the deep brown veining of the wood grain. Why, that must be from one of Sylvie's magnificent old hickory trees. Is that correct, Benton?"

"Yes," Benton said. "It is hickory."

"Well, what an excellent choice," Worthy said. "Hickory is known the world 'round for its strength and durability. I think it's perfect, a thoughtful gift."

Max dabbed at the corners of his mouth with the napkin again. "Pardon me," he said. "I did not mean to imply that it was not well crafted, nor that Benton must have been, uh, otherwise distracted when he presented Nealey with such a gift. Truly, I meant no harm. Perhaps I'm limited by an under-active imagination," he said and smiled at Nealey.

"I'm afraid you've misunderstood, Max," Nealey said and ran her fingers along the smooth edge of the wand. "This isn't just a stick."

"Well, of course not!" Worthy said. "Don't you recognize what it truly is, Max?"

Max held out his hands. "I am afraid that its nature escapes me."

Sylvie swallowed a bite of pancake and laid her fork down across her plate. "Ah, Max," she said, "not everyone can see the value so readily. It is, in fact," she said and motioned toward it, "a magic wand."

Max let out a throaty laugh. "A magic wand?" he said.

In spite of his outburst a moment before, his face showed no hint of a smile as he got up from the table and walked toward Nealey.

"Surely, you do not put your faith in those old superstitions. May I hold it?" he asked.

Nealey held the wand more firmly. "No, I don't think so. It's a very special gift from a very special person."

As soon as the words were out of her mouth, Nealey glanced at Benton.

Benton nodded at her. "Perhaps you could share it just for a few seconds."

Benton's voice echoed in her mind. *Let him hold it, Nealey.*

Startled, Nealey blinked. Then, she looked directly at Benton.

He returned her gaze. His eyes did not leave hers.

Let him hold it.

She heard it as clear as day.

She forgot momentarily about the wand. Her fingers loosened.

Benton smiled.

"Very well," Nealey said, obeying the voice in her mind, and held out her hands.

Max took the wand from her. With a great gesture and a theatrical voice, he cried out and waved the wand: "I'd like to hear a great roar of thunder!"

"A great roar of thunder? In this beautiful weather?" Worthy said. "The sky is perfectly clear. I don't think you'll be hearing thunder, Max."

Benton slid his chair back, but Worthy laid a soothing hand on his arm.

Benton winked at him. Then, he stood, drawing himself to his full six feet four inches. He straightened his shoulders and flexed his fingers.

Nealey thought he stood as if he were preparing for battle.

He looks like a warrior.

Benton's eyes met hers again. He gave a slight nod. Then he

lifted his chin.

Suddenly, a great clap of thunder roared. It shook the table and seemed to rumble along the floor.

Nealey jumped and slid her chair back from the table.

Sylvie gasped when one of the purple tapers toppled out of the candelabra.

She reached to set it back in place and frowned at Benton.

Another roar of thunder sounded in the distance.

Max glared at Benton, then grimaced and dropped the wand as if he'd been burned.

"Excuse me," he said as he walked toward the archway that separated the dining room from the foyer. "I'm leaving today and there is much to do beforehand."

"Let me know if I can be of any assistance in your packing, Max," Benton called after him.

Sylvie let out a sigh.

Nealey picked up the wand off the floor and with trembling fingers, managed to put it in her lap.

An awkward silence followed as they continued their meal.

"That thunder came out of nowhere," Nealey said, her voice higher pitched than usual. "It's uncanny the way it roared just as Max called for it. This magic wand," she said as her still trembling fingers stroked it, "might really be magic after all."

"Well, most certainly it is magic, dear," Worthy said. "Benton doesn't do shoddy work. Perish the thought!"

As she ran her fingers over the wand, Nealey relaxed. She took a deep breath, then chuckled. "Did you see Max's face? He looked petrified when he heard that thunder."

Then Sylvie chimed in. "Nealey, darling, while we're talking of magic wands and the great power yours holds, might I mention something of importance?"

Nealey looked at her, puzzled.

"But of course, Aunt Sylvie. Mention whatever you like. I feel strong enough now to handle just about anything."

She stole a glance at Benton and smiled.

"Wonderful. Now, my dear, you've noticed the three empty places at the table, haven't you?"

Nealey turned to her. "Yes, Aunt Sylvie, as you've said, we must always be prepared for unexpected guests."

"Quite right," Sylvie said. "We must always be prepared. Now, darling," she continued, "I feel it necessary to make a few introductions. Your third day with us is just beginning now. Much has happened in that time."

"A great deal," Nealey said and looked at Benton.

Beneath the table, she slid her hand over until it rested next to his. Immediately, she felt his hand wrap around hers.

Sylvie moved her chair away from the table and walked to the double doors at the archway. She closed them quietly.

"Well, now," she said as she turned around, "would you like to meet the other members of our family?"

Worthy dropped his fork.

"Oh, my," he said.

Sylvie nodded at him.

Nealey scanned the people sitting at the table. Worthy, Noble, Benton, Aunt Sylvie.

She leaned forward to find Lulu.

"Where is Lulu?" she asked.

"She's probably gone out through the doggie door to have a romp. She comes and goes as she pleases," Benton said.

"Are there members missing?" Nealey asked. "I know there are no guests because of the renovations, but it seems that we're all here. The three empty places are for guests who happen to drop in, right?"

Worthy cleared his throat. "Perhaps this isn't the proper time."

Nealey felt Benton squeeze her hand gently. With his hand on hers, she felt stronger than she had in months.

"Darling," Sylvie said, "as it happens, those who are attending today are not what you'll expect them to be. Please summon all of your courage and understanding. Will you promise me that?"

Nealey looked at her, puzzled by the request.

"I'll try," she answered.

"You know, my child, that you have had some past experience with things of a spiritual nature."

Nealey frowned.

"Forgive me for treading on your past, but I think it might make things a bit easier for you now."

Nealey felt Benton squeeze her hand again.

"I'm not sure I understand what you're talking about, Aunt Sylvie. Why on earth would my studies be important if I'm simply meeting other members of the family?"

The delicate scent of jasmine wafted through the room.

Sylvie wrung her hands.

"They're here," she said.

Chapter 23

Max gently slid open the drawer of the tall bureau in his room until he felt it lift off the tracks. He set it on the bed and examined the inside, then he slipped two fingers around the underside of the drawer and found a tiny button. He pressed it and watched as the center of a panel in the inside drawer popped open. He smiled and drew out the papers he'd stowed there years ago. A broad smile formed on his lips. He had hidden them just right, behind a removable panel in the bottom of the drawer so that they would not be disturbed by curious owners.

For a moment, his reflection in the small mirror atop the bureau caught his attention. He cocked his head this way and that, admiring himself.

"I rather like the blond hair," he said. "Suits me. And this nose, these high cheekbones," he said as he leaned in toward the mirror. "I get better looking with each new century!"

He straightened his tie and gazed affectionately at the gold cufflinks.

"These, yes, solid gold, a gift from the Royals in Amsterdam. Priceless."

He rifled through the papers and drew out several clippings, then laid them carefully on the bed beside his open wallet. Carefully, so as not to destroy the more delicate of them, he arranged the coated clippings by place and date:

Amsterdam, 1786, a son born to Alderman Joshua and Emma Wolcott

Britain, 1790, twin boys born to Royal Statesman Isaiah and Adelaide Wolcott

"Ah," he said, "such fond memories."

He read aloud from the next clipping.

"Ireland, 1830, a girl, Marguerite born to The Honorable Alton and Adelaide Wolcott, and in 1831 twin girls also born to same, and Ireland, 1884, twin girls born to Sir Henry and Lady Anna Wolcott."

"Lady S. Anna Wolcott," he repeated. "Anna, beautiful Anna."

"And the last of the treasures," he said as he looked down at them.

North Carolina, 1920, a son born to Bishop John and Marguerite Wolcott Sanders Tennessee, 1957, twin girls born to Congressman Edward and Ida Wolcott Hollady

Tennessee, 1976, a daughter born to Mr. Lyle Martin and Charlotte Wolcott Martin Tennessee, 1976, a daughter born to Sylvia Wolcott

"Sylvie," he said. "The great Sylvie Wolcott. Yes, but we have secrets, don't we, Sylvie?"

He collected each paper, slipped it into the specially-treated archival envelope and restored each to its place beneath the hidden panel of the drawer.

He glanced out the window and saw Lulu sniffing at some flowers.

Max eyed the dog and frowned.

"Damnable creature. It will be such a pleasure to do away with that one."

Then he looked once more into the mirror. He ran a finger over the arch of his eyebrow.

Chapter 24

When Nealey saw the three members of her family, she pulled her hand out of Benton's grasp and slid her chair back so fast that it slammed into the wall. In an instant, she felt her throat close, and she gasped for breath.

"Oh dear," Worthy said. "Poor child, it's all too much for her."

Benton moved like lightning. He stood beside her and put one hand on the back of her neck.

Nealey tried to inhale, but all she could do was wheeze.

Then, with his thumb, Benton rubbed a tender spot between her shoulders.

"You have nothing to fear," he said. "Trust us, please."

Nealey felt a soothing sensation course throughout her body, almost as if she'd slid into a tub of deliciously warm bath water. She breathed easily, and for a moment, she closed her eyes and imagined herself floating in the calming waters, small waves lapping at her chin.

Her pleasant daydream was interrupted by a soft—and familiar—voice.

"I am Anna, your great-great grandmother, child. I would never do anything to hurt you."

Nealey opened her eyes.

The beautiful young woman from the portrait stood before her, a consoling smile on her face. Around her neck, she wore the stunning necklace Nealey had found.

"My great-great grandmother?" Nealey asked softly.

She looked at Sylvie. "I, uh, I don't understand."

"Yes, but you will, darling. You will."

Anna's delicate fingers fluttered to the necklace then down again to the ribboned waistband of her skirt. "And these are my girls, Maggie and Mae."

Nealey's eyes went immediately to the little girls, the two she'd seen in the kitchen and in the portrait upstairs. They stood hand in hand, their eyes lowered. They appeared no different from any two human children.

She felt Benton gently ease her forward.

And then, to her relief, she felt Lulu lick her hand. "Lulu!" she cried. "When did you come back in?" Nealey bent down and hugged her.

Sylvie motioned to Nealey. "Come, darling, they are family. Let us greet them properly."

Sylvie put her arm around Nealey's shoulder as they walked toward Anna, Lulu trailing behind.

"Anna, this is our Nealey."

Nealey stood and stared. At first glance, Anna looked utterly human, but a faint rippling around her feet made her appear to be standing in a shallow pool of water.

"Forgive me," Anna said, glancing down. "I haven't the energy I once had."

"But *we* do, Mama," Mae said with a smile. "We have plenty!"

"Nealey," Sylvie said, "Don't the girls look simply divine today? Anna takes such good care of her little ones."

Anna smiled and patted the side of her upswept hair. "One tries her best under the circumstances."

Nealey said nothing. She could see that everyone was staring at her. With a quick glance over her shoulder, she saw, too, that Benton, Noble, and Worthy were standing beside the table, all of them watching, as well.

They want me to say something. But what? I'm looking at ghosts. What am I supposed to say?

"Perhaps you could simply say hello, Nealey," Benton said. "Greet them as you would any member of your family."

When Nealey felt her heart begin to race, she wrapped her trembling fingers tightly around her wand. She swallowed hard.

Lulu whined beside her then licked her hand again.

"Hello, Anna. It is very nice to meet you," she said in a faint voice.

Then she looked down at the girls. She felt the strain in her face and knew she wasn't smiling. She tried to smile but couldn't manage it. She opened her mouth to speak but no words came. She closed her eyes, took a breath, and tried to calm herself.

She tried again to speak. "Hello," she said, her voice so soft it was barely above a whisper. "It is very nice to, nice to, uh, meet you, too."

Mae burst into tears and buried her face in her mother's skirt.

"She didn't even smile. She hates us!"

Maggie began to sob, then, and huddled next to her mother.

Lulu gave a gentle bark.

On a nearby marble and wood plant stand, a crystal vase with a single red rose in it toppled onto the hardwood and shattered into several pieces.

Anna gasped, and then both girls cried even harder.

"Oh, dear," Sylvie said.

Benton came forward. "It's all right. I'll get it."

Sylvie looked at Nealey as if pleading with her to soothe the children.

Nealey wrapped her fingers tighter around the wand. Then, with all the courage she could summon, she knelt beside Anna, Maggie, and Mae.

"I'm sorry," she said, her voice stronger. "I didn't mean to hurt your feelings. Really, I don't hate you."

She reached out a trembling hand and touched Mae's back.

She expected her hand to go right through her. The girl was a ghost, after all, but to her surprise, the child felt as substantial as any human.

Nealey smoothed the ruffled tiers on Maggie's skirt. "I'm sorry," she whispered.

Benton knelt beside the broken vase.

On his knees, Benton waved his hand across the broken pieces. The pool of water dried. The shards of glass lifted off the floor and followed the movement of his hand. He picked up the vase and guided the broken pieces into place. Then, with his large hands wrapped around the crystal, he closed his eyes. A sheer golden light swirled around the crystal then faded away.

He smiled.

He set the perfectly restored vase back onto the stand and blinked his eyes. The vase filled with a dozen bright yellow roses.

"Benton, dear, they are quite lovely," Sylvie said.

"You fixed it!" Mae said, peeping at him from the folds of her mother's skirt.

"He's magic," Maggie said softly then put a finger to her lips and shook her head. "We're not supposed to tell."

Nealey showed them the wand. "Yes, I know," she said with a slight smile. "He made this for me."

Mae held out her small hand.

"Can I hold it?"

Anna corrected her. "*May I* hold it?"

"May I?" she said.

Lulu scratched at the double doors.

"Lulu, darling, come away from there and visit with our guests," Sylvie said.

"What is it?" Maggie whispered.

Mae turned around to face Nealey, then glanced over and frowned at Maggie. "Don't you know?"

Maggie shook her head.

"It's a magic wand," Mae said. "Can't you tell?"

Maggie beamed. "A *real* one?"

"Yes," Nealey said. "It's the real thing."

Worthy walked up beside Anna and the girls.

"Ah," he said, "it isn't often one has the opportunity to see a true magic wand. We are quite fortunate, indeed!"

"Does it do any tricks?" Mae asked. "I mean, can we do something magic?"

Nealey looked at the girls, the two of them with eyes sparkling. Their sweet, innocent faces tugged at her heart.

They're ghosts. Remember ... they're not alive.

But Nealey dismissed the thought. To her, they certainly seemed alive. Precious little girls excited about something new. She reached out and stroked Mae's shiny red curls.

"My mama brushes my hair every day," Mae said. "Sometimes, I don't like it, but I have to sit still anyway."

"Me, too," Maggie said and twirled a curl between her chubby fingers.

Tears welled in Nealey's eyes.

"My little girl didn't like to have her hair brushed, either," she said.

"What is her name?" Mae asked.

Sylvie covered her mouth.

"Children," Worthy said, "we must get Benton to show us how that wand works. Wouldn't we all like to see a bit of magic?"

"Did I say something wrong?" Mae asked, looking up at Sylvie. "Did I do something bad?"

"Oh, heavens no, sweetheart. You have been a perfect little lady. I am so proud of both of you."

Mae stepped away from her mother's skirt and put her hand on Nealey's face.

"Then why is she crying?"

Anna knelt down, her feet still surrounded by a rippling pool. She touched Nealey's shoulder. "You are family, Nealey. We love you."

"Mama, did I make her cry?" Mae asked.

Nealey wiped her eyes and sniffed.

"No, Mae, you didn't. I was remembering about my little Lauren."

Benton knelt beside her as she wiped away the remaining tears.

"Where is your little girl?" Mae asked.

Benton took the wand from Mae's hand and said, "Okay, who wants to see a magic trick?"

Maggie tugged at Mae's sleeve.

"Stop it," Mae said and brushed Maggie's hand away.

"I want to know where the little girl is. Is she coming for a visit? I've got some toys we can share, but she can't play with my favorite doll, my good one. Mama will get mad."

Nealey stood, Benton right behind. She leaned back slightly until she could feel his body next to hers. She inhaled a deep breath, then let it out slowly.

"Now," Worthy said to the girls, "how about that magic trick? Benton, show the girls something spectacular, won't you?"

"How about this?" Benton asked.

He waved the wand, and the room filled with bright balloons in every color of the rainbow.

Maggie squealed with delight as one of the rosy red ones drifted down to her. She wrapped her arms around it.

But Mae frowned at him, then looked up at Nealey. She put

her hands on her hips. "Isn't anyone going to tell us about Lauren? We want to meet her."

"Mae," Anna said, "I have heard quite enough from you. You and Maggie go upstairs to your room."

Mae folded her arms across her chest and frowned.

Anna raised one eyebrow.

Mae's shoulders slumped. "All right."

As she started to walk away, Anna brushed a balloon away. She stopped Mae with a hand laid gently on her shoulder. This time, she raised both eyebrows.

Mae balled her fists, but let them hang at her side. She turned and faced Nealey.

A balloon drifted in front of her.

"I'm sorry," she said, brushing past the balloon. "I just wanted to know about your little girl, that's all. I didn't mean to be rude."

Mae glanced up at her mother.

Anna nodded once and smiled.

"We must be going now," Anna said to the group. "It was a pleasure to meet you at last, Nealey. We'll see you again, I hope."

Nealey smiled at them. "Yes, of course," she said and waved away a balloon.

Then she called to Mae. "You weren't rude, Mae. My sweet Lauren died last year. She was murdered."

A collective sigh of sympathy came from Sylvie, Anna, Worthy, and Maggie.

But Mae said, "Like us?"

"Yes," Nealey said, her voice strong, her fingers wrapped tightly around the wand, her body leaning against Benton's, "just like you."

As Mae walked toward her, Nealey noticed that her form seemed to have changed. Her little arms and legs looked fragile, now, as if they had lost some of their fullness. And then, she realized that the child was fading away. Her feet had disappeared altogether. She glanced at Anna who now had no form below her waist, only rippled air surrounding her.

"Did she get to go to Heaven?" Mae asked.

"Heaven?" Nealey said.

Mae nodded and smiled.

Lulu scratched at the doors once again.

Cradling a balloon, Worthy knelt down next to Mae. "Well now, what do you think, my dear?"

"We're going someday to see our Papa," Mae said. "He's waiting for us. Benton said so, and Benton never lies."

"How right you are, my dearest. Only a little while longer," Worthy said, "and you three beauties will be on your way just as soon as we get rid of that pest."

Mae furrowed her brow. "You mean that bad man?"

"Most certainly. We are going to displace him very soon."

Mae turned and looked at the large arched doors.

Lulu stopped her scratching, sat at the doorway, and barked.

"Well, you better hurry," she said, her voice trembling now.

"What dear?"

She pointed to the doorway.

Suddenly, all of the bright balloons began to pop, one by one. The room filled with the sounds of mini-explosions.

Maggie and Mae shrieked and covered their ears.

"Hurry, let's go, Mama. Hurry!"

"What's happening, Benton?" Sylvie asked, her face betraying her fear.

Benton shook his head. "I'm not sure."

"He's here again," Mae yelled. "He's here. He's coming to get us! He'll take us to that bad place!"

The noise of the popping balloons ceased. The room took on a deathly silence.

The girls disappeared.

Anna left, as well, but in the spot where she had stood lay her stunning necklace.

Nealey scooped it up at once.

Lulu pawed at the doors again. She turned her head toward Benton and whined, then looked back and growled.

The huge double doors under the archway rattled.

Lulu stood her ground, her mouth pulled back from her teeth, as she continued the low growling.

"Benton, what's wrong with her?" Nealey asked.

He made no response.

Nealey saw that his gaze was riveted on the archway.

All of them watched as the doors rattled again, the sound of it like thunder.

Suddenly, the handles clicked, and the doors eased open.

Chapter 25

Outside the archway doors, the group stood gaping at an empty space.

"Well, now, that's certainly odd," Worthy said. "Nothing at all out here."

"It is odd, isn't it, Benton?" Sylvie asked. "After such horrid rattling, as if it were a matter of life or death for someone to get those doors open, it's quite bizarre that there was no one there."

From the top of the stairs, Max chuckled.

"My goodness," he said. "Don't you all look like a sad bunch?"

He sauntered down the steps, his hand on the banister, and walked toward them.

Sylvie stood with her fingers wrapped around Lulu's collar.

"It's so aggravating when things don't turn out as we planned them. Isn't that right, Benton? We make the best of plans, include our most exciting tricks, but for some reason, things go awry. Terrible feeling, isn't it?"

Max winked at him but didn't smile.

Lulu growled as he came closer.

"Easy, my sweet," Sylvie said to Lulu.

"I beg your pardon, Max? I'm not sure I understand," Benton said.

Max moved toward the double doors leading outside. "It's just that when we are trying to entertain little ones," he paused then snapped his fingers as if he'd remembered something. "Never mind. I must go to my car," he said. "So much to arrange before this evening, and I must be sure to gather *all* of my belongings. Can't leave anything behind, you know." He reached for the door handle and turned back to them. "I will be a little sad to leave the Playhouse Inn, Sylvie. Even with that growling beast underfoot every minute. I am afraid that I must make a negative remark on the comment card about her, or perhaps I'll write my friend at the Post. 'Guests beware' and all that sort of thing." He smiled a truly insincere smile. "Nevertheless, there is always something exciting going on here," Max said.

"Ah, yes," Sylvie said, "but I'm sure your business is just as exciting."

Max pointed at her. "Of course, you're always right, Sylvie. Yes, I have exciting plans!"

He shut the door behind him.

Noble tapped twice on the floor with his cane.

"Oh, I quite agree with you, Noble dear. He is an odd sort," Sylvie said. "Very odd, indeed. And frightening, though I can't for the life of me think why. I must admit that I will be relieved to see him go."

Noble tapped again with his cane and looked toward Worthy.

"Certainly, Brother," Worthy said. "Noble suggests that while Max is out, we should confer in private with the girls."

Worthy put an arm on Nealey's shoulder. "My dear, would you be so kind as to serve as hostess?"

"I think he means in your room, darling," Sylvie said. "Could we meet there for some privacy?"

"Yes, it has such lovely windows, doesn't it, dear? Why, a curious person could see every little thing that's going on outside," Worthy said.

Nealey nodded. "Oh, I understand," she said, her eyes sparkling.

They want to watch Max.

"You're catching on, dear," Worthy said and winked at her.

Nealey put both hands to her mouth.

Worthy motioned toward the stairs.

"Lead the way, my dear."

Nealey grinned.

"Certainly," she said. She held Anna's necklace gingerly in her hands. "It's so stunning."

"You must take care of it," Sylvie said. "Anna will be pleased."

"Really?"

"But of course, darling. It is a part of your legacy, after all," Sylvie said.

Nealey smiled and led the way up the stairs, down the long hall, and through the double doors to her room.

"I believe there is seating enough for everyone," she said as she placed the necklace on her dresser top. "Aunt Sylvie, you and I can sit on the side of the bed, okay?"

Lulu walked to the end of the bed and flopped onto the floor.

Sylvie chuckled and pointed to Lulu. "She is such a precious girl. Maggie, darling, will you and Mae join us?"

Nealey sat on the edge of the bed and shivered at the sudden drop in temperature.

"You'll get used to it, darling," Sylvie said to her and slipped an arm around her shoulder. She rubbed Nealey's arm briskly. "Better?"

Nealey nodded.

"Boo!" Mae said when she and Maggie appeared directly in front of Nealey.

Nealey jumped.

Sylvie shook her head and sighed.

"These children!" she said. "I remember once, Nealey, when you would have done exactly the same thing. You were about three, I think, and for some reason, you loved to pretend you were a ghost. You'd jump out from behind every stick of furniture in this house with your little hands wiggling in the air and yell 'boo!' at every innocent passer-by. Scared me more than once."

Nealey just stared at her. "Here? In this house? I don't remember it."

"No, of course not," Sylvie said and parked a few strands of hair behind her ear. "Perhaps I'm mistaken. Perhaps it was Charlotte's house. You were so young then, darling, and so was I. No matter."

"We were just playing, Aunt Sylvie," Mae said. "We didn't mean to scare anybody."

"Yes, yes, I know," Sylvie said.

"Girls," Benton said as he walked closer to them, "can you help me?"

"Help you? You want *us* to help you?"

Both girls beamed.

"We love to help!" Mae said. "Isn't that right, Maggie?"

Maggie nodded.

"Fantastic," Benton said. "I need to ask you a question, and I want you to think about it carefully before you answer, okay?"

"Yes, my dears," Worthy said, "you must think before you speak. That's always a good idea, now, isn't it?"

Maggie and Mae looked puzzled. Maggie twirled a dangling red curl. Mae put her small hands together and rubbed one thumb with the other.

Benton knelt between them. "Now, here's the question. When you speak about the bad man, do you mean someone who is a guest here?"

Maggie and Mae glanced at each other, then shrugged.

Benton continued. "More specifically, girls, is the bad man the one outside right now?"

The two of them, their feet slightly off the ground, moved almost instantly to the window. They hovered there and glanced down. Then, they leaned forward and looked to the right then to the left.

"We don't see anyone," Mae said, "just that scraggly cat by the red car."

Benton and the rest of the group huddled at the large picture window.

"Where's Max?" Nealey asked. "Aunt Sylvie, is that your cat?"

"Goodness, no," Sylvie said. "I am a dog person. My precious Lulu is all I need."

"It's gone anyway," Mae said. "Just went poof."

Nealey broke away from the group and went to the window on the other side of the wall. As she stood and surveyed the driveway, she saw a small boy on his knees beside the red car. He seemed to looking for something underneath it.

"Aunt Sylvie, who is that little boy? Is he a neighbor?"

Sylvie and Benton joined her at the window.

"Who on earth could you be talking about, darling? My nearest neighbors are quite far away. They are a retired couple whose children are grown and gone. Arizona, I think."

"Then, what is he doing here? Looking for the cat, maybe?"

"Can we see?" Maggie asked, scooting in front of Nealey.

Sylvie tapped on the window once very lightly, then a second time with more force.

The little boy stood up and turned his head toward them.

Nealey gasped.

"Nicholas? Nicholas? Oh, God, it's my Nicholas."

Nealey rapped on the window pane.

"Stay there, Nicholas," she yelled. "Mama's coming."

As she turned to run downstairs, Benton stopped her and took her in his arms. He rested his chin on the top of her head.

"No, Nealey, no," he whispered. "It isn't Nicholas."

"Get out of my way!" Nealey yelled and tried to push away.

But Benton wouldn't let go.

"That's my boy down there!" Nealey cried.

Benton held her by the arms and turned her toward the window.

"Look, Nealey," he said. He moved behind her and wrapped his arms around her. "Don't be afraid. I'm here. I will keep you from harm."

Nealey leaned into Benton, felt the power of his arms around her, and stared down at the child.

As she watched, his smile turned to a sneer, his face and hands turned a putrid yellow-green color, and his blond hair suddenly black and hanging in thick mats. He rose from the ground, rose higher and higher toward the tree tops.

"Leave us, girls," Worthy said. "Hurry on, now."

Maggie and Mae vanished.

Outside, with clawed hands, the hideous boy grabbed a tree branch and swung up on it. Like a cat, he perched on the branch. His head turned this way and that, his eyes black as night.

Even inside, Nealey could hear a hissing sound when he opened his fanged mouth. It grew louder and louder until it thundered throughout the room.

Suddenly, the boy jumped from the branch, flew through the air, and stopped short just outside the window.

Lulu sat up and barked viciously.

Then, as they all watched, his form changed again. His face smoothed, his hair took on perfect curls, and his body grew long and lean.

Hovering in front of them was a woman smiling sweetly.

"Charlotte?" Sylvie said, her hand at her throat.

"Mama?" Nealey said, her fingers on Benton's hands.

The woman cocked her head to the side, the sweet smile gone.

"Tell her, Sylvie," she hissed. "Tell her everything."

That said, the creature held out her arms, cackled, and disappeared.

In her place was left only a single black feather that drifted to the ground.

Chapter 26

A loud banging on the door startled them all.

"Yes, who is it?" Sylvie managed, her voice cracking.

"Sylvie?" Max called. "Is everything all right?"

Benton opened the door so that it was slightly ajar.

"May I help you, Max?"

Max craned his neck as if to look into the room.

A sudden strong gust of wind swept across the room.

Max took a step backwards. "The windows must be open," he said. "I didn't notice such a stiff breeze outside."

He sniffed the air. "What is that terrible smell?"

"I believe it's roses," Benton said.

"Come in, Max. How may we help you?" Sylvie called.

"I simply wanted a cup of tea," Max said, "yet when I came in, the whole place suddenly seemed deserted. I thought I heard some rather disturbing sounds coming from up here."

Benton stepped back and swung the doors wide open.

From her seat on the side of Nealey's bed, Sylvie looked toward the door.

"Disturbing noises? Putrid smells? Why, Max, have you been into the wine this morning?"

Then she turned to Benton.

"Why don't you be a dear and take Nealey to see your new project? She hasn't been out that far on the grounds yet."

Then she hugged Nealey and kissed her forehead. "He's always building something. I haven't even seen it myself, so you'll be the first. Let him show you what he's working on. He lives for it!"

Benton extended a hand to Nealey. "May I accompany the fair lady on a tour of the hills?"

Clutching the wand in her hand, Nealey felt relaxed but couldn't muster a smile.

Sylvie chuckled and said, "I'll expect a full report when you return."

"I thought I heard voices," Max said. "But, there's no one here except you and Nealey, and Benton, of course. He seems to be everywhere."

"Max, I believe this is the second time you've thought you heard voices and strange sounds," Sylvie said. "Obviously, the Playhouse Inn doesn't agree with you. It is not, shall we say, your kind of place. Come," she said, "I'll make you a cup of tea before your journey."

"I hadn't planned to leave until after our evening meal, Sylvie, if that meets with your approval," Max said. "My destination tonight is only a two-hour drive from here. If I leave by 8:00, I'll have plenty of time to get settled."

Sylvie looped her arm through his. "All right," she said. "I always have a place at my table for those unexpected diners. Now, about your tea."

"That delicious Earl Grey would be wonderful," he said as they walked through the double doors.

Sylvie smiled at Benton as she passed.

Take her out of here.

Benton nodded at Sylvie.

"Max," he said as the four of them descended the stairs, "we were looking out into the driveway. We thought you'd gone to your car, but we didn't see you."

"That's odd," Max said. "I retrieved a case from the trunk, rearranged some stacks of papers. It took a much shorter time than I expected. So, I came back in and waited in the sitting room. I was thumbing through a magazine when I thought I heard some sounds from upstairs."

"Well, that explains it," Sylvie said. "We must have just missed you. Now, Max, if you'll be seated once again in the parlor, I will make your tea. Benton, I trust that you and Nealey will have a pleasant afternoon excursion."

She motioned toward the parlor. "Max, if you please."

When he'd left, she looked at Nealey and held out her arms. The two embraced.

"Benton will keep you safe, my darling. Later, you and I will have a nice long chat. Are you quite all right, my dear?"

Nealey hugged her tightly. "No, I'm not all right. I'm scared."

"As am I," Sylvie said. "As am I."

"Ladies," Benton said as he led them into the kitchen, "Max is waiting. Sylvie, the kettle is on, scones are warm."

"Where's Lulu?" Nealey asked.

"My heavens, I don't know," Sylvie said. "Poor dear. I forgot about her."

"She didn't follow us down the stairs, did she?" Nealey asked. "Is she still in my room?"

Nealey put a hand to her forehead.

"What is it?" Sylvie asked. "Headache?"

"No, no. I suddenly had a dreadful feeling of doom, like the one I had ...."

"Oh, no, darling," Sylvie said. "That won't do, now. Lulu is fine. Our friends are here. We will all be fine. I promise."

Images of that horrible night a year before flashed through her mind. Hank in the chair, dead. Her sister, Naomi, and her children on the bed, dead. Her own children huddled next to her.

"I said the same thing to them," she said, her voice flat and hollow. "It was a lie then, and it is a lie now."

Tears rolled down Nealey's cheeks. The wand slipped from her hand and fell to the floor.

The scent of jasmine wafted across Nealey's face.

An icy-cold hand brushed her shoulder.

A cold breath rushed across her ear.

She found herself frozen at the foot of the staircase, as if encased by an enormous block of ice.

The tea kettle gave a high-pitched wail.

Chapter 27

Maggie and Mae sat on the sofa in the guest house. Mae popped the toes of her shoes together while Maggie simply twirled a strand of hair.

"We have to be nice to her," Mae said, "but we don't like her. She makes scary things happen. I want her to go home, Noble."

"Now, girls," Worthy said as he stoked the fire, "this *is* her home."

Noble nodded at the girls.

"But we don't *like* her," Mae said.

Worthy folded his arms across his chest. "What is it that you don't like about her, dears?"

"She's weird," Mae said.

"Weird," Worthy repeated with a chuckle.

"Uh huh," Mae said and jumped up off the sofa. "And, she cries all the time."

"All the time?" Worthy asked.

"Well, not ALL the time," Mae said, "but a lot. Isn't that right, Maggie?"

Maggie nodded.

"But wasn't she very nice to you today?" Worthy asked, brushing a speck of lint from his white jacket.

Mae sighed.

Maggie twirled her hair.

"Now, children, be honest. Didn't she treat you very well today? She even showed you her magic wand. That was very nice of her, don't you think?"

Mae rolled her eyes then let out an exaggerated sigh.

"Okay, it was nice," she said.

Worthy bowed slightly. "Well done, little ones. Now, I must go and check on our Sylvie. She had quite a fright only moments ago. She will need the encouragement of her old friend. You two can remain here with Noble if you like."

Mae smiled up at Noble. He nodded.

"We want to go back with Mama," Mae said. "She might need us."

"Fine, then," Worthy said, straightening his white silk tie. "Allow me to escort you ladies to the inn. Our good Noble, then, can go and keep Max company."

"He's scary," Mae said. "We'll be glad for him to go."

"Is that so, girls?"

Both of them nodded.

"He frightens you, does he?" Worthy asked. "He seems a bit odd to me, as well. Come, then, let's be off to assist our Sylvie."

Mae tugged on his jacket sleeve.

"Yes, dear, what is it?"

"When he goes," Mae said, "I hope he takes the bad man with him!"

Chapter 28

"Come with me," Anna said when she found Nealey at the foot of the stairs. "Let's go to the kitchen."

Anna sat beside Nealey at the kitchen table, stroking her hair.

"You'll be fine, dear," she said as her fingers ran through the girl's thick red curls.

Nealey had her arms folded on the table, her head resting on them.

Sylvie stood at the sink and ran her fingers through the dish-water.

A gust of wind brushed across her face. The fragrance of roses lingered in the air.

"Ah, you've returned," she said.

"Indeed, I have," Worthy said. "I trust you missed me while I was gone?"

"I'd hardly noticed," she said and smiled at him, then nodded in the direction of the table.

Nealey raised her head and wiped tears from her face.

"Is everything all right?" Worthy whispered to Sylvie. "Nealey looks quite pale."

She washed one of the china plates, rinsed it, then handed it to him. "Careful," she said. "That's my good Haviland."

"Yes, yes, I know," he said as he rubbed the plate gently with a soft dish towel. "I'll treat it with kid gloves. Goodness knows, I shudder to think what would happen if I broke one of these jewels."

"Oh, mercy!" Sylvie cried. "Perish the thought."

"Sylvie, dear," Worthy whispered again. "There is a matter of urgency that we need to discuss. Could we pause for a moment?"

Sylvie stopped her washing.

Worthy motioned toward the dining room door.

"Pardon us for one moment," Sylvie said to Anna and Nealey.

Once inside the dining room, Worthy spoke.

"I've just come from the guest house. Mae said something quite alarming."

"Tell me," Sylvie said.

"She said, in reference to our guest, that when he left tonight, she hoped he took the bad man with him."

"What? Why, that makes no sense!"

"Shh," Worthy said. "It appears, my dear Sylvie, that there is a villain lurking about that we've quite overlooked."

"But who? Who could it be?"

"I have no idea. I must tell Benton. For now, though, let us get back to our Nealey and Anna."

Sylvie followed him back into the kitchen and resumed her washing.

"Anna, darling," Worthy said. "You look lovely, as usual. The girls wanted to go to their room, so I saw them safely there."

"Thank you," she said. "I was telling our Nealey not to worry, that all would be well. I hardly think she's heard a word I've said. I am afraid that I frightened her. Perhaps my unexpected presence caused her more grief. She stood like a statue and simply shivered. Mercy me. The tea kettle wailed and nearly frightened me to death. So to speak."

Nealey sniffed and rubbed her temples.

"I did hear you, Anna, and I appreciate your coming to help me. And yes, I was scared until I realized it was you. I'm just having a little trouble getting over the sight of my little Nicholas. I miss my children so very much."

Sylvie dried her hands on her apron and nudged Worthy toward Nealey.

"Why, most certainly you do!" Worthy said and put his hand on Nealey's shoulder. "Of course, it's only natural, my dear."

"You've been so strong, such a brave girl," Anna said. "We are all very proud of you."

Benton came in from outside carrying a bouquet of flowers.

"Well," he said, "quite a gathering we have here."

"Benton, how lovely!" Sylvie said, "Oh, you know how I love fresh flowers on my kitchen table. Bless you. Now, if you will, put them in the vase on the table. I've just removed the old ones, so our vase is in need of replenishing. As usual, you've brought new ones just when they were needed."

Benton walked to the sink, filled a glass with water, then waited for Sylvie.

"Oh, my yes," she said as she reached for a tin box on the window sill. She opened it and took out a small amount of some gold powder. She sprinkled it into the water. "Just a pinch is all we need. Too much would be disastrous for those beauties."

Benton poured the contents into the vase on the table then put the flowers down into the water.

"Roses and lavender," he said. "Always soothing, especially to our ghosts. I thought they might help with the anxiety that seems to be spreading."

"You are absolutely right, my dear. What better for frayed nerves than the soothing scent of roses and lavender? You are a wonder, Benton."

"They are simply perfect on that table," Worthy said. "Our Benton has such an eye for color."

Nealey inhaled. "Oh, they smell wonderful. So relaxing."

Anna smiled.

"Now, Benton," Sylvie said, "why don't you do as I suggested and take our Nealey to see the new project you've been working on? I believe some fresh air might serve her well."

Nealey stood and stretched. "I'm feeling much better," she said. "I could use a walk. Besides, I'm a little curious about this new project of yours."

Nealey glanced around the kitchen. "Where's Lulu?"

"Lulu!" Benton called. "Time for our afternoon walk. Come on, girl."

Lulu burst through the double doors and sat at Benton's feet. Her pink hat hung from her mouth.

"Oh, how precious!" Sylvie said. "She's brought her cap with her. Such a brilliant girl you are!"

Lulu looked at Sylvie. Her mouth spread out and she nodded her head.

"Why look at that!" Sylvie said. "I think she smiled at me. Oh, you're such a darling," Sylvie gushed and kissed her on top of her huge head.

Lulu gave a soft little bark and dropped her cap on the floor.

She bounded past Sylvie and out the double doors.

"Now, what is that all about I wonder?" Worthy said.

In a moment, Lulu came through the doors again. In her mouth, she carried Nealey's jacket.

Worthy and Benton chuckled.

Sylvie shook her head. "My, my," she said.

Nealey took her jacket and slipped it on. "If you aren't the smartest dog I've ever seen!" she said and ran her hand along Lulu's head. "Such a good dog you are!"

Then, she turned to Anna. "Thank you for trying to help. I feel much better now."

"You are most welcome. You are family, dear," Anna said. "I must go and check on the girls."

With that, she disappeared.

"Now, you two scoot," Sylvie said. "Worthy and I will get this kitchen in tip-top shape. Isn't that right, Worthy?"

"I imagine it is," Worthy said and waved a hand. "Oh, Benton, one little item for your consideration before you leave."

Benton nodded.

"Well, you see, the girls made an interesting comment just a few moments ago."

"They do that frequently, those two," Benton said.

Worthy straightened his dish towel and moved to the sink. He picked up a rinsed cup and dried it carefully. "The good Haviland," he said. "I know."

Still holding the cup, he said to Benton, "They said that when our *guest* left, they hoped he took the bad man with him."

"Interesting."

"Am I missing something?" Nealey asked. "I don't understand."

Benton took her hand. "I'll explain it as we walk."

Lulu barked a tiny little feminine bark.

"Well, whatever Lulu says is fine with me," Nealey said. "Just let me fix her hat."

They left through the door that led outside, Benton holding Nealey's hand, Lulu trailing alongside, her pink hat perched daintily on her head.

Chapter 29

Standing together, Worthy and Sylvie gazed out the kitchen window.

"Just look at the two of them, Worthy. What a splendid couple they'd make." Worthy smiled.

"Perhaps you're getting a little ahead of yourself, dear Sylvie. Benton is …."

Sylvie waved a hand at him and kept watching.

"Oh, goodness, Worthy, I know what Benton is. Still, he and Nealey, under the right circumstances, would make a wonderful story, don't you agree?"

"Yes, certainly, I agree. However, in my experience, these types of … unions … rarely occur. They're frowned upon."

Sylvie sighed and shook her head. "I know all that, too. Immortal, mortal. It's never encouraged, for obvious reasons. But aren't there exceptions? Aren't rules meant, at perfect opportunities, to be broken?"

"Some rules can't be broken, Sylvie. Benton can never tell Nealey the whole truth of what he is. It is forbidden. If he breaks that rule, then God forbid, he will lose his place here, especially in light of the fact that he has already broken one of our supreme rules."

"Benton? I can hardly believe that."

She handed him the last of the dishes. "Careful now. That's our final piece."

Worthy dried it carefully, stacked it with the others, then laid aside his towel.

"Yes, dear, when our Benton was first assigned to us—after he'd completed his training—he was such a grand specimen, so full of himself, so full of pride in his accomplishments. He was quite puffy about it, really."

"Benton? Puffy?" Sylvie asked. "I can't imagine such a thing."

"His pride led to arrogance, I'm afraid, and worse. In a critical moment, he underestimated the power of an enemy—one of our own, actually, who'd turned to the darkness. Benton could not defeat him as he'd done in training so many times. The enemy proved the stronger foe."

"So, our Benton lost the battle? Isn't that common? Even the bravest of our warriors lose an occasional fight, don't they?"

Worthy nodded.

"Yes, you're right. But in this case, three souls hung in the balance, innocent souls who could not fly homeward. They were bound, after that, bound here and trapped."

Sylvie looked at him, puzzled.

"Surely, you don't mean ... no, not our Anna and the girls."

"The very same, I'm afraid. And now, our Benton must make amends. He has suffered mightily for that wrong."

"Oh," Sylvie said and waved a hand, "but certainly he could not help it. Everyone makes mistakes. You and all of your rules!"

He pointed upward. "Well, they are not exactly MY rules, now are they, dear?"

Sylvie sighed.

"When Henry Wolcott built this house and Anna named it the Playhouse Inn, the two of them had no idea that it would, indeed, become a playhouse for the girls," Worthy said.

The kitchen door swung open.

Max stood there.

"Yes, Max? I trust you're enjoying Noble's company. He is not much of a talker, but he is a great listener," Sylvie said.

"Another cup of tea would be lovely, if it wouldn't be too much of an inconvenience. I wouldn't want to interrupt anything, well, so cozy."

"Nonsense!" Sylvie said. "I'll bring you a cup. More scones?"

"They're quite delicious," Worthy said.

"Shall I bring them for you?" Sylvie asked as she turned on the tea kettle.

But Max didn't respond. His attention seemed riveted on the window.

Sylvie glanced out herself and saw Benton and Nealey, hand in hand, their feet hardly touching the ground, traveling up the hill.

The tea kettle whistled.

"Well," she said, "the tea is calling."

Max turned and left.

"Would you hand me a cup and saucer?" Sylvie asked Worthy. "And that tin of scones beside you?"

Worthy did as he was asked.

Sylvie grabbed a white serving tray from one of the lower cabinets, placed the cup and saucer on it and poured the tea. She arranged three scones around the saucer, then set one crystal dish of sugar cubes off to the side with a small pair of tongs atop it. A crystal pitcher filled with cream sat next to the sugar.

"Napkin, please," she said to Worthy.

She tucked the edge of the napkin neatly under the saucer, and topped it with a sterling silver spoon. A slim crystal vase with a single yellow rose in it finished the setting.

"Oh, my, I almost forgot these," she said. "They've not even cooled sufficiently, but perhaps they'll do."

Beside the pitcher of cream, she set a dish of her still-warm candied apricots.

"You are a genius in the kitchen, my dear," Worthy said.

"I'll dip them in my homemade chocolate as a special treat for dessert this evening. Now, I'm off to deliver the goodies to our guest."

Sylvie picked up the tray then hesitated and set it down again.

"You know, Worthy, Max was nowhere to be seen when that vile thing appeared at the window. I was convinced that our troubles centered around him, but the girls said ...."

Worthy put his fingers to his lips and nodded his head.

"Oh, mercy me," Sylvie said. "I'd better get this tea to him, keep him pacified if possible."

Worthy smiled at her and nodded again. Then, in a soft voice, said, "No harm will come to you, Sylvie. But *you* must tell the truth. The evil here spoke directly to you. It knows. You must tell Nealey the truth. She deserves it, and you, my dear, deserve to be free of your burden at last."

With the back of her hand, Sylvie wiped at a few dots of perspiration on her forehead.

Chapter 30

Outside in the chilly afternoon air, Nealey, Benton, and Lulu walked along the flagstone garden pathway. Nealey delighted in the waist-high purple and red azaleas, the lush, head-high pink and blue hydrangeas, the fragrant peach-colored roses, periwinkle coneflowers, and even a whimsical patch of jack-in-the-pulpit, its tall red and white flowers so thick they hung in spirals.

"These flowers are magnificent," she said, "but it's October. They shouldn't be blooming now."

Benton shrugged. "Very rich soil," he said. "And a special food your Aunt Sylvie created. Brings them right out."

At the pathway's end stood a tall white gazebo, richly carved from wood, with brightly-colored hanging baskets filled with draping vines lush with flowers. A wind chime mounted on a white wooden pole played at the entrance. Two steps led up onto the shiny hardwood floors where three ornate benches sat along the spacious interior. From the high ceiling hung a crystal chandelier.

"It's beautiful," Nealey said as she looked around. "I saw it my first day here but didn't take the time to come this far out. I wish I had."

"I'm glad you like it," Benton said. "Want to sit?"

Nealey shook her head. "On the way back, it will make a nice resting place."

Beyond the gazebo, the open spaces lay in vast verdant waves of rolling hills.

"C'mon," Benton said and gently grabbed her hand. "Let me show you what's over that tallest hill."

"Okay, Lulu, are you ready?" Nealey asked.

Lulu barked and trotted in front of them.

"She's such a dear," Nealey said, "and she always seems to make me feel better."

Benton smiled.

"She's got a bit of the magic in her, always has, ever since she was just a pup. Sylvie found her wandering up there."

He pointed to the steep hills.

Nealey covered her forehead with her hand as she gazed in the direction of the lush green slopes.

"That little pup was probably only ten weeks old, then," Benton continued. "It was just after Sylvie's husband died eight years ago. She'd been withdrawn, depressed."

"Aunt Sylvie?"

"It was a hard time for her. They'd been married only a few short years. When he died, she kept busy with the inn, answering letters from her fans, going to book signings. Still, when she was here and alone, she didn't seem her usual spunky self. Then one glorious day, she found Lulu. They fell in love at first sight."

"You must have been working here then," Nealey said.

"Yep, I'd been here a while,"

Nealey frowned. "I didn't even know about it until after the funeral when she sent me a letter and told me he'd passed away. I had never even met him." She lowered her head. "I'm ashamed, now, that I didn't call her or offer to come and stay with her."

"Don't be," Benton said. "She wouldn't have wanted you to drop everything and come up here, Nealey. She grieved on her own, privately, the way she thought she should."

"Still, I could have done something, anything to let her know I cared. We drifted apart once I left the convent. I've always regretted that I didn't try harder to be a part of her life. She was so good to me. I should have done something when he died. I've always loved her so dearly."

"Sylvie already knew that."

Nealey gazed out at the steep hills that rose in the distance to the right of the inn. She had seen them every time she looked out her bedroom window. At the crest of one of the hills sat the large boulder she'd seen when she first arrived only three days ago.

Has it been only three days? So much has happened.

She remembered the man who sat atop the boulder and the two golden orbs that he'd spun around and played with almost like a yo-yo.

Benton held out a hand. "C'mon, we'll be there before you know it."

She took Benton's hand and followed.

Well ahead of them, Lulu stopped and looked back in their direction.

"She loves a good run," Benton said. "Let's catch up."

"I don't think I can. It's such a steep hill."

"Do you see that boulder?"

Nealey nodded. *Oh yes, that boulder. I saw it my first day here.*

"You haven't seen it up close," Benton said.

Nealey looked at him. *Wait. Did he know what I was thinking? Again?*

"So, that's where we're headed. Now, just start running, then hold tightly to my hand, okay?" Benton said.

Something in his tone convinced Nealey that she could make it up that hill.

She shrugged. "Okay. I'll trust you." *Or maybe I won't. Maybe I'll just go along for the adventure. I mean, if you can read my thoughts, then ….*

Benton chuckled.

Nealey took a deep breath and ran alongside him for a yard or so, but then she had the peculiar sensation that her feet weren't hitting solid ground. They were moving, but the effort of running had vanished. Instead, she and Benton seemed to be gliding.

In only a moment, Nealey felt the ground beneath her again as she stood in front of the boulder.

"See?" Benton said. "That wasn't so bad, was it?"

Nealey laughed. "It was perfect."

Lulu sat beside the boulder and barked loudly.

For the first time, Nealey saw her panting.

"She's not getting any attention, no accolades for her sprint up the hill," he said as his fingers fished in his jacket pocket. "How about a little treat?"

Lulu sat up and begged, pink hat askew, her spindly front legs dangling in front of her, her tongue hanging out.

"Close your mouth, dear," Nealey said imitating Sylvie's voice. "It is not proper for a southern belle to go around with her tongue sticking out," Nealey said and put her hands on her hips, Sylvie style. "No, no," she said and moved her index finger back and forth. "It just won't do!"

Benton laughed a hearty laugh. "You're good," he said. "Sylvie would be impressed."

"Or appalled," Nealey said.

Lulu wolfed down the treat as soon as Benton gave it to her.

"She's just a bit spoiled," Nealey said. "But she's oh, so worth it!"

"Benton," she said in a sudden change of mood, "on my first night here, I saw this boulder back there from my window. And I saw a man sitting on top of it. He played with two orbs. Is that the right term?"

"Orbs of light?" Benton asked.

"Yes, exactly. Orbs of light. He played with them like a yo-yo."

"Hmm," Benton said. "Interesting."

Nealey brushed aside a large purple aster as she walked. "What is most fascinating is that I saw those same orbs once before," she said. "On that night a year ago. They wrapped around my feet and the children's, and they felt warm and soothing. I don't remember much after that."

"Trauma," he said, "often erases memory. Maybe that's why you can't remember."

Nealey nodded.

"We've only a little farther to go," Benton said softly.

Nealey straightened Lulu's pink hat and patted her on the back.

"It's just down in that valley," Benton said.

They walked through thick, ankle-high grass. Native flowers grew in abundance. Large showy purple asters, slender red bleeding hearts, tall white shooting stars, and pink geraniums filled the landscape of the hills. Several groves of native hickory trees and magnificent old oaks dotted the verdant slopes.

"Such a gorgeous place," Nealey said as she fingered one of the white flowers of a shooting star.

"Careful," Benton said. "It's poisonous."

Nealey wiped her hand on her jacket.

After only a few more feet, Benton stopped and pointed to a large white building that looked brand new.

Scraps of wood lay around it, but in its newness, the bright walls and glittering shingled roof shone against the deep green of the valley. A semi-circular stand of tall old oaks guarded the perimeter.

A church? Yes, it looks like a church.

"Here, let me help you cross," Benton said and extended his hand to Nealey. "Watch your step. This new construction isn't quite finished. I see a few nails lying around."

Nealey hesitated.

"Is something wrong?" Benton asked.

"This is what you wanted to show me?"

Benton nodded.

"You're building a church?"

"Yes," he said.

"I haven't stepped foot inside a church since ..." Nealey stopped. "I'll see it another time," she said.

Benton lowered his eyes.

"I'd love to show you the stained-glass window. Won't you just take a quick look?"

Nealey shook her head.

"I can't. I just can't."

"Not even a peek?" Benton asked and smiled at her.

His smile made her feel so good that she stepped forward and walked to the doorway. "Okay, a peek. That's all. I'm not going inside."

Benton opened the double doors for Nealey.

A flurry of wings blinded her.

Chapter 31

Maggie and Mae rocked back and forth in the small chairs in their room on the third floor.

"She wouldn't know," Mae said. "If we're quiet and don't make any mess, Mama would never know. Let's do it."

Maggie frowned and shook her head.

"You're a 'fraidy cat, that's all."

Maggie lifted her feet and popped the toes of her shoes together as she rocked.

"There's nothing to do," she said. "Please go with me?"

Maggie shook her head again.

"Fine, then," Mae said. "I'm going by myself."

Mae stopped rocking and hopped out of the chair. She gave one last plea to Maggie.

"We won't get caught. I promise. She's outside with Benton, and Mama's talking to Aunt Sylvie. I want to see if she has a picture of her little girl, that's all. *Please*."

Maggie shrugged.

Mae lifted her arms. "Yippee, you're coming?"

"Now," she whispered, "if Nealey comes in, we can hide behind the curtains or disappear if we have enough, well, you know."

Maggie stood up and put her hands on her hips.

"Okay," Mae said, her shoulder slumped. "We'll just disappear, but it's way more fun to hide!"

At the door, Mae turned to Maggie.

"The easy way or the way *real* girls would do it?"

Maggie rolled her eyes and sighed.

"Fine!" Mae said and balled her hands into fists. "We'll go the easy way, but I don't like it. If we want to *be* real girls, we have to *act* like real girls, and real girls don't ... get ... invisible!"

Maggie put her finger to her lips.

Mae screwed up her face and stuck out her tongue. Then she held out her hand.

"Well, are we going or not?"

Maggie put her hand in Mae's. Maggie closed her eyes.

Go.

And the two little girls disappeared.

Only a few seconds later, they appeared inside a bedroom, but it wasn't Nealey's.

They blinked.

"Huh?" Mae said as she glanced around. "This isn't Nealey's room."

Suddenly, her eyes widened.

Maggie covered her mouth with her small hands.

"Well, now, girls," the deep voice said. "To what do I owe this unexpected pleasure?"

Maggie and Mae stared open-mouthed at the familiar man who stood in front of them. He brushed at his sleeve, straightened a gold cufflink, and smiled.

"Please," Max said, gesturing toward the chairs in front of the window. "Take a seat. We'll have a nice chat."

Maggie took Mae's hand and closed her eyes.

Go!

When she opened her eyes again, she and Mae were still standing in the same place.

"Have a seat, won't you?" Max insisted.

"We, we were trying to find our mother," Mae lied and glanced at Maggie. "Isn't that right, Maggie?"

"Yes," Max said. "But if I understand correctly, you must go where you are summoned. Is that correct?"

Maggie tightened her hand around Mae's and closed her eyes again.

Go, now!

Max inched closer to them and laid a hand on Mae's shoulder.

"I'm afraid it's useless, you see," Max said. "You cannot disappear from this room as long as I desire your company, and at the moment, I desire it. Don't worry. We won't be here long."

He nodded toward the chair.

"Sit down."

He brushed at his other sleeve and adjusted the gold cufflink.

Chapter 32

Nealey gasped as three white doves flew past her.

"Are you all right?" Benton asked. "Here, let me see."

He bent and examined every inch of her face.

"I'm okay," she said. "I'm fine, really."

He kissed her lightly on the forehead. "Just making sure. I'm sorry. Doves just seem to like it here."

When Benton moved away, she looked inside the church.

Her eyes were drawn immediately to the back of it.

An enormous stained-glass window depicting a host of angels graced the wall. In the center of the window stood a lone angel with enormous white wings that spread the length of the window. He held a dove in one hand, a shield in the other.

"It's beautiful, Benton," she said.

"I'm glad you like it."

"You built this yourself, all of this?"

"I love working with wood," he said and ran a hand along the door facing.

"What about the stained glass? You didn't make *that*, did you?"

He shrugged and grinned sheepishly.

Nealey stared at him, her arms crossed in front of her.

"I can't believe you did all this by yourself. Is there anything you *can't* do?"

"I can't swim," he said softly.

"What?" Nealey said and cupped her hand over her ear. "I couldn't quite hear you."

"I, uh, I can't swim. I sink like a rock."

Nealey laughed.

"You're kidding me, right? A big, outdoorsy guy like you?"

He shook his head and stuck his hands in his pockets.

"There's one other thing I want to show you, if you'd care to look," he said softly. "It's around back, just in front of that stand of trees."

"Okay," Nealey said.

They walked around the side of the church, stepping over stacks of wood, until they came to a clearing with a large building in the middle of it.

"My workshop," Benton said.

"It's pretty big for a workshop," she said. "It's almost as big as the church!"

Benton opened the door.

The enormous shed was filled with natural light from windows all along its walls. On one side to her left, Nealey saw various tools. On the other side, four long tables lay side by side. On each table was a massive wooden structure.

Nealey looked at Benton and held out her hands, palms up.

"It's going to be the steeple," he said sounding to Nealey as excited as a boy with a new toy. "I'll finish each piece then assemble it when I mount it on the roof. Look at this one," he said and ran his hand along it. "It's almost done. It's the top piece."

Nealey walked the length of the cone-shaped structure. Her fingers flowed along the smooth, dark wood.

"It's beautiful," she said.

Benton stood beside her. "Thank you."

As her fingers ran across the wood, she stopped. She flattened her hand against it and closed her eyes. Warm to the touch, it seemed to pulse beneath her hand. For a moment, her heart raced. She wanted to step away, but the warmth of the wood on her hand held her. She leaned in closer and listened to a distinct but barely audible humming sound.

Benton slipped his arm around her waist.

"Can you hear it? It's almost as if low voices are reverberating from deep in the earth," she whispered.

"All the time," he said. "Sometimes, I think it's singing to me."

"I feel that way about water," she said.

Benton cringed, then shook his head and chuckled.

"Let's go outside and let some sun shine on our faces."

Lulu ran over to the doorway and barked softly. Her hat was askew again and covered in bits of weeds and flower petals.

"Ah, you've been having a run, I see," Benton said.

"Doesn't she look precious?" Nealey asked.

"She looks as if she's just about had it for the day. Guess it's time we head back."

Benton held out his hand to Nealey. "Ready?"

Before she could answer, she felt a swift wind across her face. She closed her eyes against it, and when she opened them again, she, Benton, and Lulu were standing in front of the gazebo.

"How?" she asked but then shook her head. "I keep asking how you do things, but so far, I haven't had many answers."

"Want to sit now?" Benton asked, gesturing toward the benches.

When Nealey had taken her seat, Benton sprawled beside her and rested his arm on the back of the bench.

"There's something I'd like to say," Nealey told him.

"Why don't you lean back? Relax. You can tell me anything."

Instead, Nealey stood up. "I talk better when I'm standing," she said.

"I'm all ears."

For a few seconds, Nealey could do nothing other than look at the man. He was so handsome. He seemed so big and safe. Now, after their kiss, every time he was near, her body ached for him. She wanted to cuddle up beside him and feel his powerful arms around her again.

Oh, I could so easily fall for him. Have I already fallen?

"Yes," Benton said.

Nealey inhaled a sharp breath.

Benton blinked.

"You were about to tell me something?" he asked.

Nealey saw the long dark lashes cover his sky-blue eyes.

"Yes, well," she said and began to pace in front of the pew. "First of all, I wanted you to know that I was not going to jump off the cliff. I went there because I heard someone calling me, or at least I thought I did, so I went to the cliff side."

Benton leaned forward and rested his elbows on his knees.

"The voice," she continued, "seemed to be coming from down in the water, so I got as close as I could to the edge and leaned over. But all I wanted to do was find out who it was. I didn't know Lulu was with me. I'd never hurt her."

Sprawled along the hardwood, Lulu raised her head and cooed.

"No, of course not," Benton said. "Do you know who it was?"

Nealey shook her head. "It sounded familiar, but I don't know. I've heard that voice before, but when I try to put a face with a voice, my mind just goes blank."

"You'll figure it out, Nealey. I'll help if I can."

"My family," she said, "you've heard about what happened to them from Aunt Sylvie? You know they were ... all of them ... my babies, my husband, my sister. Murdered. I saw it. All of them shot down, killed." Tears welled in her eyes. "I can still see it, just like it was yesterday."

"I'm sorry about your loss," he said. "Truly sorry."

"I haven't been inside a church since. I don't intend to step foot inside one ever again because I know it's just a sham. There's no God up there watching over us, and if there is, if there is some *being* controlling our lives, then I want nothing to do with Him."

Nealey felt her hands trembling.

"Thank you," Benton said softly.

Nealey frowned.

"For what?"

"For telling me," he said. "It means more than you know."

"I have something else to tell you, too," she said as she paced across the gazebo.

"I'm listening," Benton said.

"I think I have some of this figured out."

"Some of this? What do you mean exactly?"

Nealey stopped her pacing and sat beside him.

"From the moment I first met you, Benton, I felt there was something a little mysterious about you. I couldn't really put my finger on it, though. Then, I met Worthy and Noble. They have that same air about them. Not quite normal. Something's a little different about all of you. Even Aunt Sylvie. She has her mysterious ways, too."

"Doesn't everyone?"

"No, Benton, not everyone is mysterious. Take me. What's mysterious about me?" Nealey shrugged. "Nothing, nothing at all, or at least there wasn't anything odd about me until I came here."

Benton frowned. "The Playhouse Inn has made you odd?"

Lulu barked with a little sound like laughter.

Nealey looked down at her, then back at Benton.

"I never saw ghosts until I came here. I didn't see hideous faces in the windows or feel floors tremble or whatever that thing was on the third floor. So, yes, it's made me odd. This place works on my mind, Benton. And today, those horrible things at the window. How I thought I saw my little Nicholas. And my mother! What did it mean when it said Aunt Sylvie should *'tell me everything.'*"

Nealey put her hand on Benton's arm.

"What is it that she's supposed to tell me? Do you know?"

"Whatever it is," Benton said, "she will tell you in her own way and in her own time. You have to accept her for who she is, Nealey."

"Right," she said. "She told me that years ago. The thing is, she has never told me who she is, exactly. I mean, she's wonderful. She has taken care of me all my life. I spent so much time with her when I was a kid that I used to think that she was really my mother, and that my real mom was just a substitute for Aunt Sylvie."

"A child would be fortunate to have her as a mother," Benton said.

Nealey scooted to the edge of the bench.

"In a way, I never felt that she was my aunt. She was my mother, just a second one. But, after I left St. Mary's, we hardly saw each other. I missed having her in my life ... and I missed Naomi, too. She wouldn't even answer my letters. But Benton, I had such a vivid memory of my mother being so scared here, and I saw what happened to her. Something terrible happened to her here at the Playhouse Inn."

"Any ideas about what frightened her so?"

"Yes, I think so," she said. "That creature upstairs, do you know how long it's been in this house?"

"A long time," Benton said.

"Well, what if my mother saw it? I mean, I don't know why or how she would have, but if she did, it would explain why she was so frightened. I remember her grabbing us up out of the bed and running to the car. She didn't say goodbye to Aunt Sylvie. She just left, and burned rubber when she did it."

Nealey stood up and folded her arms in front of her.

"She couldn't get out of there fast enough. And she made me and Naomi promise never to come back here. Naomi never did."

"How old were you then?"

"Just a child, eight or so."

"You and your sister had to take care of her after that?"

Nealey nodded.

"She wouldn't speak to Aunt Sylvie, but I remember staying weeks at a time with her here." She lowered her head. "Naomi refused to come back here. She stayed with the neighbors. She believed Aunt Sylvie was ... evil."

"That's a shame," Benton said.

"And when I arrived a few days ago, I stood outside and put my hand on the door, and I heard my mother's voice telling me to promise not to come here ever again. It's very confusing, Benton," Nealey said, unfolding her arms. "I mean, why would she allow me to come here so often with Aunt Sylvie?"

Benton propped his elbows on his knees, his hands under his chin. "Would you like the truth now, Nealey? I know why. Your Aunt Sylvie told me. Your mother was alone in one of the bedrooms when Anna appeared to her and asked her not to be afraid. Your mother was horrified and convinced from then on that this house was evil, that it entertained spirits from Hell."

Nealey clasped her hands in front of her. For a few seconds, she looked around the gazebo.

"So, in all those years, Mother never said a word about that, but she believed this house was evil. She allowed that 'evil' to take over her life. She was obsessed with it, and she saw evil everywhere after that. But yet she let me come here all the time and stay with Aunt Sylvie?"

"I believe," Benton said, "that she thought Sylvie was evil, too, and that you would grow up the same way. Basically, she gave up, Nealey. She felt she couldn't fight it anymore where you were concerned."

Lulu came and stood beside her.

Nealey smiled and rubbed the top of the dog's head.

"You know, when I met Maggie, Mae, and Anna today, at first, I was terrified of them."

She reached up and ran her fingers over a hanging wisteria bloom.

"I couldn't accept that I was seeing ghosts. My mind just wouldn't believe it. My mother's mind wouldn't have accepted it, either. Her faith was really all she cared about, and when it was truly tested, she just gave up."

"Sadly," Benton said, "it happens to many. Some never regain their faith."

Nealey lowered her eyes.

"Today, after only a little while, I felt such sympathy for the girls and their mother. Sort of like they were versions of me, Naomi, and my mom."

Benton nodded.

"It's hard to explain," Nealey said and looked at him. "They must be trapped here. Is that right? And it has something to do with that creature upstairs, doesn't it?"

"Impressive," Benton said. "The thing upstairs has haunted the girls and Anna for years."

"What will release them?" Nealey asked. "Is there anything that can help them?"

Benton smiled.

"Well, for one thing, there's the Wayfarer's Sky."

"What?"

"The ancients believed that a certain coloration and formation of the sky would set lost souls free. It's called the Wayfarer's Sky. We haven't had one in many years."

"The Wayfarer's Sky. I've never heard of it. But if the girls and Anna are truly stuck here, or haunted as you say, how could a sky help them?" she asked as she got up to walk around the inside of the gazebo.

"It isn't just the sky but a combination of things. And they are haunted. Trust me."

"Ironic. Ghosts that are haunted," she said.

"It happens more than you'd think," Benton said.

"My mother was haunted. I just never thought of it before. She was haunted by whatever she saw here. My sister Naomi and I called it the Unspeakable because my mother wouldn't let us talk about it."

Nealey stepped around Lulu and slid onto the seat next to Benton. "Before I came here," she said, "I hardly thought about ghosts. I studied about such things in school, took a few courses that went into some gruesome details about the supernatural."

"Not all schools teach about the supernatural," Benton said and edged forward on his seat. "You were fortunate."

"Fortunate, yes."

"So, after your schooling, what turn did your life take?" Benton asked.

"You'll laugh," Nealey said.

"No, I won't laugh. Trust me."

"I was a nun for a while," Nealey said.

Benton's eyebrows shot up. "A nun?"

Nealey nodded.

"Aunt Sylvie insisted on sending me to St. Mary's Convent. I hated it at first, and I was furious with her. But I missed her terribly. I took my vows and lived there until I was almost twenty. When I first left for the convent, Naomi and my mother were appalled. I don't think either of them ever forgave Aunt Sylvie for sending me there. But my mom was too sick, Naomi too preoccupied with her gardens. We hadn't been close in a very long time, even before I went away."

"Why were they appalled about a convent?" Benton asked.

"They called it a pagan cult and said I was doomed to Hell."

"I don't get it," Benton replied.

Nealey stood up and brushed at her jeans.

"My mother and Naomi were staunch fundamentalists, Benton. Any religion outside of that they considered pagan and of the devil. That's why they hated Sylvie, even after all that she'd done for us. My mother and sister were sure she was a Satan worshipper. And when I went to the convent, that meant I was following in Sylvie's footsteps.

"I loved the convent, but then, it seemed as if overnight, I just wanted a different life. I thought Aunt Sylvie would be furious. And I was absolutely right!"

"What happened?"

Nealey fiddled with some dangling wisteria.

"She was angry, or at least I thought so. Now, when I look back, I don't think she was mad, Benton. I think she was scared to death. But I didn't see it then, and I left the convent."

"What did you do next?"

"I went to college, got a degree in theology, and met Hank.

Naomi came to the wedding, but she didn't speak to us. I hardly saw her again until she married Brian and moved into the house next door."

The mention of his name made Nealey's stomach turn. She leaned against one of the posts on the gazebo.

Benton jumped up from the bench.

"Are you all right?"

Nealey nodded.

"I'm okay."

"Are you sure?" he asked and put a hand on her shoulder.

Nealey smiled up at him.

"I'm sure."

"Come sit beside me," he said and led her to the bench. "Now, what happened then?"

Nealey chuckled.

"Well, after Nicholas was born," she continued, "I finished the last course in my Masters of Divinity. Then, I spent a great deal of time thinking about Aunt Sylvie."

"Really?" Benton said.

"Yes, the last course was all about the supernatural. My mother always said Sylvie was a witch who dabbled in black magic. I never believed her, but Naomi did. I knew that Aunt Sylvie was sort of mysterious. The more I know of you, Worthy, Noble, and Aunt Sylvie, the more I'm halfway convinced that you *might* be Wiccans."

Benton seemed uneasy. He grimaced.

"Is that right?" Nealey asked. "I'm not being judgmental. I mean, it's fine if that's what you believe in, some sort of earth magic. I'd just like to know, that's all."

Benton looked uncomfortable. He hugged his arms in front of him and rubbed his back against the railing of the gazebo.

Lulu walked to the bench and whined.

"Are you okay?" Nealey asked him.

"My back," he said.

"What's wrong with your back? Here, lean forward and let me take a look."

"No, it's okay. It just itches."

Nealey held out her hands and wiggled her fingers. "Long fingernails," she said. "Great for scratching backs. Take off your jacket."

"No, it's fine. I don't want to trouble you."

Nealey put one hand on her hip. "Off."

Benton slipped off the jacket and draped it across Lulu.

Lulu cooed at him.

Nealey put her hands on his broad back.

"Tell me where," she said as she moved her fingers along his shirt.

"Oh, there, right there," he said and scrunched up his shoulders. "Oh, God, right there, yes."

While she scratched, she felt the rippling muscles.

He must work out all the time!

"Hauling wood and keeping these grounds will bulk you up in a hurry," Benton said. "Oh, yeah, that's it."

Benton let out a long sigh of relief.

Nealey smiled.

"Better?" she asked.

"Much," he said. "Thank you. Now, about the Wiccan idea."

"Yes?"

"Nealey, we aren't Wiccans."

She narrowed her eyes.

Benton rolled his shoulders, sighed again, and stood up. He pulled Nealey up beside him. As he slipped on his jacket, he said, "The supernatural always defies logic. If you studied theology, you know that. At the convent, surely you must have run across things you couldn't explain."

"No, the convent was structured and rigid. But before that ...."

"You *have* had experience with the inexplicable. Paranormal, supernatural, whatever you want to call it?"

Nealey turned away from him.

"Years ago," she said softly.

Benton turned her toward him.

"Tell me, please, Nealey. When did you experience something you couldn't explain?"

"I was only a child, but when I was here with Aunt Sylvie, we would stand at the cliff and listen to the water. I could hear those mighty waters singing to me."

"How lovely," he whispered.

"Many times when I was with Aunt Sylvie. Many times. Then,

later, when I took my first church."

"Your first church?"

"Yes, Benton, my first church," she said and drew him close to her. "I was called to a house where a young man had been doing strange and terrible things. His family was afraid of him, and they wanted the house blessed."

Benton gently brushed a stray hair from Nealey's forehead.

"You were the priest."

"Yes," she said. "When I first saw him, he seemed familiar, in the same way that Max sounded familiar, as if I'd heard the voice before. But, of course, I hadn't. So, I went through the house and followed the ritual blessings, yet when I stepped into his room, he lashed at me with a small knife and cut my finger. And then, he did the strangest thing."

"Tell me."

"He sliced his own finger with the knife."

Lulu turned and ran down the steps, Benton's jacket still on her back.

"Then he grabbed my hand and held it. He held it so tightly that I wanted to scream. I tried to wrestle away from him. I pulled and strained, but his grip was superhuman. No matter how hard I tried, I could not pull away. I watched him when he put our hands together." Nealey trembled. "In that growling voice of his, he said that we had *shared blood.*"

Benton slipped an arm around her and pulled her close.

"He said I was his forever."

Chapter 33

Anna stood in the kitchen doorway, a sheaf of papers in her hand.

"She's been reading my work, Sylvie. I am not pleased."

"You startled me, darling," Sylvie said. "Whatever is that you're holding?"

Though her appearance brought a chill to the room, Sylvie had grown accustomed to it and shivered only slightly.

She took a seat at the table and motioned for Anna to do the same.

"Now, dear, is something bothering you?" Sylvie asked Anna.

She held up the yellowed papers. "Nealey has been reading my work. No one reads it without permission."

"Well, she is family, Anna. She meant no harm," Sylvie said. "Please, may I have those so that I can put them up for safekeeping?"

"But they're my stories," Anna said.

"Yes, dear, I know, but I fear that unless we take steps now, the papers will be damaged beyond repair. I can have them copied onto archival paper and bound in leather so that they will remain in perfect condition. Wouldn't you rather like seeing your work in a rich leather volume?"

Anna's face brightened. "I would, yes, and Nealey is such a nice girl, isn't she? I just felt strange about having her read my stories. I've never let anyone read them. There is one in particular that is quite private."

"I will take supreme care of them."

"We've been so happy here, Sylvie. The time has flown so quickly."

Worthy sat at the table. "You don't mind if I join you, do you, Anna, dear?"

She smiled at him as her arm began to fade.

"You have given us everything we could hope for," Anna said.

Sylvie waved a hand.

"Good gracious, this is your home. The girls were born here."

Anna stared down at her lap.

"Anna, is something wrong?" Worthy asked.

"Why do you suppose he murdered us? Did he just go mad? What made him hate us so much that he could kill us? I've turned the questions over in my mind for a hundred years. Each time I look at the portrait and see his face, I am unable to make sense of it."

"Worthy," Sylvie said, "would you give Anna your thoughts on this matter?"

"Yes, of course," Worthy said. "Well, it seems to me that the young man was simply jealous of his older brother who had the good fortune to marry a gorgeous young woman of means and have three beautiful children with her."

"It wasn't painful, you know, the way I'd thought it might be. He pointed the weapon, but before the shot fired, I saw a golden sphere of light at my feet. It wrapped itself around me and the children. We felt so light-hearted, so warm and safe that we giggled, all four of us. Thank God for that light and for my precious little Marguerite who survived."

"My grandmother," Sylvie whispered. "Bless her soul."

"When we woke in this house, I was a bit perplexed and have been since. Weren't we good enough to go to Heaven as our Bible taught us?"

"Oh, my goodness, yes!" Worthy said. "You and the children were wonderfully good, yet you have been trapped here these years by one who was not so good."

Worthy reached out his hand. "Do not worry, my sweet Anna. We'll dispose of this evil very soon, and you and the girls might just be Heaven bound."

"Heaven bound," Anna whispered. "I fear the twins will not be pleased at leaving their home."

"Worry yourself not, my dear," Worthy said. "Noble, myself, and Benton. We will try our best, I promise you."

"Benton, yes, quite the handsome fellow, he," Anna said and smiled. Then, she held up an index finger.

"Though not as handsome as my Henry, of course." As soon

as she'd said the words, Anna lowered her head. "Henry's brother was troubled, you understand. On the day of the portrait, Henry and I spoke of it at some length, of his strange behavior over the last few days. He wasn't always that way. He was usually so light hearted. He seemed quite the pleasant fellow. But during the week of the portrait, he changed. He seemed angry. I thought—oh, surely it was my imagination—I thought I heard him growl."

Anna shuddered.

Sylvie wrung her hands. "Anna, I don't recall your mentioning that detail before."

Anna lowered her head. "I was ashamed to speak of it."

"Perhaps, Worthy, it is a detail worth considering, yes?"

"Anna, had you heard that sound before?"

"Oh, no, never—well, there was one other time," Anna stopped and covered her face with her hands.

Sylvie got up and knelt beside her. "Anna, darling, you've nothing to fear. Please, there is no need to hide anything from us. We love you."

"Just after I married Henry—oh, it's been ages ago—I met a man at a charity event we held here. He was a handsome man in a fine suit, gold cufflinks. We talked of art and writing."

"Yes, dear, go on," Sylvie urged.

"I don't know what came over me, but I felt, oh, mercy, forgive me, I can't go on!"

"Yes, Anna, you can. Now, please tell us about the man," Sylvie said.

"No, it's too horrid, too shameful!"

"Come now, Anna," Sylvie said. "Nothing is so horrible that it would affect our love for you."

Anna looked at Sylvie. "You'll think me a disgrace to our family."

"Nonsense," Sylvie said with a wave of her hand. "I believe I already hold that title!"

Anna smiled.

"Very well," she said. "He offered me a glass of wine, sweet red wine that tasted like raspberries. It tingled in my mouth and felt very pleasant. Why, I think I must have drunk the entire glass. It was delicious. So, I had another."

"That's hardly shameful, darling," Worthy said.

"As I put the second glass to my lips, I felt such a sting. And at that precise moment, my gentleman friend must have felt the same thing, for he held the glass away from him."

"We examined the glasses together and found tiny chips on the rim of each glass. I was astonished, and I could still feel the sting on my lip. When I touched it, I knew it was bleeding, and as I looked at my friend, I saw that his lip, too, was cut."

"Oh, my," said Worthy.

"Why, I could hardly believe it. I reached to get a napkin to wipe our lips, but as I moved, my friend grabbed my arms."

Anna covered her face again.

"Come, dear, you must tell us," Sylvie said. "Please."

Anna put her hands in her lap.

"He bent down, Sylvie, and I thought he was going to wipe away the blood from my mouth. I reached to do the same for him, but—oh, mercy—he didn't. Instead, he pressed his lips to mine, full on." Anna stopped. "What came over me, Sylvie?"

"What do you mean, dearest? Please, it's time to let go of this thing that's kept you so burdened."

Anna moved her hands and talked, staring down at the floor.

"After the kiss, he said something about sharing blood. He said that now I was his forever. And then, he left. He left me standing there. I felt dizzy, so I went to my room, carefully feeling my way up the long staircase. By the time I'd climbed the stairs, I could hardly move one foot in front of the other. I must have fallen asleep quickly. My memory fails me."

"When I woke the next morning, Sylvie, his words wouldn't leave my mind. *I was his forever. His forever,*" Anna said. "But that's not the worst of it, Sylvie."

Worthy urged her on. "Please, dear, if it doesn't pain you too much."

"As I lay there on the bed, I felt a stirring in my stomach. I knew immediately."

Anna burst into tears.

"What did you know, my darling girl?"

"I knew that I was with child, Sylvie, and that my gentleman friend, in some way I'll never be able to understand, fathered the child, the twins, my precious twins. How?" she said between sobs. "How could it have happened?"

Sylvie's hands trembled. "Oh, Anna."

Slowly, a tear trickled from Sylvie's eye. She brushed it away with the sleeve of her tunic.

"Oh, my, no," she whispered.

Worthy moved his chair and sat between them. He draped his arms around their shoulders.

"My precious girls," he said.

Sylvie laid her head on Worthy's plump shoulder.

"Dear God," she whispered. "It happened to me, too."

Chapter 34

He shifted in his chair and brushed at the sleeve of his silk designer suit.

"I'm Max," he said. "And how are you two lovely girls today?"

The two girls said nothing. They simply held hands and blinked.

"Come now," he said. "Hasn't that beautiful mother of yours taught you proper etiquette? It is quite rude not to speak when someone introduces himself. As I said, I am Max."

"You know our mother?" Mae asked softly.

Max raised his eyebrows.

"But of course," he said. "She is, in fact, a very special friend."

Still holding hands, the girls looked at each other then back at him. Their eyes narrowed.

"Ah, I can see you don't believe me," he said and rose from the chair.

The girls scooted back in theirs.

Max got up slowly, opened a dresser drawer, and took out an envelope. Carefully, he removed a clipping from inside.

"Here," he said. "Do not dare touch it, but I will allow you to look at it. You can see your mother's name right along this line."

The girls leaned forward.

"See?" he asked and pointed to it with his index finger. "There. It says, 'Sir Henry and Lady Anna.'"

Mae let go of Maggie's hand and stood beside the chair.

"That's our Mama and Papa," she said and stared up at Max. "Did you know our Papa, too?"

"Not as well as I knew your mother," he said and put his hand on Mae's shoulder.

She flinched.

"But I do remember the day that you and your sister were born," he said.

"You do? You knew us when we were babies?"

"I most certainly did," he said and sat on the end of the bed facing the girls. He nodded in Mae's direction. "You were named Maebelle Anna, and your sister," he said nodding at Maggie, "was Margaret Anna. Both of you have your mother's name as your middle name."

Mae smiled and nodded her head. "We do! Isn't that right, Maggie?"

Maggie grabbed her hand and pulled her back into her chair.

Max smiled at them.

"Well, now," he said, "since you know I truly am a friend of your mother's, then perhaps you'll allow me to share a little secret?"

Maggie blinked and tightened her fingers around Mae's hand.

"A secret?" Mae asked.

"Oh, yes," Max said. "A very special secret. Perhaps I shouldn't," he said and steepled his fingers at his chin. "You might inadvertently tell someone."

"No," Mae said, "we won't tell. I promise. We're good at keeping secrets, aren't we Maggie?"

Maggie frowned at her.

Max leaned forward on the edge of the bed.

"Are you sure I can trust you?"

Mae put her hands to her chest. "Trust *us*? We're the best secret keepers ever!"

"Hmm," Max said.

He rubbed his chin with his thumb and index finger and glanced up at the ceiling.

Mae squirmed in her chair and grinned at Maggie.

Max sighed.

"After a short but deliberate consideration, I have decided that you might be trustworthy. Given your family heritage, perhaps you are telling the truth."

With her index finger, Mae drew an imaginary mark over her chest.

"Cross my heart," she said.

Then she looked over at Maggie.

"Yours, too, Maggie. We have to swear."

"Maggie, do you swear not to tell?" Max asked in a soft voice.

Maggie's shoulders slumped, and she nodded her head slowly.

"Perfect!" Max said. "Now, my children, here is the secret."

He leaned even closer to them, his face next to Mae's, and whispered.

"I've brought a friend with me."

Mae's eyebrows shot up.

"A friend?"

"Yes," he whispered, "a dear friend."

Mae wrinkled her nose.

"Max?" she asked.

"Yes?" he replied.

"Your breath stinks."

Max balled his fists, then inhaled slowly. He scooted back onto the end of the bed, crossed his legs, and wrapped his hands around his knee.

A tiny puff of smoke streamed from his mouth.

"Is it a boy friend or a girl friend?" Mae asked.

Max cocked his head to the side.

"A boy friend, quite young, in fact. Just about your age."

"Oh," Mae said and frowned. "We'd rather have a girl to play with. We don't like boys very much. They can act stupid."

"Well, this boy is not stupid. But he is very lonely because he has no one to play with, and he's very shy ... very shy."

"Well?" Mae asked. "Where is he? We'll play with him if he's nice. Won't we, Maggie?"

"As I said, he is very shy. So, I'm afraid he's hiding."

"Hiding?" Mae asked. "Oh, we love hiding!"

Mae walked to the side of the bed. She got on her knees, lifted up the bed skirt, and looked underneath.

"No one under here," she said.

Then, she opened the bathroom door and looked inside.

"Nope," she said. "Come on, Maggie. Help me."

Maggie didn't budge.

Finally, Mae saw the closet.

"Aha," she said. "Bet he's in here."

She walked straight into the door but could not pass through. Startled, she glanced back at Maggie and whimpered.

"Help me, Maggie."

"Come now," Max said. "Let us not have any childish whimpering. I can assure you that my friend is not in there."

Mae frowned and folded her arms across her chest.

"Ah," Max said and stood up, "but I know where he is."

Mae looked up at the ceiling, arms still crossed.

Max stood and turned toward her.

"I will not tolerate childish behavior. If you choose to act like a child, then I will be forced to treat you as such," he said. "I would much prefer to think that I could share my secret with you. I can't, you understand, share it with someone who sulks," he paused and waved a hand as if to dismiss the sulking.

Mae lowered her head.

"I'm not sulking now," she said. "But I couldn't get through the door. I can always get through *doors*."

"Yes, well," Max said. "When you are in my company, I will say when you may pass through doors. Do you understand?"

He smiled at her and folded his hands in front of him.

Mae didn't answer. She continued looking down.

"Do ... you ... understand?"

"We understand!" Maggie said and got up. She walked over to Mae and took her hand.

"Ah, she speaks yet again," Max said. "Well, that is grand. Now, are you still interested in finding my little friend?"

Mae nodded and looked over at Maggie.

Max clapped his hands. "Fine, then I will tell you where he is."

Mae smiled.

"Where?" she asked.

Max wiggled an index finger. "Not so fast. If you want to find him, you'll have to follow me."

"But where is he?"

Max shook his head.

"Now, if I told you, that would give you an unfair advantage. No, if you want to find him, I'm afraid you'll just have to come with me."

"But where?" Mae asked.

"Upstairs," Max said and held a hand to each of them. "Are you ready, girls?"

"Upstairs in our room?" Mae asked.

"Of course not," Max said. "You two would surely have found him by now. Am I correct?"

Mae nodded.

Maggie squeezed her hand.

"But we can't go in that other room," Mae said. "It's dangerous. Benton said so."

Max sighed. "Benton, yes."

Max walked to the door. "Very well. I will go and play with him myself. I'll give him your regards. It's such a shame, too. Up there you could be *real* girls."

"Real girls?" Mae asked.

Max nodded. "Of course, can't you already feel a difference? In my presence, you are almost fully human. Feel your skin, girls. It's soft, is it not? And warm to the touch?"

Mae ran her fingers along her arm.

"Why, it is. It really is!"

Max smiled.

"Now, do you believe me? If you go with me to meet my friend, you will very nearly be real girls."

Mae looked at Maggie. "Can we? Just this once? I'd love to be a *real* girl. And that boy is up there. We can play with him."

Maggie shook her head.

Mae jerked her hand from Maggie's and put both hands on her hips.

"But if *he's* up there, it can't be dangerous. Max wouldn't leave his little friend up there if it was dangerous, would he?"

Max smiled at them. "Certainly not! What sort of friend would I be if I left the boy alone in a place where he could be harmed?"

He held out his hand. "Join me?"

"We'll just go see him, and if we like him, we'll play. Okay? And we can be real girls!" Mae tugged at Maggie's hand and smiled sweetly. "Please."

Maggie sighed.

Hand in hand, the girls stepped beside him, Mae in the lead.

"My little friend will be delighted to see you both," Max said.

He flipped the lock, put his hand on the handle, and pushed gently on the door.

It didn't budge.

"We're gonna be real girls, Maggie," Mae said. "Isn't it exciting?"

"Quiet, please," Max said.

He pushed on the door once more, this time with more force. Then, he sniffed.

"What is that horrid smell?"

"Roses," Maggie said softly.

The door began to rattle, vapors of white mist streaming under it in waves.

Max backed away, coughing and sputtering.

"That smell," he said, "it's suffocating me."

Wide-eyed and trembling, Mae and Maggie stood motionless.

The white mist poured in under the door filling the room from floor to ceiling.

Come, children.

Maggie and Mae looked at each other and at Max, still coughing, slouched on the side of the bed.

Quickly, come out of the room.

Mae looked down at her arms. They had begun to fade.

Hurry, children!

The mist seemed thinner now, the smell of roses hardly detectable.

Max took a deep breath and stared at them. His eyes had turned solid black.

He held out a clawed hand.

"My little friend is waiting for you," he said as he stood and reached for their hands. His voice sounded like a low growl. "He'll be so disappointed."

The girls looked at Max and screamed.

Hurry!

With both her hands, Maggie grabbed Mae's. They vanished into the hallway.

Noble stood at the landing. He smiled at them and stepped aside. With his cane, he motioned down the steps and nodded.

"We could have been real girls again, Noble," Mae said and sniffed back tears.

Noble held out his arms and embraced them.

When the door of Max's room flew open, the two girls gasped and disappeared.

Max, looking his dapper self, stared at Noble.

Noble straightened and lifted his chin.

"Well, well," Max said as he brushed past him and headed down the stairs. "I'll be quicker about it next time, my friend."

Noble put a hand to his sunglasses.

Max stumbled on the steps but caught himself on the railing. He did not look back.

A slight grin formed on Noble's face.

Chapter 35

Sylvie sat at her handcrafted roll top desk writing a thank you note to a fan whose kind letter and weighty compliments about her latest book nearly moved her to tears. When she'd finished the note, she waved it in the air to dry the ink and slipped it into an embossed, gold-foil lined envelope.

She ran the sticky triangle over a damp sponge housed at the corner of the desk in a Waterford crystal bowl. In a finishing touch, Sylvie dropped a dab of bright red, hot wax then pressed into it an ornate W, a custom-made stamp given to her by her late husband, Sir Martin Ellis Williamson—Marty, as she called him.

Though he had loved her dearly, he had hated the Playhouse Inn. It made him uneasy he'd said numerous times, almost weekly. He complained of hearing strange noises, said he felt like he was being watched all the time. He swore that the house would suddenly get so cold in places that he shivered.

His pleas to sell the Playhouse Inn and move back to his beloved Ireland Sylvie understood, but largely ignored.

How could I sell this house? How could I leave?

She had tried but failed to convince him, just as he had tried and failed to convince her. They came to an impasse: he wanting to be with her but hating the house; she wanting to be with him but hating to leave. There seemed no compromise.

Yet, in each other's arms, they were deliciously happy.

Sylvie glanced at the framed photo of him on the desk and smiled.

"I miss you, my darling," she whispered.

A pang of guilt suddenly stabbed her through the heart.

I killed him.

A tear formed in the corner of her eye.

If I had told him everything, he might still be alive.

A sweet breeze blew, just then, across Sylvie's face. The scent of roses filled the air.

"Hello, my dear," Worthy said, silk handkerchief in hand.

Sylvie smiled up at him, took the hanky, and dabbed at her eye.

Worthy seated himself in the overstuffed leather chair opposite Sylvie's desk. "Forgive my barging in unannounced. I trust I am not intruding."

"Nonsense, you've come at the perfect time," Sylvie said. "You can help me with these letters."

She waved her hand across a plastic postal box on the floor filled to the brim with envelopes, some white, others ivory, pink, blue, and green.

"Just look at them, Worthy. Perhaps I should hire an assistant. The fan mail should be answered in much faster fashion. My readers depend on it. And where would I be without my readers? Sylvie Wolcott would be no one without them."

"Ah," Worthy said as he brushed a speck of lint from his white suit coat, "I beg to differ, my dear. The Sylvie Wolcott I know could never be 'no one.'"

Sylvie folded her hands in her lap and stared at them. A warm golden glow came across her hands.

"I have come to bring you a gift," Worthy said.

A small framed photograph appeared in her hands. Engraved along the gilded bottom edge were the words, "Family Portrait, 1787."

"Have you seen that photograph before?" Worthy asked.

Sylvie shook her head.

"The family is that of Alderman Wolcott, his wife, and their son. The portrait was painted in, as it says, 1787, in a castle in Amsterdam."

"Wolcott?" Sylvie asked.

"Yes, my dear, your ancestors. When their home was destroyed, they fled to Ireland where the Wolcotts remained. Though many of their possessions were damaged, the portrait was unscathed. They took it with them to their new home place—a lovely castle atop a hill—which still stands, though it has been through many renovations."

"Who took the photograph of the painting?" Sylvie inquired.

Worthy stood beside her and laid a hand on her shoulder.

"When they arrived in Ireland, they purchased land from a man who had befriended them. He sold them quite a number of acres, which was the custom at the time. Five hundred, I believe, of beautiful Irish hills and valleys."

Sylvie looked at him, puzzled.

"You see, my dear, the man who befriended the Wolcotts was a man of some rank, a baronet named Williamson. Centuries later, I believe that young Martin Williamson took that photograph of the portrait that still hangs in Castle Wolcott, as he had also befriended many of their descendants."

"Are you saying that my Marty took this photograph?"

Worthy smiled.

"He was a photographer by trade, was he not?"

Sylvie nodded.

"He mentioned to me once that he knew some of my distant relatives and that he'd visited them often," Sylvie said. "He didn't mention the photograph. Odd, don't you think, that he would not tell me about it? He was such a wonderful photographer."

"And afflicted, my dear, with the same heart ailment that claimed his father and brothers. You did not kill him, Sylvie."

Sylvie brushed a few stray hairs from her face.

Worthy smoothed his coat.

"Sylvie, dear, I hesitate to bring up this most delicate subject."

"Now, really, Worthy, when has that ever stopped you?" Sylvie said as she gazed down at the photo.

"Yes, well, there is the matter of your inheritance from Marty."

Sylvie did not look up but simply set the photo carefully on the writing desk.

"That matter is closed."

"But Sylvie, wouldn't you just want to take a peek? A short trip, my dear, and of course, you'd need your most faithful companion along."

Sylvie looked at him with narrowed eyes.

"You want to go to Ireland? Then, go. What on earth is stopping you?"

Worthy leaned forward in his chair. "But Sylvie, dearest, he left you his family's castle and five hundred acres! Just think what a lovely B & B you could create there. Oh, my goodness, you'd give it such life!"

Sylvie did not respond.

"In my inquiries, I have discovered that your very castle has of late been the subject of much gossip."

Sylvie did not look up.

"What sort of gossip, not that I'm in the least interested."

"No, I suppose not," Worthy said. "It is situated not far from a docking station for tourists, and though the caretaker and his wife are faithful and well provided for, they are refusing to stay beyond another month."

"And why should that concern me? Surely, there are others who would take the job."

"There are rumors," Worthy said.

Sylvie shook her head. "I have no reason to leave the Playhouse Inn right now, Worthy, none at all. Everything I love is here. Besides, Nealey must be taught how to manage things."

Worthy said nothing. He simply scooted back in his chair and straightened his white tie.

"All right," Sylvie said, "what sort of rumors?"

"Sounds of children crying, women screaming. The villagers say it is haunted. Tourists have left quite agitated, and the villagers are angry that the American owner won't at least come to see for herself what is going on."

Sylvie removed another letter from a green envelope. She read it, set it aside, and glanced at her watch.

"Just look at the time, Worthy. I must begin preparations for our evening meal."

Worthy stood up.

"Then, I shall join you," he said. "An extra hand in the kitchen can be helpful, wouldn't you say?"

Sylvie smiled at him.

"Yes, my friend, always helpful."

He smiled.

As they walked to the door, Worthy paused.

"You know, my dear, with your knowledge of earth magick, I believe you will make an interesting discovery when you examine that little photograph carefully."

"Marty's photograph of the portrait?"

"The very same," Worthy said. "Now, I will agree that your modern heritage is right here within these walls. However," he said and leaned closer, "your—shall we say—*provenance* lies in the hills of Ireland. But no more about that for now. There is, after all, an evening meal waiting to be born!"

Sylvie walked to the desk, picked up both photos, and held them in her hands.

"My dear Marty," she said.

"You know, Sylvie," Worthy said, "precious memories are said to lift the spirits."

He opened the door for her.

"And some of them need it so desperately, dear. So desperately."

Chapter 36

By 6:00, Sylvie had the evening meal underway.

"Anything I can do?" Benton asked as he and Nealey walked in from outside, Lulu right behind them.

"Ooh, it smells delicious, Aunt Sylvie," Nealey said. "What is that heavenly aroma?"

Sylvie wiped her hands on a dish towel.

"A new recipe," Sylvie said and winked at her. "Apple butterscotch pie, with just a touch of lavender."

"Mm," Nealey said.

"Benton, dear," Sylvie said as she picked up a small mixing bowl, "would you spread this parsley butter over the salmon fillets? They're laid out on that rack on the table. Oh, one moment. Dear me, I almost forgot!"

She reached into a small jar on the counter and sprinkled its gold powder over the parsley butter.

"Now, that should be divine."

She handed the bowl to Benton. "Once you've finished, I'll put the tarragon, bacon, and caramelized onions on top. Then, into the oven they go."

"Worthy?" Sylvie called.

"Where are Worthy and Noble?" Benton asked.

"They've volunteered to set the table," Sylvie said.

"Yes?" Worthy called from the dining room.

"Don't forget the soup bowls," Sylvie replied. "We're having your favorite: cauliflower and bacon soup topped with Parmigiano Reggiano."

Worthy stuck his head in the door.

"I am not at all certain that I can bear it, Sylvie dear. It simply sounds too delicious!"

"Then perhaps I shouldn't mention the warm spinach salad with cherry tomatoes, avocado and smoked bacon."

From the doorway, Worthy smiled and shook his head.

"Sylvie, you are a hungry man's dream!"

Lulu gave a delicate bark.

"Oh, forgive me my precious," Sylvie said. "Was I ignoring you? Goodness gracious. Let's see what we have here," she said and handed her a piece of crisp bacon.

"She's so spoiled," Nealey said, "but such a good girl."

Lulu looked up at her.

"See that?" Nealey said. "I swear she's smiling."

"But of course," Sylvie said, "she smiles all the time. She's a happy girl, yes she is."

Lulu flopped down in the middle of the floor, right in front of the kitchen table.

"Lulu, sweetheart, I'm afraid you're going to have to scoot," Sylvie said to her.

Lulu raised her head then let it flop down again.

"Please, dear," Sylvie said. "I must get this meal finished."

Lulu huffed but got up and moved closer to the door leading outside where she flopped down and huffed again.

"Oh, just look at that angel," Sylvie said. "Isn't she wonderful?"

Lulu wagged her tail. It thunked on the linoleum floor.

"Now," Sylvie said, "let's get this show on the road."

Benton buttered the salmon fillets.

"Thick or thin?" he asked Sylvie.

"Thick," Sylvie said. "We want that flavor oozing all over."

Nealey held Lulu's pink cap in her hands.

"I'll hang this up," she said. "Then I can help, too."

She took a few steps, then stopped and turned toward Benton. He looked a little different. His face seemed pale.

"Are you feeling all right?"

Benton looked a bit shocked. "Sure, I'm great. Why?"

"I don't know," Nealey replied, twisting the strings of Lulu's hat. "I thought, for just a moment, that you looked pale."

Benton shrugged. "I'm fine."

"Oh, darling," Sylvie said, "as long as you're going that way, would you look around for Max?"

"I thought he was leaving," Nealey said.

"Yes, yes, he is," Sylvie said, "after dinner."

Nealey shuddered. "He gives me the creeps."

Sylvie took the rest of the bacon from the pan and drained it on paper towels.

"I think we all feel the same," she said to Nealey. "But, he is our guest, and we must do our best to represent the Playhouse Inn. Don't you agree?"

Nealey shrugged.

"I have a lot to learn," she said. "I'd have thrown him out yesterday after he acted like such a jerk about my wand."

"Yes, dearest, I understand," Sylvie said as she washed the baby spinach. "But you are responsible for *your* actions, not his. As an innkeeper, you must be prepared to deal with guests who may or may not be altogether likeable. The Playhouse Inn is partly yours now, dearest. As co-owner, you must learn how to handle any situation with grace and finesse."

Nealey narrowed her eyes.

"Are you planning on leaving, Aunt Sylvie? I thought you'd be here to help me. I can't run this place by myself."

"Oh goodness no, I'm not leaving, dear, at least, not right away, but you know, there are those book signings. I must attend each one. I'd never dream of disappointing my fans. I have a new book in the works. And, perhaps one day, I might like to travel abroad for a few months, in the future, of course. One never knows where life will lead."

"Well, right now," Nealey said, "the only place it's leading me is to the foyer to put up Lulu's hat."

Benton chuckled.

"If you don't mind, sweetie," Sylvie said, "could you run upstairs and bring me my reading glasses? I need to check one tiny detail in the cookbook. I think they're on my writing desk. If not, then I haven't a clue where they might be."

"I'll find them," Nealey called as she walked out the kitchen door, twirling Lulu's pink cap.

"These fillets are ready, Sylvie," Benton said. "Anything else I can do?"

Sylvie motioned toward the dining room and smiled.

"You might check on the progress of our table setting."

"We can *hear* you," Worthy called in a melodic voice.

"You'd better go help him," Sylvie said. "Everything should be just right for the grand celebration tonight."

"Celebration?" Benton asked. "I didn't know we were celebrating."

He motioned for Sylvie to go ahead of him into the dining room.

"Did I hear correctly, dear Sylvie?" Worthy asked as he placed the last piece of gold baroque flatware.

He looked at it, straightened it once, then straightened it again.

"We're having a celebration tonight?"

Sylvie smoothed an edge of the royal blue tablecloth.

"Magnificent," she said. "Exactly what I wanted for celebrating the safe journey and speedy exit of our departing guest. He'll be leaving immediately after dinner."

"Noble, isn't this the most stunning table setting you've ever seen?" Worthy asked.

Noble turned his head toward them then went back to staring out the window.

"My word," Worthy said, "just look at how excited he is! He's been staring at some fascinating scene on the side lawn since we came in."

"How could I have done it without you?" Sylvie asked and laid a hand on his arm.

"I think he's blushing," Benton said.

"Nonsense," Worthy said and waved his handkerchief at them. "I am simply quite proud to have helped."

Noble tapped his cane once on the floor.

"Oh mercy, yes, you were a great help, brother," Worthy said to him. "Why, you've stood guard and kept us safe for well over an hour."

"My goodness," Sylvie said. "I'd be lost without the three of you. Now, time to get the salmon in the oven."

In the kitchen, Sylvie pulled a cookbook off the shelf and fanned through it.

"I need my reading glasses!" she said, sounding a bit agitated. "These words and numbers look like big black blotches. What can be keeping our Nealey? I was certain my glasses were on the desk. Surely, they can't be that hard to find."

"Benton, would you be a dear and ..." her voice trailed off.

"Benton?" Sylvie said and clutched at her chest.

"Benton?" she called louder. "What on earth is happening to you? Dear God, what is wrong?"

Chapter 37

Nealey found her Aunt Sylvie's reading glasses on the writing desk, just where Sylvie had said they'd be. She stuck them into the pocket of her hoodie and was about to leave when she paused, her eyes fixed on an ornately framed photograph.

She stared at it, then moved it closer to her face.

Family Portrait, 1787.

"Who *are* these people?" she muttered.

Just as she leaned over to replace the photograph, she noticed the rounded end of what looked like a small pink and green duffle bag tucked at the edge of the writing desk.

Is that my bag?

Nealey stepped to the side of the desk and looked down at it.

It looks just like mine.

She picked it up, set it in the desk chair, and unzipped it.

When she saw what was inside, her hands began to tremble. She braced herself on the edge of the desk.

One by one, she removed the three items from the bag and laid them in the chair.

The first was a necklace, a weighty gold Celtic cross hung on an ornate chain.

The next was a stole, white brocade embroidered along its edges with small gold crosses and green trinity knots.

The last, a Bible of rich brown leather, the words *Reverend Nealey Monaghan* inscribed in gold across the bottom.

All three had been gifts from Sylvie when Nealey had been ordained.

Impossible! I threw them away. How did they get here?

She recalled those hazy months after Hank and her children had been killed, remembered how much she had hated God for taking them away. One vivid memory stuck with her.

On a freezing cold night in her bare feet, she'd taken the small duffle that housed what she once considered sacred items–the cross, the stole, and her Bible—and walked to the edge of the driveway. She stood there for a few minutes, looked up at the sky, and yelled, "This is what I think of you!"

Then, she removed the top of the largest garbage can and tossed the bag inside.

The thudding sound when it hit the bottom brought a smile to her face. It made her feel good, really good. It hadn't mattered that she'd worked so hard to become ordained or that Aunt Sylvie had bought her the treasured gifts, or that the cross and chain were solid gold or that the stole was hand-made from Irish linen and brocaded satin, embroidered with a special Carrickmacross Irish lace entwined among the designs.

Nothing had mattered one bit except tossing them all into the trash.

She remembered walking back inside and going to the living room window. She'd paced in front of it all night waiting for the garbage collectors to come early the next morning. She'd wanted to see them pick up that trash and haul it away.

And once, while she paced and watched, she'd seen the lights.

Two golden orbs spinning beside the trash can, the same lights she'd seen the night of the murders.

The lights.

Now, Nealey remembered seeing those same lights on her first night at the Playhouse Inn.

The lights.

She slid down onto the floor and sat there thinking.

Years ago, when she was fourteen, she took her mother's car keys and drove the old Nova to the store to get a loaf of bread and some milk. There was nothing in the house to eat, so she convinced Naomi that she knew how to drive well enough to get them to the store and back. On the way to the store, they were laughing and talking about a boy Naomi liked. The car stalled at a red light, but Nealey managed to get it started again.

An unexpected rain shower made the winding road slick, but Nealey drove carefully. She heard the train in the distance.

"Hurry up," Naomi said. "Johnny's supposed to call. Come on. Gun it and get over those train tracks. We'll be stuck here waiting for that God-awful slow thing to go past."

"Johnny won't call you," Nealey had said. "And if I gun it, the engine will stall."

"Scaredy cat," Naomi said.

"Scaredy cat. Me? I'll show you," Nealey had said and floored it.

The car shot onto the train tracks then died.

She tried to start it again but couldn't.

Naomi began screaming when they saw the train barreling down the tracks at them. They tried to open the doors, but with their trembling hands, they couldn't budge the locks.

Nealey tried again but couldn't get the motor started.

Naomi was hysterical by now, and all Nealey could do was pray.

She prayed aloud, the most fervent prayer that had ever crossed her lips. And while she prayed, she felt as though she'd stepped outside of herself. She saw and heard nothing except the sound of her voice calling to God for help. The outside world simply faded away.

As the train sped closer, Nealey opened her eyes and saw the lights, two golden orbs hovering just outside the windshield. They glowed and spun.

"God? Is that you?" Nealey had asked.

The car rolled backwards, safely off the track as the train sped by, the wind from it rocking the car from side to side.

The lights.

God.

Now, sitting on the floor in Aunt Sylvie's bedroom, Nealey leaned her head against the wall and let the sweetness of that long-forgotten memory wash over her.

"God," she whispered and closed her eyes.

God, are you there? Can you hear me?

A cold nose nudged the side of her head.

Nealey opened her eyes and smiled.

"Lulu, where did you come from?"

Lulu glanced back at the door.

"Oh, right, you came in the door," Nealey said as she got up and brushed off her jeans.

Then she put her hands to her face.

"Oh, my gosh," she said. "Aunt Sylvie's reading glasses! I forgot all about them."

She repacked the duffle bag carefully, lingering a bit over the cross. She put the bag back by the desk and headed for the door. She flung it open and ran into what felt like a brick wall.

Startled, she gasped and stepped back.

Lulu gave a low growl.

"Max, you scared me half to death!" she said. "What are you doing standing at Aunt Sylvie's door?"

"I was just about to knock. Then, the door flung open. It startled me a bit, too," he said as he glanced down at Lulu while taking a step back.

Nealey forced herself to smile.

"Aunt Sylvie's downstairs in the kitchen, just where you'd expect her to be."

Did that sound sarcastic? He's a guest. I need to be polite.

"I'm headed to the kitchen, now," she said. "I'm in quite a hurry to deliver something, so if you don't mind, I really need to go."

"Fine, I shall accompany you."

No. Leave me alone!

"All right," she said as her smile faded.

With one hand on the banister rail, Nealey walked quickly down the steps, Lulu right beside her, still growling. Nealey patted Lulu's head.

"It's okay, girl," she said. "We're fine. You're such a good, brave girl, aren't you?"

Nealey thought she heard Max grunt.

When she reached the bottom, she glanced toward Max. He was standing midway up the stairs, his hands folded in front of him, a broad smile on his face.

"What?" Nealey asked. "What are you doing?"

"Just enjoying the view," he said.

As she tightened her hand around the banister, she winced and shuddered.

Nealey let go of the banister when she heard Max walking down the steps toward her.

"I have something delicious for your brave dog," Max said and held out his hand, "a treat. She likes treats, doesn't she?"

Nealey eyed it closely.

Looks like the ones Sylvie gives her.

"Where did you get it? I thought you didn't care for dogs."

"I know the dog doesn't like me, so I thought perhaps I might entice her with one of her treats."

Lulu still growled and moved close to Nealey. The huge head at her waistline nearly knocked her over.

Max stepped down until he was only an arm's length away. Then, he held out his hand to Lulu.

Nealey snatched the treat away.

"I'll give it to her later," she said. "It's almost time for dinner. We can't let her ruin her appetite, now, can we?"

"Come on, girl," Nealey said to her.

Max frowned and turned to go up the stairs.

"It's very rude," he said, "not to allow a guest to enjoy sharing a simple treat with the beast of the house. Very rude, indeed."

Nealey ignored him and she and Lulu hurried into the kitchen. She put Sylvie's reading glasses on the nearest countertop, and glanced back to see if Max was following, but there was no sign of him.

Thank goodness.

Aunt Sylvie was standing by the sink. Noble and Worthy flanked her on both sides, Worthy's hand on her shoulder.

Then, Nealey saw something that made her heart feel as if it had dropped into the pit of her stomach.

"Benton?"

She ran over to him as he leaned against the door frame.

"What's wrong?" she asked.

Benton groaned.

"Tell me what's wrong!" Nealey demanded. "You're in pain. I know it. Aunt Sylvie, what has happened to him?"

"It will pass, my dear," Worthy said. "Noble and I are going to make sure he gets safely back to the guest house for a short rest. He will be fine, I promise you."

Nealey slipped her arms around Benton.

"Please, let me help," she whispered.

Then she stepped back. His face appeared drawn and haggard,

so she put her hand on his cheek.

"I couldn't stand it, Benton, if something happened to you. Please, just tell me."

Benton managed a weak smile.

"Don't worry. Back pain. Comes and goes."

He winced as he straightened himself.

"But you're so pale," Nealey said.

"Come now," Worthy said and tugged Nealey away from Benton. "He needs a bit of rest. Then, he'll be fine and dandy."

With Benton in the middle flanked by Worthy and Noble, they walked through the door that led outside.

Nealey rubbed her eyes, then blinked.

They didn't open the door. Walked right through it.

"Nealey, darling, come here and sit with me," Sylvie said. "There are things I need to say. Please, while I have the courage to say them."

Nealey slid into a chair.

Maybe she wants to explain to me how my duffle bag got into her room, and why she's never mentioned it to me.

"Worthy assures me that Benton will be fine," Sylvie said. "We must have faith in him. He knows far more than we do."

The worried look on Aunt Sylvie's face didn't convince Nealey that Sylvie believed what she'd just said.

"Now, dear, I feel that I must reveal some things to you that might be unsettling. Nonetheless, it is my responsibility to be truthful, especially with you."

The cross, the stole, the Bible. Here it comes.

Sylvie ran her fingers along Nealey's cheek.

"You are so very precious to me," she said. "Every decision I've made since the day you were born has been for your good, Nealey, or at least, I told myself it was."

Nealey looked at her aunt, puzzled at the intense expression on her face, the shakiness of her voice.

Both hands on the table, Sylvie laced her fingers together. She took a deep breath and exhaled slowly.

"Nealey, darling," she said without looking at her, "Charlotte, my sister ...."

"Yes," Nealey interrupted, "What about her? Do you know

what frightened her so when she came here?"

Sylvie did not reply. She simply closed her eyes and took another deep breath.

"What is going on, Aunt Sylvie?"

"Well, now," Max's voice called from the kitchen doorway. "Doesn't the kitchen smell wonderful? Surely, it is almost time for dinner. I cannot wait to sample some of this aromatic fare, and then, I'm afraid, I must be going."

Sylvie put her hands in her lap.

"Max," she said and glanced up at the wall clock. "Dinner will be served in thirty minutes, promptly at seven. Perhaps you'd care for an aperitif before dinner while we wait for the others to arrive?"

Max cocked his head.

"What did you have in mind?"

"I have a lovely lime cordial, non-alcoholic but superb," Sylvie said and rose from her chair.

"Sounds quite nice, actually."

"Wonderful. Now, please have a seat in the parlor. Having people milling about the kitchen can be nerve-wracking for a chef," Sylvie said.

"Very well," Max said. "I do look forward to tasting your lime cordial."

When Max had left, Sylvie bent and kissed Nealey on the top of her head.

"I promise you that we will continue this directly after dinner, my darling girl. Now, I need your assistance. Bring me a cocktail glass from the china cabinet while I ready the cordial."

For a few seconds, Nealey didn't move. She glanced at the door that led outside, then looked again at Sylvie.

"Please, darling," Sylvie said. "It is much better to serve our guest in the parlor, isn't it?"

"Yes, I suppose so, but we need to talk."

"Of course, we will, dear, just as soon as I get this prepared. Your guests must always come first, Nealey, no matter what the circumstance."

"He's not a guest, Aunt Sylvie. He's an unwelcome intruder."

Just as the words came from her mouth, she glanced at the door.

Max stood there, his hands folded in front of him, his face devoid of expression, his dark eyes glaring at her.

Chapter 38

After clearing the dishes and straightening up in the dining room, Nealey sat at the kitchen table and watched as Sylvie dried her hands on a dish towel then put a finger to her lips.

"Shh," she said very quietly to Mae.

Sylvie motioned toward the dining room and shook her head.

Nealey smiled a weak smile at Anna, Maggie, and Mae, all seated with her at the kitchen table. Not one of them uttered a word.

"Max," Sylvie called, "while you finish your dessert, I'll prepare the invoice for your stay with us. I have all of your information at the front desk. Shan't take long. It's almost eight o'clock. I'm sure you want to be on your way."

She stuck her head into the dining room doorway and smiled. "Everything all right?"

"Just perfect," Max said. "Thank you for a lovely meal. Perhaps Benton wouldn't mind fetching my bag for me? It's just inside the door in my room."

"Benton is a tad busy at the moment," Sylvie said. "But perhaps Nealey wouldn't mind."

Nealey grimaced.

She felt Mae's little hand on her arm, and when she looked at her, Mae was shaking her head.

"No," she mouthed. "No."

In spite of a gnawing fear of having to go into his room, Nealey patted Mae's hand and got up.

Then she smiled and lied, "It's okay."

I said the same thing to my precious babies. I lied, told them it would be okay, and then Brian murdered them. My last words to them were lies. Lies.

Nealey felt sick. She bit at her lip and balled one fist.

As she left the kitchen, she glanced back and forced a smile at Mae again. Then, she lowered her eyes and hoped that Mae couldn't sense her apprehension. She didn't want to go into Max's room. She didn't want to be anywhere near him, but she also didn't want to alarm Mae.

On her way up the stairs, Nealey could understand the little girl's fear. But Nealey wondered if Max had done anything to hurt Mae. She didn't think Max knew about Anna and the girls, but she couldn't be sure. She told herself again that they were ghosts. Ghosts!

How could he hurt them?

She took a deep breath as she climbed the stairs and tried to tell herself that everything would be okay, but the feeling in the pit of her stomach warned her that it would not be okay.

Then, she stopped midway.

They're trapped here. Could Max know about them? Could the girls have accidentally appeared to him?

Nealey rubbed her temples and continued up the steps.

She had an eccentric family. She had grown so fond of them, almost as if she'd known them all her life. Now, she wanted more than anything to get to know them better, spend time with them, learn all about their favorite things.

What do they love? What do they hate? And what are they afraid of?

Nealey stopped when she reached the second-floor landing.

They're afraid of Max. Has he done something to them?

"Can't blame them. He gives me the creeps, too," she whispered.

She hesitated outside the door of Max's room. She didn't want to go in, but the sooner he had his bag, the quicker he'd be out of the Playhouse Inn for good. Instinctively, and before she could stop the movement, she crossed herself.

Then, with her heart pounding, she opened the door to Max's room and stepped inside to grab his bag. It was just where he said it would be, on the floor near the doorway. When she bent to pick it up, something on the edge of the bed caught her attention.

With the bag in one hand, she walked to the edge of the bed and looked down at a piece of paper. It looked like a fragment of the stationery from the Playhouse Inn. The top edge of the paper was ragged, as if it had been torn away hurriedly. Notes handwritten in an elaborate script filled the page.

Nealey picked it up and read:

Tennessee, 1976, a daughter born to Mr. Lyle Martin and Charlotte Wolcott Martin Tennessee, 1976, a daughter born to Sylvia Wolcott

"What?" she said, "this can't be right."

She read the last two lines again, this time pronouncing each word carefully.

"Tennessee, 1976, a daughter born to Mr. Lyle Martin and Charlotte Wolcott Martin."

It can't be right. I was born in 1976. Naomi and I. We're twins.

Then she read the second line again.

"Tennessee, 1976, a daughter born to Sylvia Wolcott."

"NO!" she said. "1976, no, that's not right. Aunt Sylvie's never had a daughter."

She flipped the paper over to see if there was a signature or an indication of who had written those lines. Nothing.

"Someone is obviously mistaken," she said and folded the piece of paper. She tucked it into her jeans' pocket.

Could I be? No, it doesn't make any sense. What about Naomi?

Nealey took a last look around the room.

Her eyes widened as she saw the portrait of Anna above the dresser. She walked over to it and stared at the woman.

So lovely. Why would anyone want to kill her? And why is she trapped here?

Above Max's bed hung another portrait of Anna. With her was a handsome, bearded man in a dark suit. Alongside him stood a priest.

The plaque beneath the portrait read: *John Wolcott, Anna, and Father Madison, The Blessing of the Playhouse Inn, 1889.*

"The year before she died," Nealey muttered and looked closer at the portrait.

"The Inn was blessed—there's the priest—the year before she died. If it was blessed, how could an evil spirit trap them here?"

She reached up and ran a finger over the glass.

Beautiful Anna.

Then, she let her finger drift over to the priest. As she blinked and focused her eyes a little better, she studied the priest's face.

Nealey gasped and put both hands to her mouth. She backed away from the portrait, knocked over the night table, and sent a vase of flowers crashing to the floor.

Oh, God! Oh, God!

She grabbed Max's bag and ran downstairs to warn Aunt Sylvie.

Chapter 39

Mae swung her legs back and forth under the kitchen table and twirled a fork in her hands. Maggie sat quietly beside her and watched Lulu, sprawled as usual on the kitchen floor, tail thumping occasionally on the linoleum.

"Can we tell her yet?" Mae asked her mother.

"No, dear," Anna said and patted Mae's hand. "We must wait for Sylvie."

"But ...."

Anna raised an eyebrow.

"No, buts. We must wait for Sylvie. Now, wipe away the crumbs from the table, if you please, and Maggie, you can ...."

Nealey suddenly burst into the kitchen.

"Where's Aunt Sylvie? Where is she? I have to talk to her, and I have to talk to her now!"

Lulu lifted her head and gave a deep bark.

"What is wrong, Nealey?" Anna asked.

"Where is she, Anna? This is no time for asking questions! I have to find her now!"

Nealey's hands shook, her voice trembled.

"Please, I must find her before it's too late."

A heady scent of roses suddenly filled the room. A slight breeze ruffled the curtains.

"Too late?" Worthy asked softly and laid a hand on her shoulder, "Calm yourself my sweet. Sylvie is occupied, but she will return momentarily. Perhaps in the meantime, I could offer you assistance?"

"No, get away! There's nothing you can do," Nealey said, her voice sharp and loud.

"As I said, my dear, your Aunt Sylvie will return in a moment. I'm afraid you must simply be patient for a little longer," Worthy said. "Please, tell me what is troubling you so."

Nealey paced in front of the kitchen table and stumbled over Lulu's long legs.

"Lulu, you're in my way! For goodness sakes, can't you find another place to take a nap?"

Lulu lifted her head then plopped it down again and made a moaning sound.

Immediately, Nealey regretted her sharp tone. She bent down and patted Lulu's head.

"Sorry, girl," she said.

Lulu got to her feet, licked Nealey in the face, and moved toward the nook by the outside door. She turned three times in a circle, then flopped down and snorted.

"Can't any of you hear me? I must speak to her NOW."

"Ooh, you're gonna be in trouble if you talk to Aunt Sylvie like that," Mae said, one arm fading quickly. "She doesn't like yelling. It's not ladylike."

Nealey turned her head and glared at Mae.

"Mae," Anna said, "you and Maggie go upstairs this minute and put your pajamas on. It's past your bedtime."

"Children, mind your mother," Worthy said in a pleasant voice. "You've been such good girls today."

Mae sighed, took Maggie's hand, and said, "She was nicer when she was a little girl. Now, she's just a grouchy old …."

"That is quite enough from you, Mae. Upstairs, now!" Anna said.

Maggie and Mae disappeared.

"What's *that* supposed to mean?" Nealey asked, exasperated.

Suddenly, she felt dizzy, so she braced herself on the kitchen counter.

"Are you unwell, Nealey?" Anna asked. "Come, sit down here at the table."

"I shall return in a flash," Worthy said. "Anna, will you take care of our Nealey?"

"Most assuredly. Come, dearest," Anna said.

Almost instantly, she hovered beside Nealey, feet encircled in the blue-green pool, and guided her gently to the table and into a chair.

Worthy helped her take a seat, then walked to the door and slipped through.

Anna put a cold, almost translucent arm around Nealey's shoulders.

"Please, dear, can't you tell me what is wrong? I love you, Nealey. There is nothing you can't share with me."

"I got a little lightheaded, that's all. I do that sometimes."

"Yes," Anna said, "you are like the rest of us, dear. When we are stressed, our bodies don't cope well. Dizziness forces us to sit and rest a few moments."

"The rest of us?" Nealey asked.

Anna rubbed the side of Nealey's cheek.

Even though the touch was icy cold, the hand barely recognizable, Nealey calmed as soon as the faded fingers stroked her cheek.

"Yes, dear," Anna said. "All of us experience it. The women, I mean. In our family. Sylvie, too, though rarely in plain sight of anyone else. She hides it well."

"Where is she, Anna? I must talk to her. I must."

Lulu lifted her head and cooed.

The outside door eased open.

"I have returned," came Sylvie's call. "Benton does not seem to be doing well at ...."

When she stepped into the kitchen, Sylvie stopped.

"My goodness, what is happening, Anna? Nealey, dear, are you all right?

"She's had a little spell," Anna said.

"Oh, those spells!" Sylvie said. "They're such dreadful nuisances. Are you better now, dear?"

Nealey nodded.

"Are the children in bed?"

"Fast asleep, I believe," Anna replied.

Sylvie smiled. "Such precious little dears."

"I see that Max's car is gone, thank goodness."

"Aunt Sylvie! You're back! We missed you," cried Mae. "We couldn't go to bed without giving you a hug."

Maggie and Mae appeared, clad in blue pajamas. They ran to Sylvie and hugged her.

"Oh, my goodness," Sylvie said as she embraced them, "I was only gone for a bit, but isn't it lovely to be missed?"

Anna stood, one barely visible hand still on Nealey's shoulder.

"All right, my little ones, it is very late."

"Anna? Will you stay just a moment?" Nealey asked. "You need to hear what I have to say. It's important."

"But we want to talk to Aunt Sylvie. And we're thirsty, too," Mae said.

"Oh, my, who could refuse such darlings?" Sylvie asked. "Give me one more big hug, then off to bed with you. Your sweet mother will give you a sip of water when she goes upstairs with you."

"No, she won't. She'll say it's too late," Mae said.

The delicate scent of roses wafted through the air. A slight breeze ruffled the paper napkins on the table.

"Ah, and I believe that she would be exactly right. Now, how about a good-night hug for your dear friend, Worthy, then ...."

"We know," Mae said, "off to bed."

The girls hugged Sylvie, then Worthy, then stood in front of Nealey.

"Good night, girls. Have a peaceful sleep," Nealey said and smiled. "Forgive me for being sharp with you earlier. I didn't mean to hurt your feelings."

Maggie and Mae smiled. Then, for the very first time, they put their arms around Nealey and hugged her.

"Thank you," Nealey whispered to them. "I needed that."

"Now, it's Worthy's turn," Mae said as she whispered something into Worthy's ear.

"I see," he said. "What vigilant children you are! Now, run along with your mother."

As Anna, Maggie, and Mae vanished, Sylvie stepped beside Worthy.

"It seems that our guest merely pulled his car to the other side of the house. He hasn't left at all," Worthy told them.

"What?" Nealey said and stood up.

"The girls said that he's hiding and that his friend is hiding with him."

"His friend?" Sylvie asked. "What friend?"

Worthy straightened his tie.

"The one the girls call *the bad man*. They said he was waiting."

"For what?" Nealey asked.

"I'm afraid, my darling," Worthy said, "that he's waiting for you."

Chapter 40

Nealey sank back into one of the overstuffed chairs and shuddered.

He's waiting for me.

"Now, isn't it more comfortable in here?" Sylvie asked. "I do love this sitting room. It's such a cozy place, don't you think, Worthy?"

"But of course, I agree," Worthy said as he eased onto the blue sofa beside Sylvie. "It is one of my favorite spots, next to the kitchen."

"Lulu, dearest, would you like to come in here with us? Come on, sweet."

Instead, Lulu sprawled in the foyer.

"I believe she's tired, Sylvie," Anna said from her chair.

"Yes, it is quite late, close to 11:00. She's accustomed to being in bed by now," Sylvie said.

Nealey shook her head and tried to push the horrifying thought out of her mind. She needed answers right now, and the only people who could give her those answers were sitting around her.

He's waiting.

"Now, darling," Sylvie said, "try to rid yourself of that unpleasantness."

Startled, Nealey looked at Sylvie.

Sylvie simply smiled.

Nealey, on the other hand, let out a sigh and wrapped the cold fingers of her left hand around her magic wand. She was thankful now that she'd taken a few minutes to get it from her room. Somehow, it made her feel a little safer.

She shook herself out of her reverie and rubbed her arms. Even in the cozy sitting room, the fireplace sending warmth throughout, Nealey shivered.

"Worry yourself not, my dear," Worthy said to her. "Benton will return to us shortly."

Nealey stared at him for a few seconds, a thin smile on her face.

Nealey fingered the wand and rubbed her forehead.

I don't understand.

Worthy smiled at her.

"Fear not, my dear. All of your questions will be answered in time."

"Well," she said, "I might as well get on with it. Here they are, Anna."

Nealey laid the photograph she'd gotten from Sylvie's room and the note from Max's on the coffee table. Though her hands trembled, she straightened each item neatly.

"Oh, dear," Anna said, "your hands are shaking. Forgive me for making the room so cold. It seems that I need the heat for energy so much more now. I am sorry, Nealey."

"Don't worry about it, Anna. I am glad you're here," Nealey said.

She tapped the photo and the note.

"Aunt Sylvie, please take a look at these," Nealey said.

"My necklace!" Anna exclaimed. "She's wearing my necklace."

"My dear Anna," Worthy said and leaned forward. "I must tell you about the history of your necklace."

"The history?" Anna asked, one hand fluttering to her neck. "My Henry gave me that necklace as an engagement gift."

"Yes," Worthy said, "but before it belonged to Henry, it had a different owner."

Anna shook her head.

"A different owner? No, that's quite impossible," Anna said.

"Now, my sweet Anna," Worthy said and stood up. He brushed at the sleeve of his white jacket and straightened his tie.

"It is high time I told you the truth," he said as he patted his pocket square. "It is high time in this house for several truths to come out."

Sylvie, Anna, and Nealey wrung their hands.

"Oh, dear," Anna said.

"What truths?" Nealey asked.

"Get on with it," Sylvie said and waved a hand in his direction.

"Anna, I think you will be pleased to know that your cherished necklace first belonged to one of your ancestors. It has been in the family since the 1700s."

"But Henry said it was made for me," Anna said. "Why would he have said it if it were not true?"

"Perhaps, dear," Sylvie said, "he did not mean it in the literal sense, but rather in a figurative way, meaning simply that it was perfectly suited to you."

Anna said nothing. She had faded, now, to her waist.

"Yes, that sounds right, Anna," Nealey said and smiled. "Maybe he meant it in the most loving way."

"Dearest," Worthy said, "what is important about this is that your Henry loved you, did he not?"

"Yes," Anna said softly.

"I doubt that even Henry knew its true history," Worthy said. "When the baron commissioned it, he did so with a two-fold purpose. One was to give his wife a most stunning piece of jewelry. The other was to make certain that the stone in the center—the beautiful emerald—was large enough to conceal a stone underneath."

From his suit coat pocket, Worthy withdrew the necklace and handed it to Sylvie.

"My dear, if you will be so kind," he said to her.

Sylvie picked up the necklace and ran her fingers across the large emerald stone in its center.

"There is a small catch on the back," Worthy said. "If you will simply press it, I think you will find the secret."

"Oh, dear," Anna said again. "I do not have much energy left."

"Stay with us as long as you can," Worthy said.

Sylvie pressed the catch and felt the large emerald slide to the side.

"What is it?" Nealey asked. "Tell us, Aunt Sylvie. What is beneath the big stone?"

Sylvie examined it carefully.

"I believe it is—yes, I'm certain of it—it is a piece of jet."

Sylvie held up a small rounded stone that looked like black glass striped with a single red line marbled through it.

"Jet?" Nealey asked. "What in the world is jet?"

Sylvie pushed a few stray hairs from her face. She fingered the stone, turned it over in her hand several times.

"It's lovely, isn't it?"

"Let us continue," Worthy said.

"What kind of stone is jet, Aunt Sylvie?" Nealey asked.

"Well," Sylvie said, "it is actually fossilized wood. It takes centuries for a piece of this to form. Black glass with a red stripe. The ancients believed the red stripe to be a blood sign. Every shaman possessed one of these. Oh yes, it was a staple in his ... tool kit, highly cherished, very powerful."

"Powerful?" Nealey asked.

Sylvie glanced at Worthy. He nodded.

"The ancients used this stone to exorcize demons, to send them back to the Underworld where they belonged. Whoever possessed one of these stones was said to be safe from the evil affectations of demons and vile spirits."

"Why cover it with an emerald?" Nealey asked.

"Ah, there was a method to it," Worthy said. "The emerald is the most highly prized stone for warding off evil, but you must remember that in order to exorcize an evil, you must first attract it."

"I don't understand," Nealey heard Anna say, though she could no longer see her.

"The Wolcott family was haunted—ages ago—cursed," Worthy said, "by an entity powerful enough to resist the emerald and hold captive the souls of many of your departed kin."

"But if the jet is capable of exorcizing an evil, why are all those souls held captive?" Nealey asked. "Wouldn't the stone drive away the spirit?"

Nealey got up from the chair.

"This curse," she said, "is it the thing that keeps Anna and the girls trapped here? If it is, what about the stone? Why doesn't it work?"

Worthy stood in front of one of the large windows in the sitting room, his hands behind his back.

"It does work, my darling Nealey," Worthy said and turned to face her. "But only in the right pair of hands."

"Aunt Sylvie, do you understand this?" Nealey asked.

Sylvie replaced the jet and slid the emerald back into place.

"I'm afraid I do," she said.

"Then, please, explain it to me," Nealey said. "Tell me why they're trapped here. It doesn't make sense. All of this for a stupid necklace?"

Nealey heard Anna gasp.

"I am sorry, Anna" she said in the direction of the gasp. She squeezed her fingers tighter around the wand.

"It is a fine, elegant piece of jewelry," Nealey said, pacing the floor in front of Sylvie. "I'm simply trying to understand what is going on, why you and the girls can't leave the Playhouse Inn. I just can't believe it's all because of a necklace! Enlighten me please, Aunt Sylvie."

Sylvie stood and hugged her.

"My precious girl," she said. "As our dear Worthy has said, this necklace is the key to releasing our Anna and her girls. It has been the key all along, for hundreds of years."

"But if you knew that, why on earth didn't you do something about it?"

"Ah, but she *did* do something," Worthy said. "She sent you to the convent. She removed you from the presence of this evil and prayed that the religious life would protect you."

"But why didn't you tell me?" Nealey asked. "Why?"

Sylvie lowered her head.

"We hoped," Worthy said softly, "that your time at the convent would steer you to God, darling. Only then could you have the right pair of hands."

Nealey looked at him and shook her head.

"We? The right pair of hands?"

"Yes, darling, we, all of us. We prayed that you would have a priest's hands. Only a priest can use the stone, a very special priest."

Nealey stepped back and slumped into a chair.

"A very special priest," she whispered.

Sylvie laid a hand on Worthy's arm.

"We're making a complete mess of this," she said.

"No, Sylvie, you're doing a perfectly fine job," Anna said. "You're telling the truth, and she was such a precious baby, wasn't she? Oh, what a delight to have in our home."

"Anna?" Nealey asked. "What did you mean by that?"

Nealey struggled out of the chair.

"Tell me, please. What did you mean?"

"Dear, dear me," Anna said. "Have I spoken out of turn?"

Sylvie stood very close to Nealey.

"Darling, please listen to me. I know that you are confused at the moment, but I am trying. Anna knows what a beautiful baby you were because ... well ... because you were born right here in this house."

Nealey chuckled and tightened her grip on the wand.

"Don't be silly, Aunt Sylvie! I wasn't born here. I was born in a hospital, only a minute before Naomi was born. We're twins. You couldn't have forgotten about Naomi."

"No, dear, I haven't forgotten about our quiet little Naomi. Do you remember–no, you couldn't possibly–but when the three of you came here, years ago now, Naomi stayed as close to Charlotte as she could get, barely let go of her skirt the whole time. Our Naomi didn't care for the Inn or for me, I'm afraid."

Suddenly, Nealey gasped and stepped away from Sylvie.

A long-forgotten image flickered into her mind.

A bedroom. A beautiful woman in a long dress, her hair swept up, was singing a sweet lullaby to her. 'Sleep, my child, in peaceful splendor all through the night.' Two little girls chimed in and sang with her.

"Anna," she whispered.

Nealey's eyes widened as yet another image came to her.

She was cuddled in a woman's lap. She could smell her perfume, and there were bubbles. Bubbles everywhere. The sounds of little girls squealing with laughter. Splashing in a bathtub. Maggie and Mae? Then, Aunt Sylvie's voice, "Time for bed my sweets."

And the last, Sylvie's voice again. "No, Charlotte, a little longer. I am her...."

"What, Aunt Sylvie?" Nealey asked, almost dazed. "You are my what?"

Sylvie put a hand on each of Nealey's cheeks.

"Sweetheart," she said. "I am ...."

Nealey's eyes met hers.

"What?" she asked.

"I am your mother," Sylvie said. "And you are my beloved daughter."

Nealey shook her head.

"Charlotte is my mother," she said, her voice trembling. "Naomi is my twin."

"No, sweetheart, listen to me. Charlotte raised you as her own. You and Naomi were born on the same day."

"Yes, I was there with you, dear," Anna said. "Such a beautiful little baby you were. Oh, it was such a splendid day for us all. The girls were delighted to have a little sister."

Nealey put her hands to her temples and shook her head.

"No, that can't be right," Nealey said. "I would have known. I mean, wouldn't I have guessed it? You have deceived me all these years?"

"A mother must do what she can to protect her child," she said softly, "and she must pray that the child will grow up with the right pair of hands."

"What?" Nealey said. "What are you saying?"

Nealey threw her arms in the air. "God, my whole life has been a lie!"

Worthy put his arm around Nealey's shoulders.

"Nealey, be honest," he said softly. "Wasn't there ever a time when you thought Sylvie was your mother? Ever? Think back."

Nealey lowered her eyes.

"There were times when I *wanted* her to be my mother."

She remembered standing at the cliff's edge beside Sylvie years ago. She could hear herself call to the waters below. She felt the sweet peacefulness of being with Sylvie and calling out to the river.

She saw the two of them in the kitchen, she playing on the black and white linoleum floor, Aunt Sylvie mixing something in a large bowl and offering her a lick of the spoon. Such happiness there was in that kitchen!

"Well, now, see?" Worthy said, his voice louder and filled with enthusiasm.

Nealey took a few steps until she was very close to Sylvie.

"You gave me away," she said. "You didn't want me?"

Anna gasped. "Oh, no, dear, that's not true at all. It was the creature."

"Darling," Sylvie said, her voice barely audible, "I always wanted you, even when I couldn't have you."

"Why?" asked Nealey. "Why couldn't you have me?"

Sylvie shook her head. "You see, dear, I wasn't married. Things were different then."

"You wouldn't have cared about that," Nealey said. "Why, why couldn't you have me?"

"I knew I had to send you away, darling. The entity upstairs, it might have harmed you. I felt it wanted you, and I couldn't risk it. Charlotte was more than happy to keep you with her, and Naomi, well, you became a precious little family."

"Yes, a precious little family," Nealey said.

She walked to the window and stared outside.

Sylvie laid a hand on Worthy's arm.

"What did you mean," Nealey asked, "when you said you hoped I'd be a very special priest, one with the right pair of hands?"

Nealey held out her hands and looked at them.

"My hands are not special," she said. "I must have disappointed you."

"On the contrary, my darling girl. You have in every way made me proud," Sylvie said. "You were everything I could have hoped for in a daughter."

"I wasn't a very special priest," she said and slid into one of the chairs close to the window.

"I beg to differ, my dear," Worthy said. "You were an extraordinary priest, quite special, indeed."

Nealey turned and stared at him.

"You have a special bond with the Upper Realm."

"What?" Nealey asked.

"You remember, don't you, my darling girl, the golden orbs?" Sylvie asked. "The ones you saw years ago on the train tracks?"

"Orbs," Nealey repeated in a hollow voice.

The lights.

Nealey's mind was reeling. Images flashed through it at lightning speed, as if she were watching a film of every moment of her life, each frame visible for only a second before it changed to another. In the mental images, she saw them now.

The lights.

At the Convent when she was so lonely. At the hospital when Nicholas was born, barely alive. At the church when a tornado ripped off the roof.

"The lights?" she asked suddenly.

"Yes, darling, yes!" Sylvie cried.

"I remember them," Nealey whispered and leaned her head on the back of the chair. "I tried to forget about them. I thought I was crazy for seeing them, and I didn't want to be crazy like my mother."

"Oh, no, sweetheart," Sylvie said and knelt beside her. "They were your guardians, my dear, there to keep you safe, to comfort and protect you."

Nealey managed a weak smile.

"Aunt Sylvie?"

"Yes, honey, what is it?"

"In one of those old photographs upstairs, there is a picture of a priest. I recognize him. It's Max, or his ancient twin."

Sylvie nodded.

"Yes," she said. "Yes, our family cannot seem to get rid of him. He's cursed us for years."

"Aunt Sylvie, I'm glad that you are my mother. I wish I'd known earlier."

"I tried to tell you many times, but I simply didn't have the courage. I knew you loved Charlotte and Naomi. I feared you wouldn't be happy or safe here with me."

Nealey reached across and brushed some stray wisps of hair from Sylvie's face.

"If you are my mother," she said, "then who is my father?"

The front double doors slammed open with a ferocious bang. Lulu yelped, and Nealey jumped up out of her chair.

Chapter 41

Wearing only a pair of boxer shorts, Benton lay on the bed in the guest house curled into a fetal position. He moaned and wrapped his fingers more tightly around a wrought iron bar on the headboard. A sudden chill forced him to pull a quilt up to his neck. He shuddered.

"God help me," he whispered.

Noble stood beside the bed staring out at the darkness.

"You must go," Benton said to him. "Please go."

Noble didn't budge. He only turned his head in Benton's direction.

"They need you," Benton said and grimaced when the pain shot up his back again. "Worthy isn't strong enough by himself. He needs you."

Noble turned his head back to the window.

"I love you like a brother," Benton said, "but go. Your stubbornness is posing a threat to the family. Can't you see that?"

Noble turned toward the door and sniffed.

"I smell him, too." Benton said and relaxed as the pain subsided. "He's in there with them. He's in the house."

When the door blew open, Noble stiffened.

Wearing their flowered pajamas and holding hands, the girls hovered an inch or so off the floor.

"Something stinks in our room," Mae said. "It stinks so bad we left. We were scared, and we couldn't find Lulu. Can we stay here with you?"

Noble held out a hand to them.

Instantly, they appeared beside him. Maggie wrapped her arms around his waist while Mae stood close by.

"What's wrong with Benton?" Mae asked. "His back is bleeding."

"I'll be fine. Don't worry," he said.

"But, you're magic," Mae replied. "You're not supposed to be sick and bleed."

Benton tightened his grip around the bar again and moaned.

"Noble, can't you fix him?" Mae asked.

"Girls," Benton said, struggling to sit up.

"I will be fine in just a little while. I promise you."

"Benton?" Mae asked in a softer voice.

He looked at her.

"Is this like the last time?"

"I'm afraid so," Benton said, his elbows propped on his knees, his head in his hands.

"When you tried to help us, but the bad man shot us all and took us?"

Benton nodded his head.

"So, now, you're turning into a warrior so you can fight?"

Noble tapped Mae on the shoulder and pointed to the door.

"But we want to stay here, Noble. It stinks in there, and we're scared."

"Don't be afraid, girls," Benton said. "We will protect you."

Mae shook her head.

"But what about last time? You didn't help us get to Heaven."

"I know," Benton said, his face contorted in pain. "God forgive me. I was too proud to believe I could be defeated. Last time, I was too late. He had already taken your sweet little souls. But *this* time, I am wiser. Things will be different. I promise you."

"We don't want anything bad to happen to you. We love you," Mae said.

Benton forced a smile.

"I'll be fine. Really."

"You won't have to go in the water, will you? I mean, since you can't swim and all. We want you to be careful."

"I'll be careful, girls."

Mae lowered her head.

"What's wrong?" Benton asked.

"We're afraid," Mae said. "Will he have a gun this time? We hate guns."

He shook his head.

"No, he will have something more powerful."

Mae stepped away from Noble and stood next to Benton.

"What will he have?"

"Noble, I must get outside now," Benton said and moved to the edge of the bed. "It's almost finished. Girls, back to the house. Noble will go with you, and he will protect you."

Noble bent down and supported Benton as he struggled to his feet. Slowly they moved toward the door.

"What will he have?" Mae asked. "You said he'd have something stronger than a gun. What?"

"The necklace," Benton said as he staggered out the door. "And Nealey."

Chapter 42

Nealey rushed into the foyer. Seconds before, Lulu's yelp and the slamming doors had made her heart skip a beat.

"There's no one here," she said, "and Lulu's gone! How could the doors have slammed by themselves? Where could she be?"

Standing beside her, Sylvie slipped the piece of jet from beneath the emerald and pressed it into Nealey's hand.

"We will find her, my dear. Now, don't let go of this. In your hands, it will protect us."

Then Sylvie put the necklace on and motioned toward the doors.

"We must find Lulu," she said to Worthy. "And Anna, dear, please stay upstairs with the girls. They may be frightened. Children always want their mothers when they're afraid."

Nealey had a sudden mental image of her own children huddled beside her, Brian pointing the gun at them. She could almost feel their trembling bodies pressed against hers. A hatred welled inside of her, hatred toward the man who frightened her innocent children and stole their lives from her. She clenched her fists.

Brian! How I hate him.

Something nagged at her, something about Brian. She concentrated for a moment.

Then she gasped.

Brian! I remember!

"Nealey, dear, we have work to do," Sylvie said and kissed her on the cheek then slipped an arm around her shoulder. "Our Lulu might be in danger. She might need us, though granted, for a woman her age, she is still quite adept at taking care of herself, but one never knows."

"Aunt Sylvie, I must talk to Anna. I must!"

Nealey's hands trembled. She felt her heart racing.

"Now?" Sylvie asked. "You look positively pale, Nealey. What is wrong? We really must find Lulu."

Nealey laid a trembling hand on Sylvie's arm then turned and raced up the stairs.

Not long after, Worthy opened the double doors to the inn and called to Sylvie.

"Come along," he said. "We will begin our search."

"Why does Nealey need to speak to Anna?"

"I am clueless," Worthy said.

Sylvie grabbed the flashlights from the bureau drawer and glanced at the antique grandfather clock.

"My gracious," she said, "it's well past midnight. I had no idea it was so late."

She slipped on her coat and stepped across the threshold.

"Let us set about to rescue our sweet Lulu," Sylvie said. "Now, where could she be?"

Sylvie handed her flashlight to Worthy then clapped her hands loudly.

"Here girl," she yelled. "Time for your bedtime snack."

She elbowed Worthy.

"That should bring her. She can't resist her bedtime treat."

The two of them stood in silence at the bottom of the steps, waiting for a response, a sound, anything to tell them where Lulu was.

Sylvie put a hand to her ear.

"What is that sound? Do you hear it, Worthy?

"Yes, yes," he said. "Is someone digging?"

Sylvie rubbed her arms.

"It gives me chills," she said. "Is it coming from the back of the house? Or perhaps around the side?"

"Well, let us investigate," Worthy said.

Sylvie hooked one arm in his and scooted as close as she could get to him.

"I'm frightened," she said.

Worthy patted her hand.

"Fear, yes, I've heard of it. Terrible thing."

They walked toward the side of the house and stopped to listen.

"Can you hear it?" Worthy asked. "It does sound like someone's digging."

"Yes, I think it's coming from over there by the old storm shelter."

They took a few more steps and Sylvie cried out then tumbled to the ground. Her flashlight rolled across the lawn.

"My word, what is wrong, dear?"

"Get my flashlight, will you? I can't see out here. What has happened to our outdoor flood light? Benton said he'd fixed it. No sign of it now, though."

Light suddenly spread across the object over which Sylvie had taken her spill.

"My goodness," Worthy said, "is that your gardening shovel?"

Worthy helped Sylvie to her feet. They both peered down at the offending object.

"Yes, it's my shovel," Sylvie said, "but what is that around the edges of the blade? Shine the flashlight closer."

Worthy cleared his throat.

Sylvie looked at his face then down along his arm. From his finger shone a bright white light that lit the entire area around the side of the house.

Sylvie smiled at him.

"Of course," she said.

Then, she bent down to examine the shovel.

"Oh, my word," Sylvie said and clutched at her chest.

She ran her hand over the edge of the blade of the shovel.

"It's blood, Worthy, and it's still warm."

Sylvie groaned.

"You don't think, do you, that someone has hurt our Lulu? Oh, please, dear God, not our Lulu."

Worthy bent down and picked up the shovel. Then, he examined the doors of the storm shelter.

"She's not here, Sylvie. Our Lulu is not here."

"Oh, dear, where can she be?"

Sylvie clapped her hands again.

"Come, girl. Come!"

They searched through the bushes at the side of the inn, walked along the back side of the house, combed the hedges in front of the garden entry.

"Come, girl," Sylvie called several times.

"Wait," Worthy said suddenly. "What is that?"

He shined his light toward the back of the house.

"There," he said. "By the greenhouse."

Sylvie opened the door to the greenhouse expecting a burst of moist, fragrant air. Instead, she inhaled cold air that smelled like rotting meat.

"Oh!" she said, almost gagging. "I cannot stand it in here."

"Let me take a look around," Worthy said. "Go back outside so that you can breathe."

Sylvie stepped outside.

"Lulu, darling, where are you?" she called, her voice trembling, her strength almost gone. "Come, precious."

She made a feeble attempt at clapping her hands.

"My Lulu," she whispered.

The scent of roses drifted past her face. Sylvie turned and saw that the greenhouse was filled with a bright, pulsating light that changed from white to gold to blue.

Sylvie marveled at the beauty of it.

A few moments later, Worthy stepped out.

"Let's go back to the house," he said. "Come along."

He took Sylvie's arm and led her in the direction of the front of the inn.

"But what about Lulu?" she asked. "You haven't mentioned her. Was she in there? Did you find her?"

Worthy said nothing. He simply patted her arm.

"Everything is coming to a head, Sylvie. You must prepare yourself. We know that Max is still here. We know that he cannot have anything good in mind."

"Yes, but," Sylvie said.

A low rumble of thunder sounded in the distance.

"There will be a fight, I'm afraid," Worthy said, "but you must trust in us. Now, let us go back into the house. There is nothing more to be done out here."

When they'd reached the bottom of the steps, Sylvie stopped.

"You've been a great help," she said to Worthy and put her hand on his arm.

A clap of thunder startled them both.

"The storm approaches," Worthy said.

The doors of the inn suddenly burst open.

"Aunt Sylvie, you must come," Nealey said.

Sylvie glanced at Worthy.

"Hurry!" Nealey yelled.

Chapter 43

Outside the guest house, Benton struggled to his knees but hadn't the strength to stand. On all fours, he stared at the soft grass beneath his hands. The pain came in nauseating waves. He knew he needed to be up, and he tried, but he couldn't manage it.

Max is in the house with them. I need to be there.

Suddenly, two feet clad in shiny black shoes appeared directly in front of him. A sickening smell overwhelmed him.

"So, he's in the house, is he?" Max asked, his hands clasped in front of him. "Did I hear you correctly?"

Benton groaned.

"Well, *someone's* in the house with your beloved Nealey. That is true. But shall we say it is someone who is not, well, one of us."

Benton lifted his head and glared at him.

"And what do we have here?" Max asked as he squatted down. "A wounded soul? An injured warrior? My, my, but it is lovely to see you in such a state, my friend. It will make my job here so much easier."

Benton tightened his jaw.

"Leave them alone," Benton said. "I know why you came here."

"Are we getting upset?" Max asked. "Aw, how sweet. To love those ... humans ... so much. Never had the experience myself."

Max stood and brushed at his trousers, then his sleeves. He adjusted his gold cufflinks. Then, he sniffed loudly and inhaled.

"Ah, the night air in October. Such a lovely fragrance."

Benton coughed.

"Well, we'll have to chat more often, my friend," Max said. "It is always so enlightening to spend time with you, but for now, I must be off. Business to attend to."

Benton raised his eyebrows.

A boom of thunder shook the earth beneath them.

Green fingers of lightning fell from a dusty pink sky and clawed the ground beside them.

Benton smiled. "God speed," he said.

Max winced then glared at him. "I think not," he said. "Your storms do not frighten me. And you might be interested to know that I've destroyed that insidious beast you seem so fond of. A few whacks with a shovel and poof! Gone to doggie heaven. And even *you* can't save her after—what is it?—yes, three hours. Once the rigor sets in, you're helpless."

Benton pushed himself up off the ground. He took a deep breath, put his shoulders back, and drew himself to his full height, a head taller than Max.

"If you have harmed her ..." he said.

"Pardon me," Max interrupted and leaned in close to Benton.

Benton wrinkled his nose.

"There is no question of *if*," Max spat, "for you are in no condition to do anything. I have been waiting for this moment for centuries, waiting for you—the favored one—to fall. My patience is paying off. Just look at you. The mighty Benton weak as an old woman!"

"I have beaten you once, Max."

"HA!" Max said. "That was a hundred years ago, and I gave up willingly. Too much trouble for too little gain. Now, though, it is a different matter entirely."

With one hand, Benton grabbed Max by the suit coat and lifted him off the ground.

"Yes," he said and pulled Max so close to him that his breath ruffled Max's hair, "this time it will be different."

Then he held him at arm's length, and with a flick of his wrist hurled him into the air.

Like a nimble cat, Max landed on his feet only a few yards away.

"Oh yes," he said and steepled his hands at his chin. "That little display means nothing. Face it, my friend, you've been abandoned by—wait, who is it now in whom you place so much faith?—ah, yes, your God and your oh-so-victorious mentor. It seems they have both decided you are not worth all the trouble it takes to keep you young and healthy."

Max brushed off his pants then cocked his head.

"If you'll excuse me, my children await. They will follow me so quickly that they'll hardly know what's happened. I can offer them so much more than you and that pathetic band of yours."

He turned and walked toward the steps of the Playhouse Inn.

Benton closed his eyes.

"Help me, please," he whispered to God.

Five luminescent green fingers of lightning burst from the sky and seared the grassy earth in a perfect circle around him.

Smoke rose from the charred ground, and when it cleared, Benton had vanished.

Chapter 44

Instead of elegant place settings and sterling silver candelabra, a single portrait occupied the dining room table. Removed from Max's room, the portrait—*The Blessing of The Playhouse Inn*—sat squarely in the middle of the table.

"There," Nealey said and pointed to a figure in the portrait. "Who is he, Anna?"

Anna peered at the figure.

"Well," she said softly, "his name is Father Madison. Quite handsome, he was, and utterly charming of manner. But now that I look closely, his face—I can't think why—but his face is somehow different. He isn't the way I remember him at all. He reminds me of someone."

Nealey shivered suddenly.

"I apologize," Anna said. "I've drawn the heat from the room again. Without it, I'd have no strength at all."

"Lulu is missing," Sylvie said as she hurried into the room. "Is she here with you, perhaps curled up snugly asleep somewhere?" Sylvie asked.

A booming clap of thunder rattled the floor.

Nealey jumped.

"We're in for a storm, I think," she said. "You didn't find Lulu outside?"

"No," Sylvie said. "I'd hoped she'd be in here."

"Oh, perhaps she's upstairs with the girls," Anna said. "She goes up there every night to check on them and usually falls asleep at the foot of the bed. Yes, she must be there."

Sylvie sighed. "Maybe you're right."

Lightning flashed across the sky.

"I hope the lights don't go out," Nealey said. "I'm uncomfortable in the dark."

"We're never bothered with power outages very much," Sylvie said, "thank goodness."

"Aunt Sylvie? Look carefully at the priest," Nealey said. "Worthy, I'd like for you to look, too."

Sylvie adjusted her glasses and leaned in for a closer look.

"Oh, my word," she said. "Worthy, dear, what do you see when you look at him?"

Worthy answered immediately.

"Max. He looks like Max."

From her chair at the head of the table, Sylvie looked up at him.

"Odd," she said. "To me, he looks like the friend I met at the charity auction years ago."

Anna laid a cold hand on Sylvie's arm.

"The one who said you were his forever?" she asked.

Sylvie lowered her head.

"Yes," she whispered.

"His face is the same as my friend, as well," Anna said. "The spitting image of that man."

The two of them glanced at Nealey.

"No," she said. "You're both wrong. The priest looks just like Brian!"

Nealey dropped down into a chair.

"And the young man who was possessed, the one who cut my hand. He said the same thing. I would be his forever. He and Brian, how could I not have remembered how much alike they were?"

Sylvie put her hands over her mouth. Then she rose and paced across the hardwoods.

"Worthy, how can this be?" Anna asked. "How can one man look like three?"

Worthy rubbed his chin.

"He is only one man, one very evil man."

"So, Anna," Nealey said, "if he's the evil entity, then the Playhouse Inn was not blessed. It was cursed, again."

"Oh, no," Anna said. "Father Madison was sent to us by a good friend. He came highly recommended. He was new to the community, true, and we knew little about him."

"So, he could have been anyone?" Nealey asked.

"But surely, he was a priest. He wore the vestments, carried the Bible, and even had some Holy Water."

"But you didn't know him before, is that right?" Worthy asked.

"No," Anna said softly. "No, we didn't.

"Ah," Worthy said.

"But why?" Anna asked. "Why would he pose as a priest? What did he want? And if he's returned, what does he want now?"

"The answer to the questions is the same, I'm afraid. Then and now, he wants only one thing. Souls," Worthy said.

Anna gasped.

Nealey and Sylvie wrung their hands.

"Mama, Mama," Mae said as she floated into the dining room, Maggie's hand in hers.

"What on earth are you two doing up so late?" Anna asked. "You were sleeping like little angels when I left only a while ago."

Noble stood at the doorway. The wind howled outside.

"We woke up. It's stormy and it smells bad upstairs. Can we stay down here with you? We still can't find Lulu."

"Lulu isn't with you?" Anna asked. "Oh, dear. Well, she can take care of herself. You two sit quietly for a little while."

Mae saw the portrait on the table.

"That's you, Mama, and Papa, too!"

"Yes, it is."

"Our Papa is so handsome, isn't he?" Mae said.

Anna smiled.

"Indeed," she said.

"Why are you and Papa standing with Max?"

Worthy moved closer to the girls.

"Come, children, let's sit down," he said. "These big chairs are terribly comfy, don't you agree?"

Maggie and Mae jumped onto the overstuffed chairs.

"Now," Worthy said. "Can you tell us more about the man in the portrait?"

Mae nodded.

"You know him. He's Max, and he has a friend with him, the bad man."

"And how would you know this?" Worthy asked.

Mae shrugged.

Thunder rumbled in the distance as a great wind blew the curtains at the open window in the dining room.

"I don't like storms," Mae said. "Maggie, come sit with me."

Maggie hopped into the chair with Mae.

"I'd like an answer, please," Worthy said.

"Okay," Mae said, "but it was an accident. We went into Max's room on *accident*. He told us about his friend," Mae said, her hands moving with every word. "That's all. Are you mad at us, Mama?"

"No," Anna said. "I'm not angry. But I'd like for both of you to sit quietly for a few moments."

"But, can I say one more thing, just one?"

"*May* I," Anna corrected. "I suppose you may, if it is important."

"Benton says the bad man will have weapons," Mae said.

"Benton? You've seen him?" Nealey asked, her tone urgent. "How is he? May I go and see him?"

"He's still a little sick," Mae said.

"But can I see him?" Nealey asked and stood up. "Please, is he in the guest house? I want to see him."

"And I am certain that he would like to see you, as well, my dear," Worthy said, "but at this time, it is not a good idea. Bear with him just a little while longer. I promise he will return to you."

"But he's sick, Worthy. Maybe I could help him."

Sylvie stood and hugged Nealey.

"He will be all right, my precious. He is stronger than you could ever imagine. You must trust him now and listen to Worthy. And sweetheart, he knows full well how you feel about it. Have no fear of that."

"I think, Aunt Sylvie, I think I ..." Nealey stopped. Ashamed for betraying Hank but overjoyed at her feelings for Benton, she lowered her head.

I love him.

"Yes, dear, I know," Sylvie said and kissed her lightly on the forehead.

Nealey nuzzled her cheek against Sylvie's.

"Shame and guilt are wasted emotions, my darling. They will never serve you well."

Sylvie patted Nealey's arms. "We must concentrate on the task at hand."

"Exactly right," Worthy added. "Now, girls, you said that this bad man will have weapons. What sort of weapons do you mean?"

"Not guns or anything," Mae said. "Just Mama's necklace and something else."

"The necklace," Sylvie said. Her hand went automatically to her neck. She fingered the large emerald and felt relieved that she had the necklace safely and securely in her possession.

"Now, girls, you were saying about the weapons. The necklace and something else?" Sylvie asked.

Maggie and Mae nodded.

"Girls?" Anna said.

They both pointed to Nealey.

Nealey looked behind her as if the girls might be pointing to something she didn't see, but when she turned back, they were still pointing at her.

"Me?" she asked.

The girls nodded.

"Oh, dear," Sylvie said.

"But, how could I possibly be a weapon?" Nealey asked.

Anna glanced out the dining room window.

"Sylvie, look!" she said. "Have you ever seen such a sky?"

Above the Playhouse Inn, the sky shone a luminescent emerald green. Waves of pink light danced inside it.

"Stunning," Worthy said. "The Wayfarer's Sky, the stuff of legend! The ancients believed that when this particular sky appeared overhead, lost souls could find their homes."

"I've often wondered what it must look like. It's magnificent," Sylvie agreed.

"Lost souls?" Anna repeated. "You mean their heavenly homes?"

"We would hope," Worthy said. "It is said that the bright colors, the unusual look of the sky, green laced with pink, attracts and guides them homeward. It is said that the Wayfarer's Sky can be summoned only by an angel."

Anna lowered her head. At her feet, the rippling pool which surrounded her moved upward.

"Oh, dear," she said. "I shan't have the energy to stay visible much longer."

"It's okay, Mama. We can hear you, and we can smell your

jasmine perfume even when you're invisible. We know you're still with us," Mae said.

"Where is Noble, by the way?" Nealey asked. "He was standing in the doorway a moment ago," Nealey asked.

"He moves quickly for an old reprobate his age," Worthy said. "Fear not."

Just as the words came from his mouth, the lights went out.

The girls whimpered.

Nealey heard but couldn't see someone moving around in the dining room, then a distinct snap as if something had been jerked quickly from ....

The necklace?

A voice called, "Well, well, it seems the entire group is here. Now, what could be better than that? My friend will be so pleased!"

Chapter 45

Nealey felt a cold hand on her neck.

"Anna, is that you?"

"Ah, the lovely Anna," Max said. "Unfortunately, she is unable to move at the moment, as are all the others in the room."

Nealey felt a hot breath on her neck and smelled rotten meat. She wrinkled her nose and coughed.

"You and I, my dear Nealey," Max said, "are the only ones free to amble about. Shall we?"

Her heart racing now, Nealey stood firmly in place, determined to show no fear. She fingered the stone in the palm of her hand then closed a fist around it.

"I'd rather not," she said, her shaky voice betraying her. "In fact, I refuse. I will stay here with my family."

"How touching," Max whispered.

He pulled her arm and dragged her backwards toward the window; then he held up the necklace.

"Dear Sylvie," he said. "I'm sure she didn't feel a thing as I took this from her."

Nealey wretched her arm from his grasp.

"Ah, a fighter. Yes, I remember how you struggled to pull your hand away. You were so young, so naïve then. It was easy to be stronger, to draw the blood, and to mark you as mine forever."

Nealey inhaled a quick breath.

"It was you?"

"But of course, dear. Who else but your own father would have gone to so much trouble?"

Nealey felt her legs shaking, her knees turning to rubber. She could hardly stand.

"I see from your reaction that you hadn't a clue," Max said and laughed. "What a delightful surprise for you, then!"

"NO!" she cried. "My mother would never have anything to do with the likes of you, never!"

"You are referring, I imagine, to Charlotte. Not my type, dear. But Sylvie? Ah yes, my dear Sylvie. Such a beautiful specimen, so full of life, and so unsure about G ... O ... D."

With the stone fisted in her right hand, the wand stuck in her jeans pocket, Nealey stuck out her left hand until she found the edge of the dining room table. She steadied herself and took a few steps away from Max.

"There is nowhere to go now, my dear," he said. "Try as you might, you cannot get away from me. And there is no one to help you. Your precious Benton is near dead, your sweet Lulu, also dead."

"Lulu? What did you do to her? She can't be dead, no, she can't be!"

Nealey felt as if Max had punched her in the stomach.

"NO!" she yelled. "Not my Lulu."

She fell to her knees sobbing.

"Not my sweet Lulu," she whispered. "Please, God, not my precious Lulu."

Cold fingers on the back of her neck tightened and pulled her to her feet.

"Enough of that nonsense," Max said. "Your God cannot hear you now. You are mine."

Nealey held fast to the edge of the table. Her eyes stung with hot tears. She blinked, as the stinging tears ran down her cold cheeks.

Benton, help me. Please, help me!

"Well," Max said. "It is time for us to go, my dear. Shall I force you, or will you be a good girl and follow your father?"

Nealey sniffed and wiped her face with the back of her hand.

"I will follow my father," she said and clamped her fist tighter around the smooth piece of jet.

When Max brushed past her, she bent her head and crossed herself. Then she slipped her fingers around the top of the wand. Feeling it in her pocket gave her strength.

"Come along," he said and took her arm. "Follow closely. I have someone who is dying to meet you."

"But, what about my family? What will happen to them?"

Max chuckled.

"They will eventually recover their senses, but by the time they understand what has happened, we will already have accomplished our purpose."

"What purpose is that?"

"Don't trouble yourself with such unpleasantness. It will be over in seconds."

Nealey stopped walking.

"What purpose? Tell me."

As they walked through the dining room arch, Nealey heard Max shut the doors and sigh.

"For one who is so intelligent, my dear, you are increasingly tiresome with these questions. Now, move!"

Max shoved her forward.

A great wail of thunder reverberated in the sky.

The double doors blew open and banged against the wall on either side.

Nealey jumped and cried out at the sound.

"Out," Max said, "to the cliff."

Nealey's heart felt as if it had dropped to the pit of her stomach.

"The cliff? But, it's dangerous out there."

"Dangerous, yes, I'd say so," Max said. "You Wolcott women, how you do ramble. The price a man pays, I imagine, for getting what he wants. Ever so tedious, my dear."

Outside, the Wayfarer's Sky, still a bright green marbled with pink, cast an eerie glow all around. Nealey blinked her eyes to focus.

Max shoved her again.

"To the cliff side," he growled. "My friend is waiting."

Nealey looked back at him and gasped.

Chapter 46

Only a few yards from the cliff's edge, Nealey glanced again at Max's face.

In the faint glow of light from the Wayfarer's Sky, she saw that his eyes had turned completely black. His face was haggard and drawn, deep wrinkles along his forehead and cheeks. His long hair was now matted in chunks of fur. His smooth hands now looked like a bird's talons.

Max no longer looked human.

What is he? Dear God, Benton, please, help me.

Nealey shivered. Out of the corner of her eye, she could see a dark shape move low to the ground and close to the side of the inn. It made no sound, but it moved as she did.

"Get on with it," Max growled. "You're too slow. My friend doesn't like to be kept waiting.

Nealey walked, her fist clenched tightly around the piece of jet.

"You don't seem the type to have many friends," she said.

Max did not respond.

When they arrived at the clearing, Nealey heard the rushing waters of the river at the bottom of the cliffs.

Mighty waters, gifts of the Creator.

At that moment, some of her fear faded way.

Mighty waters soothe me.

Her hands stopped trembling. Her heartbeat returned to normal, and her knees no longer seemed like rubber. She inhaled, turned to face Max, and bumped right into him.

He stood so close that she could feel his breath on her face.

"Goodbye, my dear," he said in a normal voice.

Nealey glanced up to see that he had returned to his former state. He looked like Max.

The ground beneath them began to tremble.

Nealey turned and looked back at the inn. From each window

streamed thick vapors of bile-colored mist that billowed out into the air. Even from twenty feet away, Nealey could smell the pungent stench of rotting meat.

"My friend," Max said. "He's so eager to meet you."

Nealey glanced toward the edge of the house. Low to the ground and next to the inn, the dark shape lurked there. Still, it made no sound.

"Hello, Mama," a young child's voice called.

Nealey gasped and stepped back.

"Nicholas?"

A young boy with tousled blond hair and deep blue eyes stood a few feet away and held out his arms to her.

"Mama, help me, please," he called. "Please, Mama."

Nealey dropped to her knees.

"Nicholas," she said. "My sweet Nicholas."

"I've come for you, Mama, so you can go back with us. Daddy's waiting, and Lauren. We miss you so much."

Tears rolled down the little boy's cheeks.

"Please, Mama, won't you come back with us so we can be a family again? It's so lonely without you."

He motioned her forward with his hands. "Come on, Mama."

Nealey got up and walked slowly toward the boy.

He smiled at her, a sweet, precious innocent looking smile.

"Little Lauren cries for you all the time, Mama. She'll be so happy to see you."

Suddenly, the wand in her jeans' pocket felt uncomfortably warm. Nealey winced and put her fingers around it. She pulled it from her pocket. It glowed a striking gold.

Warm energy tingled along her fingers, traveled up her arm, and soon filled her body with a sweet sensation of soaking in a warm bubble bath. She could smell the fragrant water washing gently over her.

For a reason she couldn't understand, she took the wand from her pocket and held it out in front of her.

"MAMA!" the boy yelled. "Please help me!"

Nealey straightened her arm and aimed the glowing wand at the little boy.

In an instant, he wailed and turned into a short, hideous

creature with the head of an old man but a body covered in thick scales oozing a slimy green substance. His hands and feet were clawed, and he was bent onto all fours.

"You are not my son," she said. "My son is in Heaven, safe and happy."

Nealey held her head high, pulled her shoulders back, and tightened her grip on the wand as she kept it aimed at the creature.

"Leave us alone," she said, her voice stronger than she could have imagined. "Get out of our house and leave us alone."

The creature turned its head and looked at her, its lips drawn back, its red eyes blazing.

"Get out!" Nealey yelled, and the wand glowed even brighter. "In the name of all that is holy, I command you to leave."

The creature crawled a few steps backward, snarling at her.

"Enough of this," Max said.

Nealey could hear his shoes crunching the dirt and rocks, but she kept the wand aimed at the creature.

He's coming for me.

Chapter 47

Sylvie stood in the dining room unable to move. She could not blink her eyes, could not feel herself breathing, could not coax even a single twitch from her limbs. She heard not a single sound, not even the steady drum of her own heart beating.

Sylvie felt as if she had turned to stone. She tried to think, but the effort seemed useless, like trying to remove cobwebs from a long-abandoned attic.

But she could see.

Directly in front of her stood Worthy, smiling, his arms on her shoulders. Though she couldn't feel them, she knew they must be there.

Worthy's lips were moving, but Sylvie could not hear or translate what he was saying.

She saw him nod his head then step closer to her, so close that all she could see was the bottom part of his ear covered in the ringlets of his hair.

Almost at once, a deep, heavy darkness overcame her, but then, almost as quickly, a glimmering golden light shone in front of her.

She blinked her eyes and felt her little finger twitch.

The light pulsated all around her, bringing with it sounds: sounds of something Sylvie could hear but couldn't identify. As the light danced around her, the sounds turned to static, a radio station too far away to come into tune.

And then ... a voice, a muffled voice.

The golden light faded as Worthy stepped away from her.

He had taken on a more serious look now.

She saw his lips moving again, but this time, she recognized the word.

"Sylvie."

She blinked her eyes again and kept them closed. She tried desperately to think, to clear the cobwebs from her mind, but they were too thick to penetrate.

When she opened her eyes again, she saw Worthy reach forward and put his hands on her face.

"Sylvie," he said.

She heard him clearly.

"Come back," he said.

Sylvie closed her eyes again.

I ... am ... here.

She opened her eyes and wiggled her fingers. Then, she took a deep breath.

I am here.

Worthy beamed at her.

Chapter 48

With the wand still aimed at the creature in front of her, Nealey heard again the sounds of Max's footsteps.

He's coming for me.

Her heartbeat quickened. Her hands trembled.

What can I do? How can I stop him?

The footsteps grew ever closer.

Her rapid heartbeat drummed in her ears.

Be brave, my precious girl.

Nealey stiffened.

Sylvie?

Yes, darling, pray. Pray out loud, my darling girl.

Nealey knew that Max was almost upon her. She turned to face him, even though she knew the creature kept at bay by the wand might attack. Just as Max was at arm's length from her, the dark figure that had been lurking beside the inn rushed out.

"Lulu!" Nealey yelled. "My sweet Lulu!"

Nealey wanted to run and hug her, but something about Lulu warned her to stay away. Lulu jumped on Max and knocked him to the ground, her teeth on his throat.

A sinister sounding laugh came from behind Nealey.

She whirled around, the wand still aimed, to see the creature now transformed into a full-grown man with wild dark hair, solid black eyes, and an oddly transparent looking skin.

The sight of him made Nealey's stomach turn. She trembled all over. Behind her, she could hear Lulu snarling in a fierce struggle with Max.

She turned around again and watched horrified as Max bucked like a horse, once, twice. On the third time, he rolled and tossed Lulu over the edge of the cliff. Lulu yelped as she tumbled down toward the rushing waters below.

"LULU!" Nealey screamed. "LULU!"

Pray, Nealey. Hold out your palm, show the stone, and pray!

Nealey closed her eyes and opened her palm.

"Our Father," she tried, but her words sounded hollow. All she could think about was Lulu.

"Our Father," she called again.

Max groaned.

"I am your father!" he shouted. "You will follow none but me!"

Nealey prayed again, the stone shining black in her palm, the wand warm and pulsing in her pocket.

"Our Father who art in Heaven," she said.

Max grimaced and fell to his knees.

Suddenly, on the other side of the Highland Rim in front of an opposite cliff, a brilliant white light formed from bottom to top.

From the depths of the rim, something rose in a splendid countenance of soft blue light surrounded by golden orbs.

The Wayfarer's Sky rumbled overhead, its lacy pink tendrils spreading out and descending toward the rising form.

Nealey inhaled a sharp breath as a figure appeared with two magnificent glowing white wings.

"An angel," she whispered as it rose to the top of the ridge.

She saw the face, the muscular body, the dark hair, and those wings, those stunning wings.

"Benton!"

As the word came from her mouth, she heard a chuckle behind her.

"Too late, dearie," the voice said. "Your magic stone didn't work, after all. Bye bye."

Max lifted her off the ground and tossed her over the cliff.

She didn't scream as she tumbled over the edge. Instead, she whispered.

"Our Father, end this evil. Please save Lulu."

From somewhere far away, she thought she heard Sylvie scream.

Chapter 49

Worthy kept one arm around Sylvie's waist as they made their way slowly around the side of the house.

"They won't work right. My legs, Worthy, I can barely move them."

"I've got you," Worthy said. "We'll make it."

"He's thrown her over. My darling Nealey. How could he?" Sylvie said, her voice quivering.

"Fear not, my dear. We will save her."

Sylvie suddenly felt very light, her legs not so heavy. She looked down at the ground and realized that her feet were not touching it, yet she and Worthy were moving quickly to the cliff side.

"You must summon all of your strength to help Nealey," Worthy said.

"But I can barely move. How can I help her now?"

"Ah, Sylvie, you have your own powers, your own brand of earth magick. Use your mind to instruct and comfort your daughter. She needs you now more than ever."

As they descended gently to the ground a few feet from the cliff's edge, a familiar voice called to them.

"Well, how nice of you to join us," Max said. "You're just in time to meet my friend. I think you will find him irresistible."

Max and his friend walked slowly toward them, their eyes aglow with a fiery red light.

Chapter 50

Nealey wasn't aware of dashing against the trees or rocks. All she felt was an incredible lightness of spirit. Even falling, she could see the beautiful blue halo that surrounded the rim, the staggering brightness of the white light, and the perfect golden sheen around hundreds of orbs.

Heaven.

It was only when she plunged into the icy, rushing waters, columns of it rising above her on each side as she broke the water's surface, that she felt her first tinge of fear.

She flailed her arms and tried to swim, but the current was so strong that she knew the fight was useless. Again and again she was dragged under, the cold water numbing every inch of her body.

Drowning.

As she drifted along with the current, she banged her head against a large rock. She opened her mouth to yell for help, but the water rushed into it and filled her throat. She tried to cough the water out, but she could barely breathe.

Drowning.

Then, she stopped fighting and let herself be dragged along. Her body went limp. As one of her hands drifted down into the freezing water, she felt wiry, wet fur.

Lulu?

The huge dog was beside her, the wand in her mouth, nudging Nealey's chin, helping her hold her head out of the water.

She's trying to keep me from drowning.

With every ounce of effort she had, Nealey grabbed hold, and as Lulu maneuvered underneath her, Nealey wrapped her arms around the dog's neck.

A brilliant light caused her to squeeze her eyes shut. A roaring wind rushed across her, and Nealey shuddered, her teeth chattering.

"Nealey," she heard from somewhere above her.

At first, Nealey thought it was thunder, a deep rolling sound that reverberated around her. All she could hear, though, was the almost deafening roar of the swift waters.

She tried to lift her head, but every muscle in her body felt as if lead weights were tied around them. She couldn't find the strength even to open her mouth, much less lift her head.

"Nealey!" the booming voice called again. "Take my hand."

Benton?

Nealey strained to open her eyes and winced as she turned her head toward the voice.

Take my hand, Nealey.

Nealey pulled one arm from around Lulu's neck and slowly lifted it upward.

A warm, strong hand grabbed hers and gave her strength.

She lifted her head and saw Benton hovering just above the surface of the water. His body shimmered, highlighting every muscle in his torso, his arms, and his legs. His thick, dark hair—short the last time Nealey saw it—now hung below his shoulders. He wore a golden vest. On his feet were sandals that laced up to his knees. On his arms were circlets of gold, and in his hand, he held a shining sword. His radiant wings moved back and forth in a rhythmic, hypnotic motion.

Glorious.

Nealey felt her hand slipping from his.

I can't. I can't.

Chapter 51

As Max approached, Worthy let go of Sylvie and stepped in front of her. Then he turned his back to Max and the friend.

Worthy held his arms outstretched at shoulder height and lifted his face to the sky.

Max and the friend were almost upon him, their clawed hands reaching for Worthy's neck. When they were close enough to reach him, Worthy called out to the sky.

"God's fire protect us!"

A shower of pink and green fire fell from the Wayfarer's Sky and encircled Worthy and Sylvie.

Max wailed and backed away as sparks of it singed his jacket sleeves.

Worthy smiled and looked at Sylvie.

Call to her. You must call to her now.

Chapter 52

Nealey fought as hard as she could, but she had no strength left. She felt her hands slipping from Benton's.

Call to the waters, darling.

Sylvie?

Yes, my precious girl. Call to the waters.

"Nealey," Benton said, his voice sounding almost like thunder, "hold on."

Nealey did as Sylvie had said and called to the waters.

Mighty waters, gifts of the Creator, be still.

The currents suddenly stopped. The still water seemed to lift her upward. With one hand on Lulu, she reached up and tightened her other around Benton's.

Almost instantly, they were both out of the water and in Benton's arms, his wings folded round them. Nealey felt them rise up, up, up over the Highland Rim.

She closed her eyes and welcomed the warm embrace and whatever came with it.

She was hardly aware that she and Lulu were now safely deposited on solid ground well away from the cliff's edge.

A heavenly warmth from the rush of his enormous glittering wings brought her back to an awareness of her surroundings. Benton hovered just beyond the trees bathed in swirls of blue and gold light.

Oh, he is magnificent!

I love you, Nealey.

She watched as he raised his arms to the heavens. Sparks of pink lightning crackled against the tip of his sword. His wings moved more rapidly, and in an instant, he had flown away to the other side of the rim.

Nealey got up, Lulu beside her, and strained to see him, but the rim was so far away that she barely saw anything. But she could hear his thunderous voice.

"Noble, it's time," he said.

Suddenly, she saw another figure emerge not too far away. He stood at the cliff's edge. Then, he reached up and removed his sunglasses. From Noble's eyes came floods of light that sparkled and shone on every surface around them. It was as if a thousand floodlights had been turned on.

The Wayfarer's Sky began to swirl above them. The emerald green sky moved almost like rolling waters, the clouds tumbling, pink fingers of lightning shooting down toward the rim.

And it sang in a melodious ring of harmony, voices of the clouds joining together. The sound echoed throughout the rim like a symphony.

Pray, Nealey. Hold out your palm and pray out loud. Fill the canyon with the sound of your prayers.

Nealey did as she was commanded. She held out her palm and yelled the prayer with all the strength her voice could muster.

She could hear Max and his friend chuckle.

As quickly as she could, she made her way along the rim. Several times, she stumbled over rocks and bushes, but she kept going until she could go no further. She slumped down onto the ground and laid a hand on Lulu's haunches.

The wand in Lulu's mouth began to glow.

"The wand!"

Nealey grabbed it and held it close to her chest.

"I need strength," she whispered as she listened to the soothing voice of the sky.

She took a deep breath that filled her lungs with warmth. Her body warmed, as well, as the healing energy flowed through. At once, she and Lulu were up and on their way again, almost running until they came to a vantage point where Nealey could see Benton. Noble's light shined so brightly that she could make out an outline of Max, as well.

Benton hovered at one end of the rim; Max stood on the opposite end.

For a few seconds, neither of them moved.

Nealey's heart pounded in her chest, and she clutched the magic wand tightly. Lulu nudged her gently.

A deathly silence crept across the Highland Rim.

Then, the symphony overhead heightened, the volume blotting out every other sound. Suddenly, Benton's wings began to move slowly back and forth.

The ground beneath her trembled.

She watched as Benton leaned forward and blew out a breath that appeared to be filled with sparkling jewels.

That breath became a mighty wind that bent the trees and caused rising waves in the water below.

On the other side of the rim, Nealey could see Max as the wind lifted him off the ground and slammed him against the side of the inn.

He howled like a caged animal as he hit.

The strong wind kept him pinned against the inn.

"Leave this place, Max!" Benton called, his voice like a clap of thunder.

Even as he flailed his arms against the blast of wind, Max laughed out loud.

"I am her father," he yelled and laughed again. "She goes with me."

"Never," Benton said.

The winds subsided, the symphony softened, and Nealey watched as Benton swooped to the other side of the rim. He hovered right in front of Max.

Nealey patted Lulu.

"Come on, girl, let's move so we can see."

The two of them scrambled across the rocky terrain. Nealey looked back once or twice trying to see to the other side, but Benton's enormous form blocked her view.

Suddenly, high in the air, she saw the glint of a raised sword's blade and the glow of an ornate shield. Then, just as suddenly, she watched in horror as Benton seemed to double over as he was propelled backward toward the side of the rim where Nealey and Lulu stood.

Something huge held Benton in its grasp. Its thin black wings stretched from the back legs to the hideous front claws, its toothed jaws open and clamped around Benton's waist.

Lulu barked then grabbed Nealey's arm in her mouth and pulled her away from the edge.

When Benton dashed against the wall of the rim, the sword fell from his hand. Huge chunks of rock exploded from the walls of the cliff and tumbled into the river below.

One of the boulders struck the creature on the back. It screeched and moved away, its jaw now gnashing at Benton's thigh.

Overhead, the sky shimmered a brilliant green, its pink fingers of lightning reaching toward the ground.

Benton shook himself, then brought up his powerful leg and whacked the creature on the bottom of the jaw. It somersaulted through the air and let out an ear-piercing wail.

Nealey covered her ears and watched as the creature careened into a tree atop the rim. It disappeared within the branches.

A low growling sound—louder now than the harmonic symphony—resonated through the canyon. From out of the tree flew the creature, now transformed into a huge, misshapen cat, its red eyes glowing, its fangs dripping with saliva, its claws extended.

It lunged at Benton's throat.

But Benton moved swiftly out of its grasp and pummeled it with his shield. The cat fell for a few feet, then flew to the side of the rim and caught hold with its claws.

The low growling turned to a sinister laughing sound.

Nealey shrank in horror as she saw the cat turn its glowing eyes on her. She watched as it scampered over the top of the rim. In only a few seconds, Nealey felts its teeth sink into her. She cried out in agony as it jerked her off the ground and flew toward the middle of the canyon.

Benton hovered in the air in front of them. He turned his head and glanced down at Noble, from whose eyes issued the gleaming white light that lit up the rim.

In the split second when Benton turned his gaze to Noble, the cat opened its drooling jaws.

Nealey screamed as she plummeted once again toward the rushing waters below.

Benton swept down after her.

The cat was then on his back, sinking his claws in and savagely tearing at the soft tissue between Benton's wings. Benton's gold vest fell away.

Falling ever closer to the water, Nealey saw a movement from the corner of her eye as something ascended rapidly away from her.

Benton's sword?

Carried on a beam from Noble's cane, the sword twirled in the air then straightened and plunged into the creature's back.

Immediately, the cat wailed in pain and let loose his hold.

Nealey felt Benton's arms wrap around her and scoop her to him just as the two of them hit the icy, churning waters.

Even as they plunged down into the water, Nealey felt the warmth of Benton's chest on her face. She could feel his heart beating. She could see the massive wings unfurling in the water.

It came to her then.

He can't swim.

An image flashed through her mind.

She and Benton walking together.

"Is there anything you can't do?" she'd asked him.

"I can't swim," he had replied.

When the swift current dragged them under, Nealey struggled to keep her mouth closed so that every bit of air stayed with her. She noticed the red swell rising beside her, blood from the places where the creature had sunk its teeth into her flesh.

She clamped her fingers tightly around the wand.

Help us, mighty waters, gifts of the Creator.

Nealey felt them both being dragged deep into the churning whirlpools, the huge wings plunging swiftly to the bottom.

He can't swim. His wings. Too heavy. Pulling us down.

She concentrated on the wand clamped in her hand beneath her.

Bubbles escaped from her mouth as the air left her lungs.

The wand. This is why I have it. To save us.

Suddenly, the wand grew hot in her freezing hands. A stream of shimmering golden light radiated from underneath her.

Benton! Benton! The wand will save us.

As they were carried deeper into the water, Benton underneath her, she saw through the murky depths the glistening golden light from the wand. It enveloped them both. Then, the water all around them took on the same golden glow.

She felt Benton move beneath her, then move again.

He's moving.

The light appeared to Nealey as two enormous hands that scooped them from the water, lifted them upright, and propelled them out of the icy river, the shimmering light shining throughout the canyon.

She heard Benton cough once, heard the great rush of his wings, and felt the power in his body return as they soared upward.

The radiance from the wand stayed beside them both, casting a deliciously hot light, and by the time Benton set her gently down on the ground, she was warm and dry. She lifted her blouse and saw that the wounds had healed.

When she focused her eyes, the emerald sky still tumbled overhead striped with lacy pink tendrils. Then, she looked at Benton and beheld his magnificent form.

Surrounded in a halo of blue and golden light, his muscles shimmering, he hovered in front of the cliff's edge.

And then she saw Max, looking perfectly human, standing feet apart on the opposite side of the rim. Beside him, with glowing red eyes stood his human-looking friend.

Benton's wings began a furious beat, and in only a few seconds, he ascended into the emerald sky.

"He's gone," Max whispered from across the canyon, yet the sound reached Nealey's ears and made her shudder. "You're mine now."

As Max let out a howl of laughter, Benton swooped down from the sky, whirling and spinning like a tornado. His form aglow, he stopped in mid-air and lifted his arms to the sky.

The muscles bulged as he harnessed two shafts of pink lightning that sparked and sizzled in his hands.

With perfect aim, he hurled one shaft at Max, the other at his friend.

Instantly, they both dropped to their knees, screaming as they caught fire. Two giant fire balls—screaming as if they were human—burned bright red and orange and then exploded.

In only seconds, it seemed, all that was left of them was a small pile of ashes and two melted gold cufflinks.

Lulu danced around in circles and licked Nealey all over.

Benton smiled at them, then disappeared into the Wayfarer's Sky.

Chapter 53

Only a week later, in the upper room of the third floor, the room that had housed the entity for so many years, Nealey watched as Sylvie worked at straightening the curtains.

The hole that had been there in the floor was now sealed and shiny new hardwood covered the entire area.

Nealey surveyed the room. Typical Sylvie style, ornate and elegant. It housed a canopy bed, a mahogany dresser and bureau, and a cheval glass full-length mirror. Portraits hung along the wall.

"A perfect guest room," Sylvie said. "Don't you agree, darling?"

"It's lovely, Aunt ... mother," Nealey said. "Simply lovely."

Sylvie beamed.

Lulu stood beside her and wagged her tail, creating a substantial breeze.

"And that window," she said, "doesn't it look stunning? When the sun's rays shine on it, well, it just lights up the room!"

"But wind chimes?" Nealey asked and ran her fingers over them, creating a sweet harmonic melody.

"Corinthian Bells," Sylvie said. "Such a lovely sound, isn't it?"

"Yes, of course," Nealey said. "But aren't they just a tad impractical up here? I always thought wind chimes were supposed to be hung outside, not inside."

The scent of roses filtered in.

"Ah, what a gorgeous sound," Worthy said. "Perfect for any comings and goings."

"Comings and goings?" Nealey asked. "As high up as this window is, I don't think many people will be coming in or going out."

Sylvie and Worthy glanced at each other.

"Well, my dear, you see," Worthy said and brushed a speck of lint from the cuff of his white silk shirt, "even though the window looks like an ordinary one—though it is stunning—it is nonetheless a portal."

"Yes, sweetheart," Sylvie said. "The Inn was built as a pleasant, happy place for wandering souls, a sort of playhouse, if you will, for those who simply could not find their way home."

"But I thought Anna and the children were the first to be trapped here," Nealey said.

"The first to be trapped, yes, but not the first to make use of the hospitality," Worthy replied. "The home had been built originally in the early 1800s long before Henry and Anna came here. They refurbished it, of course, almost rebuilt it entirely. But on the advice of Henry's grandfather, they left the portal as it was and as it is now."

Nealey looked stunned.

"So ... so there have been ghosts here for ...."

"Oh, for ages," Worthy said. "But there have also been others, too, like me! So, all is well. Now, it is time, my sweet."

Sylvie wrung her hands.

"Oh, dear," she said.

"It's for the best," Worthy said.

Sylvie shot him a sharp look.

"I know that," she said, "but they've been with me for so long."

Nealey walked over to the duffle bag and drew out her stole, her cross, and her Bible. She draped her stole around her neck and patted the lined pocket Sylvie had sewn into it, just the perfect size for the wand. She slipped the wand into its place, dropped the piece of jet in with it, and put on the gold cross.

When the temperature in the room began to drop, she smiled.

Lulu gave a soft bark.

"Anna, you look lovely," Nealey said.

Anna smoothed her skirt.

"One does her best," she said.

"Well, what about us?" Mae said. "Do we look pretty?"

Lulu wagged her tail even harder and licked the girls on the hands.

Nealey walked over to them and hugged them both.

"Your yellow dresses are simply divine! And those matching socks are perfectly wonderful," she said. "You look like little angels."

"Do we, Aunt Sylvie?"

Sylvie dabbed at her eyes with a tissue.

"You most certainly do," she said. "And Anna, I don't think you've ever been any more beautiful. You're simply radiant!"

Anna smiled.

"Thank you, Sylvie. I, we, I appreciate you, more than you could ever know."

"It's almost time, darlings," Worthy said.

Lulu made a sound like a moan.

"But wait, where's Noble?" Mae asked.

"He'll be along shortly, my little ones," Worthy said. "He has a grand surprise."

Both girls clapped their hands.

"We love surprises!"

"You'll love this one more than any you've ever had!" Worthy said.

"More than the balloons?"

"Oh, yes," Worthy said and gathered them into his arms. "Much more than the balloons."

He kissed each one on the cheek.

"But first, we have a surprise for our precious Nealey."

"Oh, goody! Nealey, did you hear? Noble has a surprise for you," Mae asked.

"A surprise for me?" Nealey asked. "Whatever could it be?"

"Now," Worthy said rather loudly as he brushed both of his sleeves and straightened his white silk tie, "let us see the first surprise!"

Lulu barked again and turned around in circles.

Noble appeared in front of the window, his white hair and white clothes gleaming. He smiled at the girls and stepped to the side.

A man came forward, but the bright light shining from Noble obscured the view. Noble nodded and motioned him forward.

As he stepped away from Noble, his form became clearer. He was dressed in khakis, a police badge prominently displayed on his shirt. On either side of him, holding his hands, was a child, one a small girl; the other, a young boy with tousled blond hair.

Nealey stared at them for a moment.

Can it be? Is it really them?

Then, when she realized it was, she began to sob.

"Hank?" she asked. "Is it you? Is it really you?"

The children let go of their father's hand and ran to their mother.

"Mama! Mama!" they cried and wrapped their arms around her.

For a split second, Nealey hesitated.

What if they're not really my babies? What if it's the creature?

But something inside her made her let go of the idea.

They are my children, precious gifts from God.

"My sweet babies," Nealey said through her sobs. "You're all right?"

Hank stepped forward and kissed her on the forehead.

"Nealey, my love," he said. "Don't cry. Don't cry, please. I can take just about anything except your tears."

"Yes, I remember," Nealey said and wiped her face with her hands.

Nealey motioned to Maggie and Mae.

"Girls, this is my family, Hank, Nicholas, and Lauren."

The girls curtsied.

"We're Maggie and Mae. We're her family, too," Mae said and smiled. "Maggie doesn't talk much. Do you like our dresses?"

Lauren clapped her hands.

"Hank, darling," Nealey said motioning toward Anna, "this is my great, great grandmother. Isn't she lovely?"

Hank nodded.

"Very pleased to meet you, ma'am."

He turned to Nealey.

"We don't have long," he said and drew Nealey close to him. "I want you to be happy, Nealey. The children and I are fine. We're peaceful and happy, the way I want you to be. Live your life as you see fit. Find some happiness, my love, however you can."

Nealey had begun to sob again.

"Oh, Hank, I have missed you so," she said.

They stood together for a moment until Hank held her at arm's length.

"Listen to me," he said. "I want you to remember all the good times we had, how happy we were. The more joyful your memories are, the better it is for us."

"I don't understand," Nealey said, hot tears still streaming down her face.

"Let your grief be done, my love. For all our sakes, focus on the positive memories. Your happiness, your laughter, will give us peace."

Nealey looked into his eyes.

"I will always love you," she said.

"And I will forever love you," Hank replied. "You have too much love in your heart to keep it from blossoming. Share it with someone who deserves it."

He kissed her once more on the forehead.

"Children," he said softly, "we need to go now. Come tell Mama goodbye."

Nealey knelt down as they approached.

"I love you so much," she said, "so very much."

"We've been good, Mama," Nicholas said. "You'd be proud of us. We help out and we always remember to say 'please' and 'thank you.'"

Lauren kissed her on the cheek.

"Love you," she said.

"Mama?" Nicholas said.

"Yes, honey?"

"Someday, you'll come and live with us again. We'll have a place all fixed up for you. Would you like that?"

Nealey hugged them both as she struggled to hold back her sobs.

Hank took the children by the hands and walked toward Noble.

"Bless you, my friend," he said, "for giving us this time."

Noble bowed.

As they stepped through the portal, the wind chimes played a sweet melody.

Sylvie walked to Nealey and embraced her.

"Hey," Mae said, "it's time for our surprise now, isn't it?"

Noble put his hand again into the portal.

This time, when the wind chimes rang, a bearded man in a business suit stepped forward.

"Henry? Henry, is that you?" Anna asked. "Oh, my Henry, is it you?"

"Papa?"

He smiled at them and held out his arms.

Sylvie blotted her eyes with a tissue.

"They've waited so long to see him," she said and sniffed daintily.

Anna and the girls rushed into his arms.

"Oh, Papa, you came for us, just like Worthy said you would."

"Yes," he said. "Now, we will be together again in our new home."

"Will we like it, Papa? Is it pretty?" Mae asked.

Henry nodded and hugged them again.

"You cannot imagine how beautiful it is, my darlings."

Noble stepped beside them.

The girls looked up at him.

"Are you coming with us?" Mae asked.

"He will make sure you arrive safely at your new home," Worthy said.

Maggie and Mae smiled.

"Well, come on, Aunt Sylvie, Nealey, and Lulu. It's time for us all to go." Mae said. "It's time for all of us to go to our new home. Papa says we'll all love it."

Mae motioned them forward. Then, she looked at Nealey.

"I'm sorry I said I didn't like you," she said. "I do like you. Do you remember when we used to play Boo together when you were little? We scared Aunt Sylvie all the time, but we had lots of fun. You were like our sister."

"I remember," Nealey said. "I love you both."

"Well, then, come over here," Mae said. "We all have to go. You're coming with us, aren't you? We don't want to go without you."

Sylvie knelt down next to them.

"Sweethearts, we cannot go with you. We must stay here."

The girls moved away from their father and stood looking at Sylvie. Tears formed in their eyes but never fell.

Lulu moaned again. She sprawled on the floor and covered her head with her paws.

"But we don't want to go without you, Aunt Sylvie. And we want Nealey to come, too. And Lulu. We'd miss you too much if you didn't come with us."

She wrapped her arms around Sylvie's neck.

"Please come," she whispered. "Please."

Sylvie sniffed back her tears.

"Oh, no, no, you mustn't be sad," Sylvie said. "You must go with your mother and father and take good care of them. Your father has missed you so. He has a place for you, my darlings, where you will be so happy."

Anna walked over to Nealey and hugged her.

"The little ones don't understand," she whispered, "but they will adjust."

Anna stood back and patted her hair.

"You will always be precious to me," she said. "And take my writings. See if you can do something with them. I entrust them to you."

Nealey felt hot tears running down her cheeks.

"Thank you, Grandmother," she said and wiped her eyes with the back of her hand.

Anna motioned to Sylvie. "Give me a hug."

The two women stood in a loving embrace for a long time until they heard Nealey whisper, "Father, we commend these souls into your loving arms."

At that, Henry, with Anna's hand in his and the girls trailing close behind, stepped through the window with Noble and disappeared.

The wind chimes rang in perfect harmony.

Within seconds, they rang again.

Expecting to see Noble, Worthy walked forward.

"Ah, my good brother, I thought you would stay longer," he began.

When Noble didn't appear, he looked at Sylvie.

The wind chimes rang twice more, but no one appeared.

"I thought those chimes rang only with comings and goings," Nealey said.

Worthy nodded.

"Indeed," he said.

Chapter 54

At 6:15 in the morning, one month after Anna and the girls had left, Sylvie stood beside the car and fiddled with her hair.

"Are we ready, my dear?" Worthy asked.

"Quite," Sylvie said and straightened her bright blue tunic.

"Now, don't forget this," Nealey said as she handed Sylvie her day planner.

"Really, darling, I don't think I need it. We'll only be gone two weeks."

Lulu barked.

"See? She agrees," Nealey said. "Two weeks in Ireland. You might need all of those phone numbers in there. You can't forget about your fans and publishers while you're away."

"Smart girl," Worthy said. "Come, Sylvie, we'll be late."

Nealey wrapped her arms around Worthy.

"Take care of her," she said. "And try to stay out of trouble."

Worthy chuckled as he kissed her on the cheek.

"Will Benton come back?" she asked him. "Will I ever see him again?"

Worthy laid a hand on her face.

"I don't know, my dear. Only one in a hundred thousand of us is chosen for it. Benton is that one, beloved of the victorious Archangel Michael. The *change*, as we call it, takes so much effort, and sometimes, it is permanent. But he risked that for you, Nealey, for all of us."

Nealey lowered her head.

"I hate to think of life without him," she said. "I do love him, Worthy."

"Yes, darling," Worthy said. "He knows."

Nealey walked over to Sylvie and hugged her tightly.

"I love you, Auntie Mother," she said. "Be safe."

"Oh, never fear, my darling. I will be safe. I am in good company. You know it was Worthy who saved our dear Lulu from

Max. He'd beaten her almost to death with that shovel, but our Worthy, he healed her."

"What would we have done without Benton, Noble, and Worthy? They saved us all," Nealey said.

Lulu barked twice and nuzzled against Worthy.

"It's quite all right, my dear," he said.

"The three of you make quite a team," Nealey said.

"Yes, well, for a group of reprobates, I guess we'll do," Worthy said.

"I wish you wouldn't call yourself that, Worthy. It sounds so, I don't know, demeaning. I don't consider you reprobates at all. You're our guardian angels."

"Ah, but dearie, there's nothing demeaning about it. It is who we are," Worthy said. "One little drop of human blood—oh, but it is a long story, my dear. Someday, I will explain it all to you. And remember, there are angels ...."

He winked at her.

"And then there are angels! You take care of yourself, and if you need anything, call us immediately."

He tapped his forehead with an index finger.

Nealey smiled and tapped hers in response.

"It takes only a thought, my dear," Worthy said. "Besides, I'm not much for those telephone gadgets. So confusing! Are you ready, Sylvie?"

Sylvie leaned out of the car and took Nealey's hand.

"Don't forget about the Sullivans and the Gradys. They'll be here next weekend. Oh, and I've called my friend Aggie to help out. She's a great housekeeper, and she'll regale you with stories, whether you want to hear them or not," Sylvie said and winked. "And sweetheart, I've left something for you at the foot of my bed, a little surprise gift."

"Ooh, a gift," Nealey said. "I can't wait!"

As they drove away, she waved.

"I love you both," she called after them.

Then, she patted Lulu.

"Come on, girl. Let's go see what we can get into."

They walked up the front steps and through the foyer.

"I guess I'll have to brush up on my cooking skills," Nealey said to Lulu, who licked her hand in response.

Nealey paused at the bottom of the staircase and looked up toward Sylvie's room.

"Hmm," she said. "I wonder what that gift could be? Come on, wanna see?"

Lulu barked and headed up the stairs, Nealey trailing behind.

"Here we are," she said as they reached the room. "Let's see what it is."

They walked to the foot of the bed and found the gift.

Nealey picked up the book, a small but thick leather-bound diary. On the cover were these words: *Sylvie Wolcott's Recipes.*

"Oh, a cookbook," she said. "Heaven knows I need one."

As she thumbed through the book, she came across an entry that caught her attention: *Recipe for Love.*

It began, "In order to create the most splendid love of all, you must have all the ingredients both on hand and in equal measure: an open heart, a willingness to forgive, a ready smile, a method of compromise, and a special touch of magic."

Nealey flipped through the other pages of the book and found it brimming with similar kinds of "recipes": *Recipe for Learning to be an Aunt, Recipe for Courage,* and *Recipe for Bathing Dirty Ghosts.*

"Bathing dirty ghosts?" Nealey said aloud and chuckled.

On the last page of the book, she discovered *Recipe for Sylvie's Secret Ingredient.*

She read the opening lines: "Sylvie's Secret Ingredient is made by mixing the freshest available coriander leaves, lavender flowers, and saffron stigmas, and one other special spice, all ground to perfection in the palm of an angel."

One other spice? The palm of an angel?

Lulu gave a soft cooing sound.

Benton? Did he grind the spices for her? Oh, Benton, how I have missed you!

She closed her eyes and fought back tears. The thought of never seeing him again made her almost sick with grief. A deep, pervading sense of loss engulfed her. Her heart ached for him.

He's gone. Oh, God, he's gone.

An image flashed across her mind. Benton, surrounded by

the halo of blue and gold light, his white wings radiant, his countenance aglow.

My Benton. My magnificent angel.

She sniffed and pressed Aunt Sylvie's book to her chest.

"I am very fortunate," she said to Lulu and forced a smile, "to have known Benton. I must remember how very blessed I've been."

Lulu barked and headed for the door.

"How about some breakfast?" Nealey asked as they walked down the stairs.

In the kitchen, Nealey got a pan from the cupboard, eggs and bacon from the fridge, and a can of fruit cocktail from the pantry.

Lulu scratched the door and whined.

"Quiet," Nealey said. "I'm going to make us some breakfast."

Lulu whined again, louder this time, and mouthed the door open.

"What now?" Nealey asked. "What is it, girl?"

Nealey walked to the door and looked out.

"Oh, oh, oh!" she said and put her hands to her face. Tears welled in her eyes as she watched him walk toward the house.

"Benton!"

Nealey charged out the door behind Lulu and jumped into his arms, her legs wrapped around his waist. His wings were gone, and he was the Benton she'd first met at the inn. He laughed and hugged her so tightly she could hardly breathe, but she didn't care. She kissed him full on the mouth. They spun around while Lulu barked and twirled beside them.

At the end of that sweet kiss, Benton set her gently onto the ground.

"Whew," he said, "that was quite a welcome home. I hate I didn't get here sooner!"

"Oh, my God, where have you been? Are you all right?" she asked.

"I'm fine," he said, a broad smile on his face. "Tell you all about it later."

Nealey slipped her arm around his waist and hugged him as they walked.

Lulu continued to bark and twirl.

"I missed you, too," he said to her and ruffled her ears.

"I was just about to fix breakfast. Are you hungry?"

"Famished!"

She smiled as she put the bacon on and broke a few eggs into a bowl. When she spied the tin in the window, she took it down and opened the top. It was empty.

"Oh, goodness," she said. "There's none of Aunt Sylvie's special ingredient left."

"Allow me," Benton said as he reached over and gently plucked sprigs of several different fresh herbs from their containers. He laid them on the counter, then from the cabinet, he took a small glass bottle and shook a small amount of its contents into his palm.

"Don't let the bacon burn," he said and winked at Nealey.

"Oh, the bacon!"

Nealey took out each slice and laid each on a paper towel to drain. She whipped the eggs and turned back to Benton.

He stood facing her with the tin in his hands, filled to the brim with a golden mixture.

"Takes only a pinch," he said.

Nealey smiled in delight.

"You're incredible," she said.

She giggled as the she put a pinch of Aunt Sylvie's special ingredient into the bowl and poured the mixture into the skillet.

"Smells good already," Benton said.

Nealey smiled at him and curtsied.

"I'm learning."

Benton opened the cabinets and took down the plates. He busied himself getting the flatware and glasses.

Nealey glanced up at him, her heart almost bursting with happiness.

Suddenly from somewhere behind her, she heard, "Hey, what about us? We're hungry, too!"

The light above the stove flickered and went out.

Nealey shuddered and turned toward the voices.

Three dirty little boys sat at the kitchen table, their clothes ragged, their bodies formed only from the waist up.

"Can't we have some food, please?"

Nealey blinked, and the boys vanished.

Sylvie's Double Crust Apple Butterscotch Pie

(Served exclusively at The Playhouse Inn, Highland Rim, Tennessee)

For the Crust:

Sift 2 cups of all purpose flour.

Add 1 tsp salt as you sift.

Cut in 2/3 cup quality shortening.

Continue until ingredients are the size of young peas.

Sprinkle 5 to 6 tablespoons cold water over mixture until dough is moist enough to hold together.

Form dough into 2 balls.

Roll out (on floured pastry board) 2 balls of approximately 11 inches each.

Fit 1 circle of dough into a substantial pie pan.

With your fingertips, gently pat our any air pockets (if left unpatted, dough will be tough). Heaven forbid!

Gently cut slits into remaining dough (to allow steam to escape).

Fold remaining dough gently in half and set aside.

For the filling:

5-6 cups Sylvie's Winter Apples[1], pared

1 cup light brown sugar, packed tightly

1 stick of butter, melted

1 cup of water

1 tsp lemon zest

A pinch of Sylvie's secret ingredient[2]

1 egg (set aside)

(optional but oh, so flavorful) 2 tsp Glenlivet Scotch, and of course, you may substitute any fine Scotch you have on hand

Instructions:

Combine light brown sugar, melted butter, water, and lemon zest.

Cook in large pan over medium heat until it boils.

Remove immediately from heat.

Add 2 tsp Scotch (optional, but if you choose a fine Scotch to use, please take a tiny sip first—just a tiny one—to ensure that its taste pleases you).

Combine sauce with pared apples, mixing in slowly but steadily, one cup at a time.

Pour into crusted pie pan.

Add pinch of Sylvie's secret ingredient, sprinkling it evenly.

Cover with top crust.

Crimp sides of crust along rim of pan with a fork, or for a more elegant touch, use your fingers to create a full fluted edge.

Bake in hot oven (450) for 10 minutes.

Remove immediately.

Mix egg wash (1 tsp water, 1 egg beaten).

Use pastry brush to baste top crust lightly but evenly with egg wash (oh, how your pie will shine!).

Return to 350 degree oven for 40 minutes.

Remove from oven.

Serve hot. (On your good china, if possible. Please, darlings, do avoid at all costs serving this scrumptious treat on paper plates. The thought makes me cringe!)

Fondest regards,

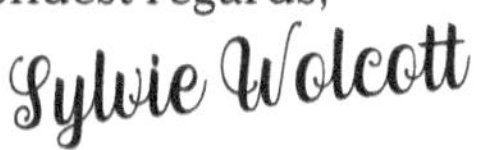

[1]*Sylvie's Winter Apples are greenhouse grown at the Playhouse Inn*

[2]*Sylvie's secret ingredient is a treasured mixture handed down through generations, a unique combination of four spices which include saffron, coriander, and lavender, specially ground at the Playhouse Inn.*

www.ingramcontent.com/pod-product-compliance
Lightning Source LLC
Chambersburg PA
CBHW030105260626
47156CB00008B/2534

* 9 7 8 1 9 5 4 3 3 2 5 7 7 *